We Danced in Venice

The Hayton Collection

Shannon Steeves

THE HAYTON COLLECTION

WE DANCED IN VENICE

In Venice, even love must learn to dance.

SHANNON STEEVES

Venice, the way you lived in this story is how you live in my heart.

Chapter One

Venice surrounded them like a lover's whisper that floated across the neck. Her grand curves, insistent like a siren's call.

Cordelia craned her neck, turning from left to right, and watching as the city emerged from the lagoon's afternoon golden haze. Terracotta buildings rose from the water as if painted by an impressionist's brush, their foundations disappearing into canals that caught and scattered the summer light. The taxi boat's engine throttled back, and the wake lapped against ancient stones with a rhythm that made her pulse quicken.

"Close your eyes," Royce said. His breath tingled against her ear as his arm wrapped around her waist.

"Why?" She turned and found him studying her with a particular intensity, a mischievous desire that still, after nine months, made her heart skip.

"Because, I asked nicely?" Royce had a hard time maintaining a poker face when eager to share something with her.

"What are you up to?"

"Trust me." His dimples appeared, undermining all attempts at seriousness.

1

"Fine." Cordelia felt the boat rock beneath her feet. The air smelled of salt and diesel, of moss, and centuries of stories soaked into stone. Royce's fingers wrapped around hers, and his thumb traced patterns onto her palm. The sensation sent shivers up her arm. "Should I be worried?"

"Shhh." His lips brushed across her neck. "Listen. What do you hear?"

"We're playing that game again, okay." She giggled, feeling his arm squeeze her closer. Cordelia rested her head on his shoulder, letting his muscular body provide support. She concentrated, filtering through the sensory symphony. "Water against wood. Seagulls fighting... over something. Someone shouted in Italian, something about a football match, I think." She smiled without opening her eyes.

"Anything else?"

"Church bells. Multiple churches, actually. And..." She paused, catching something underneath it all. "Music? An accordion?"

"Perfetto amore mio." The Italian rolled off his tongue with surprising fluency. Royce spun her around and pulled her into himself. "Alright, open your eyes."

She found his face inches from hers. Behind him, Venice sprawled with impossible beauty, but she couldn't look away from his eyes. Dark and warm like aged whiskey, they held something more intimate than the impressive architecture.

"Now, what do you hear?" he asked again, but this time his voice sounded deep, almost introspective.

"I just told you."

"No, what do you really hear?" His hand rested on her chest. "In here."

She felt her pulse thump against his palm.

"I heard your breathing change as you listened. My guess is the sounds of Venice surprised you, and you're falling in love."

"I think you should've been born a poet in the 19th century." She cupped his face in her hands. "And what's not to love about this city? Look at it."

"I'll be a poet if you're my muse." Royce's kiss barely lingered, not nearly as long as she wanted. "Mio amore." He brushed back her hair that flopped across her face as the boat maneuvered around canal traffic. Their bodies swayed together, maintaining balance as the driver shouted an apology in Italian. Royce waved and replied, "nessun problema."

"I didn't know you spoke Italian?"

"Un po'." He shrugged. Languages had always come easy for him, more as a tool to impress than reveal anything about himself. But with Cordelia, he wanted the words to convey his heart.

"Now you're being haughty. What does that mean?"

He laughed. "Haughty? I haven't heard that word in a while."

"Guess you needed a reminder." Cordelia playfully tapped Royce on the butt, generating a whistle from a gondolier as their boat slowed past a family of four. The gondolier and their taxi driver conversed and gestured in Italian.

"That's my cousin." Their driver shouted over his shoulder.

"La famiglia e tutto," Royce replied.

"Okay, what did you say this time?"

"Family is everything." He said casually, as if family bonds were uncomplicated.

"French. Italian. What other languages do you speak?"

"That's all, unless you want to include Latin and Greek."

"That's it? I barely speak English." The boat engine throttled down, and the sound of lapping water subsided as their taxi pulled alongside a private dock with bright turquoise and gold canal poles.

The dock belonged to Palazzo Li Fonti, their home for the

next two weeks. Not a hotel but a converted 15th-century palace that made Cordelia's breath catch. Deep green ivy climbed weathered stone walls, and the home's Gothic windows reflected the canal like eyes hiding secrets. Royce handled the boat fare, switching between Italian and English with ease, while a young porter disappeared with their luggage. He gave Cordelia a nod before rolling an ornate brass cart through haphazard vines that dangled above an arched doorway.

"How do you say 'you've lost your mind' in Italian?" Cordelia asked Royce as they approached massive wooden doors. "Because this is..."

"Spectacular? Overwhelming? Exactly what you deserve?" He pulled her close, wrapping his arm around her waist. She felt the heat of his desire against her back. "The last one, definitely."

A thin woman in an elegant black dress greeted them. Signora Benedetti, the palazzo's manager, wore her blonde hair swept up into a tight chignon, yet her eyes crinkled with warmth when Royce introduced Cordelia in perfect Italian.

"Ah, la fidanzata del Signor Brownell." She clasped her hands together. "Che bella!"

Cordelia understood the word for 'beautiful' but looked to Royce for the rest.

"She says you're my..." He paused and whispered in her ear. "You're the beautiful girlfriend."

"She says it as if I'm the flavor of the month."

Royce tightened his squeeze around her waist while smiling at Signora Benedetti, "Well, you're certainly not vanilla."

"I hope not." Cordelia greeted the Signora and exchanged pleasantries with her in English. She discovered the woman spoke four languages, had grown up in Milan, and had managed the Palazzo for twenty years.

As Signora Benedetti escorted them through marble corridors, her heels clicked against the floor. Cordelia noticed how the frescoes seemed to dance across the ceilings and Murano chandeliers cast prisms onto rich paneled walls. The signora chattered in perfect English, mentioning amenities as the walked: breakfast on the terrace provided scenic views, their kitchen was equipped with everything a chef would need, and somewhere amid her enthusiastic gestures was a comment about ghosts and a recommendation for the best spa.

The private elevator delivered them to their apartment, which occupied the palazzo's top floor. The modern space sprawled before them with exposed beams, soft Persian rugs, and glass doors that opened onto private terraces. Vases of white flowers bloomed in every corner, their perfume mixing with canal air. But it was the bedroom that made Cordelia pause. The canopied bed dominated the room, burgundy silk cascading from heights that made her dizzy, while windows framed the Grand Canal like living paintings. Even more impressive was the black-and-white marble bathroom with its steam shower room, which contained a freestanding tub made for two.

"Royce," Cordelia returned to the living room just as Signora Benedetti stepped onto the elevator. "I can't believe all of this is just for us." She paused, catching her breath. "I take that back, yes, I can. You practically grew up in a castle."

"It belongs to a friend." He crossed to where she stood by the window, framing her face with his hands. "I wanted to make it special."

"I know, but."

"Before you tell me it's extravagant," he pressed a finger to her lips, "It's a trade between friends. I use his palazzo for two weeks, and he borrows the Highland cottage."

"You have a *Highland* cottage?"

"My family owns it."

"Of course they do."

"And now we have a bed suitable for a Doge." His thumb traced her lower lip. "Perhaps we should test its structural integrity. Make sure it's safe."

"Safety is important." Her lips moistened the tip of his finger, and she watched as his pupils dilated. Weeks of pent-up desire rushed upward, reminding Cordelia how work had kept their schedules hectic, denying them precious time. His finger traced her slightly parted lips, dipping in-and-out to feel her tongue. But suddenly, her stomach chose that moment to growl loudly, like a roaring lion claiming its meal. He snickered, she giggled, and both laughed.

"Right. Feed the chef first, seduce her after."

"Solid plan." She reluctantly stepped back. "Although I should warn you, a good pasta dish might challenge your seduction skills."

"Is that a bet, Ms. Dyer?"

"Possibly."

"Then Venice will be my greatest ally."

"How?"

"This city is nothing but passion. And by the end of the night..." He kissed her neck. "I will be the only thing on your mind."

"Mmmm, challenge accepted." Her stomach growled again.

"Alright, let's get you fed before there's a revolt."

Cordelia's laughter tumbled into agreement, declaring food the absolute winner. For the moment.

Outside the palazzo's gated garden, Cordelia felt the delicate power of Venice settle around her with a light breeze that maneuvered through narrow streets like a silk scarf resting against the skin. At every corner, the wind unwrapped the city, inviting her to peek inside its mysteries. Her pace slowed as they crossed a bridge, and she memorized the late afternoon light as it cascaded onto the canal, turning it into molten gold. Above ornate windows gazed down on gondoliers who called to each other in rhythmic voices. A sound that echoed off the ancient stone, and mingled with distant accordion music.

The intoxication of Venice seeped further into Cordelia's senses with the scent of garlic and fresh seafood. She tightened her grip on Royce's hand and breathed in the salty air. The city's rhythm absorbed her, leaving her invigorated. Life felt eager to expand.

Royce watched as the Biblioteca Marciana rose before them like a temple to knowledge, its Renaissance white facade sparkling in the late afternoon sun. He noticed Cordelia's face transform at the sight of the historic buildings surrounding Piazza San Marco, the same expression she wore when tasting a perfect soufflé. Pure, undiluted joy.

"That's a library?" Her voice held a reverence most people reserved for the cathedral that cast shadows across the vast square.

Royce couldn't resist her enthusiasm. "Your research home for the next two weeks. Would you like to go in?"

"Now? I'm sure they're closed."

"To the public, yes, but I know someone..."

"Of course you do." Cordelia gestured with a playful curtsy. "Lead the way."

Even though Royce had visited the library many times before, the barrel-vaulted entrance hall always stole his breath with its soaring ceilings that made the basilica look understated. Gold-leaf frescoes caught the lamplight and scattered it across the walls. The air held a floral mustiness, an earthy scent that mingled four hundred-year-old architecture with modern perfumery.

"Royce!" A voice called from the main desk. "Benvenuto!"

He turned to find Dr. Alessandro Fabaligo approaching, silver-haired with a crooked nose that matched his smile. It had been five years since Royce had seen him, but he still walked with a dignified swagger.

"Alessandro, may I introduce Cordelia Dyer, the chef who's joining you this week."

"Ah, the chef!" Alessandro took Cordelia's hand with continental flair and held it between his palms. "It is a pleasure. He speaks highly of your work, but he did not tell me I would be working alongside such a beautiful woman."

Cordelia blushed, cutting her eyes at Royce while smiling at Alessandro. "Well, he didn't mention your charm either."

Royce watched Alessandro's appreciation of Cordelia with a recurring unease. Not jealousy, just an old protective instinct that encouraged management.

Alessandro chuckled and leaned toward her, "Maybe he's jealous." The two laughed, almost oblivious of Royce's presence.

"Maybe I was wrong to trust you two together." Royce snaked his arm around Cordelia's waist, resting his fingers on her hip. "How's Catarina? Will we see her this trip?"

"Oh, she's beautiful as ever, but she is in Rome this week." He looked at Cordelia, "My wife is a cardiologist. The best in all of Italy." He beamed with pride.

Soon their conversation became more serious, discussing access protocols and manuscript availability. Royce found himself distracted by how Cordelia's entire being seemed to vibrate with excitement. Her hands moved as she talked, describing her research goals, and he recognized the enthusiastic gestures from late-night kitchen conversations. This was Cordelia in her element, just with books instead of butter.

"If you would like," Alessandro offered, "I can show you the reading room now? It's closed for the day, but if you would like, I can show you."

Cordelia and Royce both agreed, acknowledging two things: one, their hunger, and two, their desire not to impose.

"Si, si, veloce!" Alessandro led them through corridors lined with portraits of stern scholars, clergy, and noble families. "The collection you want, the merchant family recipes, they are in a vault. But when you come, I'll have them ready."

The reading room silenced their conversation. Rows of dark wood desks stretched beneath an expansive ceiling, and one could imagine the centuries of whispers that filled the ornate space.

"Incredible," Cordelia said.

"Wait until you see the manuscripts," Alessandro promised. "Fifteenth century, some older. The Morschella family, they documented everything. Feast menus, household accounts, overnight guests, everything. And now, we benefit from their meticulous journaling."

A movement near the far wall caught Royce's attention. A familiar figure, one he hadn't seen in several years, stowed a binder into a camel-colored bag. Long black hair escaped from a loose bun. His stomach tightened at the unwelcome sight.

Evie Lin looked up as if sensing his gaze. Her ebony eyes widened, then warmed with surprised pleasure. Her rose-tinted lips smiled.

Royce touched Cordelia's elbow. "We should go. I think we've stayed long enough."

"Royce? Dr. Brownell?" Evie's voice carried across the

sacred silence. She hurried toward them, leaving her bag on the table. "I can't believe it! What are you doing in Venice?"

There was no avoiding it now. Royce felt Cordelia's back stiffen beside him as Evie approached. Her five foot two-inch stature radiated enthusiastic energy. The same charisma he remembered from university—before Gavin. He mentally noted that she looked well, no longer carrying the shadows of grief in her eyes.

"Evie." Royce winced, feeling the tension in his voice. "It's good to see you." His eyes met Cordelia's, who took a step back as Evie planted an Italian greeting onto his cheeks. "Oh, um, yes, hello."

"I didn't know you were coming."

"Evie, this is Cordelia Dyer, my partner. Cordelia, this is Dr. Evie Lin, from the uni—"

"The university, right." Cordelia extended her hand, only to be ignored by Evie.

"Partner?" Her smile flickered but held. "I didn't know. What are you doing here?"

"Cordelia's working on a cookbook," Royce explained, aware of the awkward air that thickened around him. "She's researching historical recipes for her second book. How are you?"

"Oh, the usual, dealing with students and chasing rumors of a lost ship's journal. You know how it is." She laughed, the sound deceptively bright. "Dr. Fabaligo has been incredibly helpful. The collections here are extraordinary. You should join me, since you obviously have some free time."

"Thank you for the offer, but my schedule is hectic, even while Cordelia's researching."

"I'm sure you can spare an hour." Her hand rested on Royce's arms but her eyes settled onto Cordelia. "He's not that busy, is he?"

"Actually, he is," she replied.

Royce felt Cordelia's hand glide across his lower back, her fingers tucking into his jeans pocket.

"Well, listen, it was wonderful to see you, but we have dinner plans. And I don't want to keep Alessandro longer."

Cordelia gracefully extended her hand. This time she wedged it between Evie and Royce. "Nice to meet you, Evie. Good luck with your Byzantine research."

"You too. Good luck with that cookbook." Evie gave Cordelia's hand one rapid squeeze. "Actually, Royce, I've been meaning to email you. About the article we discussed six months ago—the discoveries off the coast of Vis, Croatia."

"Right."

"I found some supporting evidence in a Venetian merchant records, and I think I could use your opinion."

"That's not my expertise. I'm sure Dr. Fabaligo would give you better advice." Royce felt trapped between politeness and the urgent need to extract himself from this situation. "Wouldn't you agree, Alessandro?"

"Of course," he said. "I would be happy to assist, Dr. Lin."

"Thank you. Maybe I'll email it to you anyway. I always value your opinion." She glanced between the three of them, and Royce noticed a shift in her expression. Her professional smile softened, and a lonely, vulnerable gaze crossed her face, causing her lips to pucker. Royce's chest tightened with guilt. "Oh, and Cordelia, I'm here most days if you need any help navigating all of this. I've gotten to know this place quite well."

"Thank you," Cordelia said smoothly. "That's very kind." Her eyes drifted from Evie, to the door and landed on Royce.

"Yes, right." He glanced at his watch. Seven PM. Early by their normal standards, but he'd promised Cordelia a romantic evening, a night Evie wouldn't invade. "Alessandro, thank you for the tour. We'll see you in two days?"

"Si, si! Nine o'clock, I'll have everything prepared for you, Ms. Dyer." He walked them toward the door, chattering about the architecture.

Royce felt Evie's gaze following them. At the door, he couldn't resist glancing back. She held her pack, appearing minuscule in the room's vastness. Their eyes met across the distance, and she offered a small wave. There, the loneliness radiated where boldness used to reside. There self-reproach hung.

Outside, Venice's evening air hit like a warm bath after the library's controlled temperatures. Cordelia walked beside him in silence as they navigated toward the restaurant, their fingers barely touched.

"So," she said as they crossed a small bridge, "Dr. Lin seems nice."

"Yes, she is."

"Very happy to see you, too."

He cleared his throat. His free hand slipped into his pocket and tapped the edge of his phone.

"I didn't know you kept in touch." Cordelia's tone dropped.

This was the moment to tell her everything: Evie's full connection to his resignation, the guilt that still occasionally woke him at three AM. But tourists jostled past, gondoliers called for passengers, and the evening hummed with possibility. Tomorrow, he decided. When they had privacy and time.

"Yes, well, she's a doctoral student—was a doctoral student. The one who worked closely with Dr. Andrews. Now, Evie's a leading expert on maritime commerce between Venice and Constantinople."

"Mmhmm." Cordelia's fingers reconnected with his—agreeable, assured. "Well, I have to say, watching you slip into professor mode was oddly attractive. Very authoritative."

"Just oddly attractive?" He pulled her into a quiet alcove

between buildings. "I'll have you know my lectures were standing room only."

"I bet they were." Her eyes danced with mischief. "All those undergrads girls swooning over your analysis of ninth-century Saxon politics."

"Actually, it was my lectures on the Treaty of Wedmore that excited them the most."

"I see."

He pressed her back against the ancient stone wall, caging her with his arms. "And I'll have you know those negotiations created political and cultural concepts that still exist today."

"Fascinating. Dr. Brownell, did you know," She tugged at his collar, bringing his mouth closer. "You're very sexy when you talk?" She ran her finger over his lip.

"You're a tease, Ms. Dyer." He kissed her, letting Venice fade until there was only the taste of her lipstick and the faint sound she made when his teeth grazed her lower lip. "If you're genuinely interested, I have slides..."

She laughed against his mouth. "Maybe later, *Professor*." She closed the space between their hips, running her hand down the side of his chest. "Right now I'm more interested in that dinner you promised. And wine. For sure, a glass of wine."

"Right. Then I guess we'll conclude this conversation later tonight."

"*Definitely*." Her teeth pressed against her lower lip's crooked smile.

His appetite longed for her. He stepped back, smoothed his shirt and watched her adjust her necklace that had shifted in their brief moment of passion. The chain glided delicately across the nape of her neck, a spot he wanted to kiss. "The restaurant's close. According to sources, their seafood is exceptional."

"A mysterious source again." She took his arm as they

emerged from the alcove. "Should I be concerned about this secret Venetian network?"

"Desperately so."

"Desperately? Sounds exotic." They paused long enough for her to wipe lipstick remnants from his cheek.

"If you must know, I'm a spy, and the archaeologist-turned-author is just my cover."

"How 007 of you. Is that why I've barely seen you in three weeks?"

"Yes, well, spy meetings and all."

"And I thought it was because you were a brilliant author."

"That, too." He pulled her to his side, feeling the tightness of her abs underneath the silk dress.

Their banter continued as they maneuvered through the narrow streets near Rio di San Moise. In silence they walked, listening to the chatter of tourists exploring the city. But Royce couldn't shake the image of Evie alone in the vast reading room, surrounded by the past and the threads that linked them. Her reappearance back into his life reminded him that what initially appears to be a simple omission can create a web of misunderstandings, and strangle the trust he and Cordelia had carefully cultivated.

Chapter Two

The gondola appeared from beneath a bridge like something conjured from dreams. Its black hull gleamed in the dim city lights. Cordelia had heard the Venetian gondoliers with their striped shirts were manufactured romance, something out of a tourist trap playbook, but her source was wrong. The slim cigar boat with its red velvet fabric and gold ferro invited her aboard. Like a siren's call, it asked her to surrender to Venice's seduction, to let the city write itself across her heart, and allow romance and clichés to merge.

Royce spoke to the gondolier in Italian, cracking a smile across the man's weathered face. He replied and then gestured Cordelia into the boat. Sante introduced himself with a bow, pushing off from the dock with practiced ease. The boat slid its way into the Grand Canal traffic, giving them a view of the Basilica Santa Maria reflecting against the navy night sky.

Cordelia settled her body against Royce's and listened to the water smack against the boat. "This is so touristy, but..."

"I told you everyone needed to experience it once."

"Once. I'm doing this every day for the next two weeks."

Sante sang, his voice rough but deep; an opera melody far

from the streets of London and routine life. The notes them-selves seemed to rise from the water. Soon the boat slipped into a smaller canal and passed under a bridge, so low Cordelia could have reached up and touched it. On the other side, a small square opened up with tables spilling out from a restau-rant. Diners raised their glasses as they passed, and someone shouted "tanti auguri". She waved and someone snapped their photo.

"Interpretation, please?"

"Best wishes, many wishes."

"For riding in a gondola?"

"They think you are honeymooners." Sante said and returned to his singing. The crowd cheered.

"Us?" Cordelia turned toward Royce, their mouths inches apart.

"Is that difficult to imagine?"

"No. I just hadn't..."

"Maybe you should."

His kiss tasted of deep, bold wine: earthy, comforting, sweet. Promises and possibilities emerged. Cordelia forgot about tourists and clichés. She forgot about everything except the warm subtly of his mouth and the way his hand cupped her face like she was something precious. When they broke apart, Sante still sang his love song.

The serenade paused as they entered a narrower canal where buildings engulfed the boat, creating tunnels of shadow and light. Open windows above them revealed an old woman pulling in the day's laundry from the overhead line, and a cat washing itself on a windowsill. Glimpses of everyday Venice carried on its evening routines, ignoring the gondola as it eased through the water. The city felt alive, fragrant with savory, spicy elements, and exhaled her centuries of stories.

"Cordelia," Royce said, his voice taking on the serious tone that usually preceded discussions about his family or career. "There's something I want to say."

Her stomach fluttered. She'd heard the stories. In gondolas, serious conversations usually went in one direction and typically involved rings and a question. Was she ready if he asked? She'd only let herself imagine it once, but fear had halted hope before it slipped into illusion. Besides, they'd found their rhythm together. Since her birthday party, they'd split their time between apartments, keeping spare toothbrushes and clothes at each other's place, while maintaining autonomy. "Okay?"

"We've been together nine months, and we've had our challenges—my title, our careers, and our mutual disagreement on what constitutes a properly loaded dishwasher."

She smirked. "The dishes face the center."

"I disagree. Facing outward maximizes water coverage, but that's not the point." He shifted, fully facing her. The intensity in his eyes made her breath catch. "The point is, despite all that, or maybe because of it, I." He paused, appearing to wrestle with his words. "I want you to know that this, us, is my future. Not in a 'let's get married tomorrow' way, but in a 'I can't imagine any tomorrow without you' way. I know you need time, we both do—but I need you to know you're not a chapter in my life. You're the entire book."

The words lodged in her chest, too big for her ribs to contain. He'd always been better with metaphors, but this one—this one she felt in her bones.

The gondola rounded a corner into a wider canal where blue and white lights hung over a balcony like majestic stars. Sante had stopped singing, quietly moving them through the water.

"Royce..." Tears pooled in her eyes, and she dabbed them

with the back of her hand. He reached into his pocket, pulled out a monogrammed handkerchief, and gave it to her. He knew exactly when to bring sentiment into a conversation. She laughed and dried her eyes.

The gondola passed under another bridge, momentarily casting them into darkness. She leaned into him and kissed him, letting the remnants of salty tears mix with the sweetness of his lips.

"I love you, Royce." She wiped her thumb across his lips, "Even though you load dishwashers like one of your barbarians."

He roared, "I love you too. Despite your need to keep spices alphabetized."

"What? It makes perfect sense." She said, nesting her back against his chest.

Sante cleared his throat and sang a song about eternal love in Venice. As the canal widened, they passed other couples embraced in kisses or sipping prosecco. The warm night air glistened on her cheeks as she focused on the stars. Royce's fingers traced circular patterns on her arm.

Their gondola returned to the Grand Canal, signaling their romantic hour-long ride was coming to an end.

"Are you tired?" Royce whispered, his lips pressed against her ear.

"No. You?"

He nibbled her ear lightly. "What do you think?"

"I think, Dr. Brownell, there are some important international relations you need to take care of tonight."

"Mmm, yes, very urgent."

The gondola pulled alongside moored boats rocking and bobbing at the Ponte San Moisè. Music drifted from an open window, a piano playing something soft and yearning.

"Thank you," Cordelia said as Sante helped her onto the dock. "Grazie. It was perfect."

"Prego, signora." He reached into his pocket, held out his hand, and extended a small glass charm in the shape of a heart. "Portafortuna. For luck in love."

She clutched the trinket and thanked him before Royce briefly talked with Sante in Italian.

They barely made it through the palazzo door before the tension that had been building in the gondola demanded release. Royce pressed her against the ancient wood, his hands entwined in her hair. His mouth claimed hers with unrelenting hunger.

"I hope we don't wake anyone," she gasped. "Signora Benedetti seems..."

"Is asleep." He traced the column of her throat with his lips and teeth, finding the spot below her ear that made her moan. Every time. "We're alone."

"You're always so sure of—." Her hands tugged at his shirt, seeking the warmth of his skin. Their mouths met. "God, it's been too long."

"We wouldn't have dry spells if you didn't work so late." Their eyes met.

"Shhh. I hear someone." They paused. Her hands rested on his bare chest. Footsteps echoed down the corridor. Cordelia held her laughter as Royce buttoned his shirt, her breath steadied despite a rising passion.

The shuffled steps moved closer and then stopped. Royce motioned upward and then softly closed the door, as quietly as anyone could be when shutting a heavy, carved palazzo door. After a few seconds, they glanced down the hallway. There was no one in sight. The footsteps had vanished. The corridor, lit by six sconces, remained empty in both directions. One of the flames flickered, as if someone had passed too close. Or maybe, Venice herself hinted that passion in ancient places included ancient witnesses.

Cordelia burst into laughter, "Was that a ghost?"

"No."

"Are you sure?"

"I think I know what ghosts sound like."

"True. But maybe Italian ghosts sound different from English ones." She snickered.

Arriving at their floor, pausing twice for kisses that threatened to derail the journey back to the apartment. By the time they reached the bedroom, their clothes had left a trail from the elevator to the doorway. The sweet smell of roses floated above the city's salty fragrance.

Moonlight spilled through the tall windows, painting Cordelia in silver and shadow. She stood before him, letting him memorize the lace that framed her hips. He felt a surge in his chest, the same rush he felt at Hayton Manor on that stormy night. How did she still do this to him? What about her made him feel lost and found simultaneously? The answer reflected back at him through her eyes. And it wasn't the image of Lord Brownell or a future Earl, it was just a man—flawed, wanting, and complete.

"You're staring," she said. A smile played on her lips.

"Simply admiring," he corrected, reaching for her. "There's a difference."

Royce found her waist and drew her close. She was perfect in her imperfections, each a chapter in her story: the small mole between her collarbone and shoulder, the kitchen scars on her right forearm, and her telltale nervous sign of biting the corner of her lower lip. He knew every inch of her, mentally mapping her curves with dedication; an archaeologist uncovering precious artifacts. Yet, each time felt like a new discovery.

"I love you." The words, incomplete compared to his feelings, were meant to describe the depth of admiration. How could three words encompass the way she'd reorganized his world? Before her, he'd been content with his carefully crafted life. Now he craved her passion, her beautifully chaotic world that spilled over and ignited even the air around her.

Her lips parted as she moistened them, and she undressed, letting the moonlight expose her nakedness.

Among the bed linens, they moved as one. Royce traced a path with his mouth: the curve of her neck, the hollow between her breasts, the tautness of her abs against his moist lips, and the place where her pulse soared like a bird.

Cordelia arched beneath his touch, his name a whispered prayer in the Venetian night. Her fingers tangled in his hair, and their eyes met. What he saw deep within them—trust, desire, vulnerability. It almost undid him.

"I'm here," he said, understanding the silent question.

"Always," she breathed, pulling him closer.

Her rhythm, their rhythm marked by the distance church bells signaled midnight—everything quieted.

Afterwards, they lay tangled in the sheets, her head on his chest, and his fingers tracing the edges of her shoulder blade.

"Do you think we heard a ghost?" she murmured sleepily.

"I doubt it. But if we did, are you afraid?"

"I don't think so. Hopefully, it's nice, whoever it was."

Royce pressed a kiss to her hair, but an odd feeling nagged at him—an uncertainty and discomfort.

Chapter Three

"Turn left at the sotoportego," Royce said, consulting his phone's map for the third time in ten minutes.

"The what?" Cordelia peered down an alley so narrow she could touch both walls. Laundry hung between buildings like pinatas, and an annoyed cat glanced up from its nap, disdain in its stare. "Here?"

"No, the covered passage. It should lead directly to Campo San Polo." He squinted at the screen. "Although according to this, we're currently standing in the middle of the Grand Canal."

"Fantastic. We're either Jesus or completely lost."

"If I recall, you're the one who suggested we venture out, and *get lost, be spontaneous*."

He had a point. She had suggested it after their morning distractions which included a chat with Jessica at BL London, a Zoom call with Bastien, and one lengthy call between Royce and the Earl. "Yes, but my idea was to wander romantically through these picturesque streets," she said, stepping over a puddle of questionable origin. "This appears to be where gondolas come to retire. Or maybe die."

The narrow canal beside them held several boats in various stages of decay. But even so, Venice worked its magic, casting the afternoon sun onto the rotting wood and turning them into works of art waiting to be photographed. "Oh, it smells fishy," she said.

"This way." Royce shoved his phone into a pocket and reached for her hand. "Fortune favors the bold, as my grandfather always said."

"Fortune favors people with functioning GPS." She sarcastically cleared her throat.

"Darling," Royce spun around and seamlessly pulled her into his arms. "You survived my family's dinners and London society. A few retired gondolas in a pool of stagnant water can't possibly intimidate you now."

"When you put it like that," she said as he dipped her. Her squeal bounced off the faded stone walls, causing a young mother to 'shush' them as she leaned from a window.

Five minutes later, they emerged into a small square, and Cordelia was certain it didn't exist on any map. A single tree dominated the center, its branches creating a canopy of green. She imagined its roots had probably pushed through the stones for centuries, fighting for dominance in a city built on water. Beneath it, an old man played an accordion while his wife sold flowers from a green cart.

"Now this is what I imagined," Cordelia said, breathing in the fragrance of potted jasmine climbing the wall outside a tiny coffee bar where men leaned against the brass railing and sipped their espresso. Colored shirts dangled from laundry lines stretched several stories above, connecting open windows like knitted yarn.

The man caught sight of them and, with a knowing smile, shifted into something livelier, a waltz that invited a response.

"I think we're being summoned." Royce said.

"Summoned for what? To dance?"

"Sure, why not?"

"We're the only ones out here. People will stare."

"No one will care."

She wanted to protest, but the music wound around them like silk ribbon, and Royce looked at her, with an expression that dissolved all objections. "Alright, Mr. Brownell, let's dance."

The longer the music played, the more Cordelia forgot about appearances. She waltzed, stumbled backwards, stepped on Royce's toe, and laughed. It reminded her of being five years old and dancing with her father. He'd hold her hands, and they'd waltz around the backyard, listening to the faint music blasting off-the-record player.

An elderly couple joined them, the man's cane abandoned against the tree as he led his wife around the courtyard in a dance they'd done for decades.

"You set this whole thing up, didn't you?"

"What do you mean?"

"This, all of this. You arranged it all."

"I wish I could take credit for it."

"Royce, this doesn't happen in real life—spontaneous dancing in a Venetian square. This is what they do in the movies."

"Tell that to them."

The song morphed into a slower, more intimate melody before they could escape. The older couple pressed their cheeks together and swayed. Their steps made a repetitive square.

"You're overthinking it," Royce said. His hand rested on the curve of her lower back, pulling her chest into his.

"Am I?"

"Yes. This is purely spontaneous."

His beard stubble rubbed against her cheek. "Then I want to memorize every moment." She closed her eyes and followed his lead. "A baby's giggling, the aromas from that old, wooden cart, and you. I want to remember how your lips feel."

She felt his full lips kiss her: one cheek, then the other.

"Like so?"

"Yes."

Their mouths met in one delicate kiss. She opened her eyes, letting a broad smile break through her cynicism. "If you didn't make all of this happen, then I want to make sure I remember it when we're back in London."

He stopped dancing, even though the music continued. "What if I had planned this, would it change anything?"

Her hands framed his face. "No. But if it's spontaneous, then thank you. It's one for the books."

"I promise, I did not plan or strategize any of this. Consider it a gift from the Venetian gods."

Her eyes glanced upwards, "Thank you." Her heart swelled in gratitude, and words failed to convey the emotions that washed over her like a waterfall. In an attempt to express them, she embraced Royce, letting him gaze into her eyes and explore what resided behind the stare.

A few minutes later, he tipped the man and asked for directions to the Campo. They left the square just as the sun began its descent behind the buildings, draping an amber and rose glow to the air. Cordelia glanced back one last time. The old couple still swayed together, and she wondered if that would be them someday, finding music in unexpected corners and dancing despite tired feet.

"Are you hungry?" Royce asked. "I know a place near the university with excellent homemade pasta."

"That sounds perfect." She glanced at her watch, her father's old one with the frayed brown leather straps.

"We'll have time to see the church tomorrow."

"I hope so. Our schedule is pretty packed."

"With what?" He raised a suspicious eyebrow.

"You'll find out tomorrow." She tugged at his hand, pulling him down a deserted narrow lane. "Now, let's see if you can navigate us to that restaurant of yours before the sun sets."

"Are you doubting my skills?"

Cordelia dropped his hand and jogged ahead as her sneakers squeaked across wet stones. Her eyes cut a playful glance back at Royce. "Let's call it a hunch."

"You doubt me?" He dashed forward, caught her, and pinned her against a wall. "That's disheartening." Their laughter echoed and merged with the wind as it whipped past them, creating a whispered howl.

"What's disheartening is that Aperol spritz that's growing warmer with every wrong turn you take."

"Every wrong turn I take? I believe you're the one who led us down this alley."

She looked around, spotted a blue wooden boat, and realized, he was right, it did dead-end into a canal. "Well then, I'll make it up to you...if you find where we're going." She felt like the Cheshire Cat plotting its next meal.

"Is that a wager, Ms. Dyer?"

"What do you think?" She rapped her fingers against his hip.

He glanced at his fancy watch with its compass and lunar calendar. "Tell you what, I'll have you at the restaurant in twenty minutes, Aperol spritzer in hand or I'll serenade you on our next gondola ride."

"Ooh. In Italian?"

"Yes, in Italian, if that makes you happy."

"It would."

"And, if I get you to your spritzer in time, then you agree to join me on a ghost tour tomorrow night."

"Seriously? That's your bet? Nothing like a massage or bath for two?"

"Of course not, that's happening either way."

She burst into laughter, "You're so cocky."

"I prefer confident."

"Fine, I accept your bet, Lord Brownell." Cordelia wedged her hand between their chests and offered him a shake.

He accepted and set his watch timer for twenty minutes. They crossed four bridges, passed through one sottoportego, and made two left turns. Just as Royce had said, the restaurant was near the university, tucked between a mask shop and a bookstore. It was so small she, like most tourists, would've walked past without giving it any thought. There was no sign outside the open door, just a chalkboard announcing the day's specials in Italian. Laughter and spirited conversations spilled onto the street.

They had made it in ten minutes and thirty-four seconds. He happily emphasized the seconds.

Three hours later, the palazzo bedroom windows stood open, allowing the moist Venetian night air to mingle with the apartment's floral scent. Royce watched Cordelia at the vanity, removing jewelry with an unconscious grace. First, the gold stud earrings her father gave her for high school graduation, then the pearl-drop necklace, (the first piece of jewelry she'd purchased for herself), and lastly, the bracelet he'd given her in remembrance of Paris. Each piece precisely placed in a black velvet travel case.

"You're staring," she said without turning around.

"Admiring. Completely different thing." Royce lounged shirtless on the bed, enjoying their domestic intimacy. Her ritual amused him. "I might also be plotting a surprise."

"Should I be worried?" She locked eyes with him. The mirror reflected the slight upturn of her mouth.

"I'm afraid so. I'm considering keeping you here with me, forever."

"Forever's a long time."

"Yes, but it agrees with you."

"Venice agrees with everyone. It's part of the marketing campaign, right?" Cordelia smirked, the one she made as she rolled her eyes, the one that appeared when she thought no one was watching. "But, if you insist, I guess I could be persuaded."

"Done. I'll call the airline and cancel our flights." Part of Royce secretly wished they could stay permanently. That day he'd watched her dance with abandon, charm strangers, and race barefoot up the marble stairs—a reminder of why he'd fallen for her in Paris. Her beauty, the way her nose crinkled with the first sip of coffee, and how her green eyes sparkled when she baked, still caught his breath. But her ability to find wonder in unexpected moments, that captured him.

She stood, dimmed the chandelier, and crossed to the window. Her pink silk robe caught the moonlight, translucent as a whisper. It draped over her curves. "Well, if you're keeping me here *forever*, then I need to hire movers, call Bastien, and tell your mother we can't make Sunday dinner... ever again."

"Better you than me."

"On second thought, I'll let you handle your *mum*."

"No, no, that's on your list."

"Chicken."

"Yes, I am. Have you met her?"

Cordelia gave a brief laugh, crawled onto the bed, and flopped beside him.

"Come here," he said, pulling her against him. With her back to his chest, they faced the open windows where Venice sparkled. "I can't believe you convinced that Italian grandmother to share her family's marinara recipe. I swear you're gifted."

"All in a day's work, my dear." She relaxed into him, her head finding the perfect spot beneath his chin. "Just my sweet, American charm."

"Is that what you call it?"

"It worked on you, didn't it?"

"Naturally. I'm British. We've been captivated by you since you kicked us out of the colonies." His fingers found the sash of her robe. "Your vast landscape, and uncharted territories."

She turned in his arms. Her eyes held a deep gaze, a look that always meant she'd decided to stop thinking and feel into the moment. "Show me," she said.

Royce had loved her hundreds of times in their months together. Quick morning encounters before work, lazy Sunday afternoons in his flat, and that very brief, yet memorable evening in the Hayton library during his brother's birthday party. But something about Venice, about the day, made everything feel brand new.

"You're still thinking," she said, unbuttoning his jeans. "I can hear those wheels turning."

"Just about you, about us."

"Well, speed it up." With one tug she exposed his hips to warm air. Her mouth drifted to the base of his neck, the curved spot that always made him groan.

"I'm done." Royce's hands moved underneath the silk, reacquainting themselves with her skin. "Actually..."

Her laugh vibrated against his throat. "Shh."

He rolled them over, pinning her gently among a dozen pillows that probably cost more than most people's rent. His mouth traced the delicate line of her collarbone, feeling her pulse flutter beneath his tongue. He paused, but words escaped him.

Cordelia's hands mapped the planes of his chest, letting her nails scrape lightly across.

Together they moved as lovers who instinctively knew each other's rhythms, but remained in the spark of discovery. Her robe dropped to the floor, followed by his trousers. The night air cooled the rising heat of their skin.

"Wait," Cordelia gasped as his mouth traced a path down her stomach. "The windows."

"We're three stories up facing the Grand Canal. Only the resident ghosts might see us."

"Seriously?"

Royce continued his exploration, gratified by her sharp intake of breath. "Quite possibly." Her abs tightened at the sensation of his hand sliding down her thigh.

Her worries dissolved into wordless sounds as he demonstrated his intimate knowledge of her.

Later—minutes, hours, he'd lost track, they lay tangled, their heartbeats returning to normal rhythms. Cordelia's touch, light enough to tickle but too pleasant to discourage, traced across his chest. Royce pulled the sheets over them, cocooning them together.

Outside, Venice continued its nocturnal symphony: a gondolier's oars splashing, young Italians debating, lovers conversing—the city's eternal dialogue.

Within minutes, Cordelia's breathing deepened into sleep, her body soft and trusting against his. Royce lay awake, watching the moonlight paint patterns on the ceiling.

It had been perfect, one that would crystallize in his

memory. The rational part of his mind, the part that had been taught caution, whispered, *vulnerability is a dream, and dreams by definition end.*

But as Cordelia slept, warm in his arms with accordion music echoing in his memory, he silenced that voice. He pulled her closer, breathing in the tropical scent of her hair.

If ignoring wisdom meant living in a dream with her, he'd happily let the Venetian waters carry caution into the depths of the Adriatic Sea.

The last thing Royce heard before sleep claimed him was the splash of water lapping against the stone exterior.

Chapter Four

The Byzantine images stared down at Cordelia with eyes that had witnessed centuries of prayers, promises, and most recently—selfies. Incense perfumed the air. She tilted her head further back, observing how a gleam of light transformed the gold mosaics into something alive, breathing.

"That one looks a bit judgmental," she whispered to Royce, pointing at a stern-faced saint. "Like he knows I ate gelato for breakfast this morning."

"In Italy, some might consider gelato a food group." Royce's hand found the small of her back, a reassuring touch that radiated through her linen dress. "Besides, that saint, over there, was known for his sweet tooth."

"Where did you hear that?"

"It's historically documented. Look it up." He tucked his hands into his trouser pockets, and his dimples deepened into a broad smirk.

"You're making that up."

Royce rocked on his heels and stared at the ceiling. His

chuckle caught the glimpses from two reverent tourists who didn't appreciate their silence being interrupted by laughter.

"Possibly." He rested his chin on her shoulder. "But you believed me for a second."

Her elbow came within inches of his abdomen, and instead met his hand, which glided down her arm until it interlaced with her fingers. Their eyes met, sharing a secret, a tactile flashback to the previous night.

As they continued exploring the church, their footsteps echoed against the ancient marble, each sound absorbed by centuries of devotion and reverence. Cordelia had expected to feel like a camera-ready tourist—strictly detached. Instead, the architectural wonder created a buzz deep within her core. She'd expected to feel like an intruder, trampling on sacred space. Instead, the beauty welcomed her, as if art transcended the boundaries of belief.

She found herself creating stories for each mosaic they passed, ignoring the traditional stories and giving each character a new life. The martyrs became spies and revolutionaries, passing coded messages in their prayer books. While the women secretly longed for distant, inappropriate men: pirates, poets, artisans. But it was the one severe-looking saint that grabbed her imagination the most. She decided he ran an underground network helping women escape overbearing husbands.

"I would never consider that an expression of compassion."

"It's his disguise. Inside, he's a very caring saint."

"Those are all very dramatic lives," Royce said as she continued her story about twin sisters who poisoned their husbands with tainted communion wine, and escaped with the saint's help. "If the pastry thing doesn't work out for you, I think you have a future in writing."

"I only tell the stories, you write 'em." She patted his chest and pointed at another cluster of distraught people. "Look at them, they're stuck in these walls forever, forced into a sad story."

"Maybe they're simply contemplating the meaning of life."

"Maybe it's an illusion forcing us to contemplate our own existence."

"Do I detect cynicism?"

"Not really. I find it hauntingly beautiful, but sad. They edited out the happy moments in these people's lives, ignoring when they felt passion so deep it exploded from their core. The only one who seems happy is the man on the cloud. And the angels."

"I didn't realize you weren't a fan of religion?"

"You are?"

"Only in the context of history and the beautiful architecture if left behind, but no, I'm not."

"Oh, good, I couldn't imagine forcing kids to—" She stopped. Heat flooded her cheeks. *Where the hell did that come from?*

"Imagine what?" His voice remained neutral despite the slight pause in his breathing.

"Nothing. It was nothing." She turned and put a few steps between them. "Hey, look at that fresco. Is that David with Goliath's head?"

Royce approached her from behind, placed his hand on the small of her back, and kissed her shoulder. They stood in silence, staring at the same mosaic. Twice their eyes met. Twice they looked away.

As they walked the outer perimeter of the church, they discovered a quiet alcove where a gold stand held hundreds of lit candles. Cordelia approached it, hesitated, and then picked up a small unlit candle.

"Is that for your father?"

"Yes." Looking over her shoulder, she invited Royce to join her. "He would have loved this. Not the religious part; he was aggressively agnostic. He would've loved the art and, of course, the history." She touched the candle to a flame and watched it ignite. Cordelia eased the candle into a holder, maintaining a soft grip, as if she held him in the palm of her hand. The ritual felt heavier than she imagined. Centuries of other people's prayers and grief held the outside world at bay.

Royce rested his fingers above hers. "Tell me about him."

"He was..." She smiled, remembering. "Chaotic. Brilliant. Never met an enemy, never disliked a place. He always found reasons to explore," she whispered as a small group passed. "He'd start telling you about cloud formations and end up at the French Revolution, with stops on jazz history and spider mating habits. He was random." The word lodged in her throat. Past tense still felt wrong, as if grammar could undo her loss.

"Sounds like someone else I know."

"I'm not that bad."

"Yesterday you went from discussing Venetian perfumeries to the famous mermaid love story of Venice. In under five minutes."

She laughed and leaned into him. "Dad would've liked you."

"Really?" Royce's fingers wrapped tighter around her hand, sending a warm sensation up her arm.

"Definitely."

"I wish I'd known him."

"Me too." She released her grip, and the candle slid into position.

For a few seconds they watched her candle flame join in a flickering dance, a release of someone's hope or remembrance.

"Ready to look at more mosaics?"

"Only if the tour includes more of your stories."

"Well, I think I can oblige you on that one...only because I like you."

"That's a relief."

They wandered deeper into the basilica, their whispers mixing with the morning prayers from a side chapel. Cordelia felt the strange duality of grief, reflecting on how it could ambush and linger alongside heart-palpitating passion without interfering or consuming. Proof that life insisted on continuation, like the tides that flow in and out of the city.

A few hours later, they found themselves walking among the souvenir shops. The vendors waved people in, luring them with trinkets and clothes emblazoned with Venetian slogans. The afternoon sun had shifted several shades of gold, painting the shadows amber.

"Oh my God, even in that you're still posh." Cordelia adjusted the neon green *Venezia* ball cap, which clashed with his forest green V-neck tee shirt. "And remember, Americans say, 'totally.'"

"Totally," Royce repeated, attempting to flatten the word into a deep, guttural sound. Catastrophic, actually.

She threw on a cheap gondolier's hat, posed, and said, "Now try, 'Dude, that's rad.'" Her laughter filled the shop, and attracted other shoppers to venture in.

"No."

"Oh, come on, just once."

Royce placed the hat back onto a shelf. "No one says that."

"Some do." She slid her arms around his waist, coaxing him to do her bidding. "Say it just once, for me."

"The words 'dude' and 'rad' don't exist in my vocabulary."

"You just said dude," Cordelia giggled, pressing her cheek against his. "Very sexy, Lord Brownell."

"What's sexier is you in that hat."

Her grin ticked sideways. "Maybe I'll buy it then...and wear it around Mayfair."

"I'm sure you will."

"Now let's buy you a cap." Cordelia reached for an orange one, "What about—"

"Do you have something against me? That's hideous."

"Posh." She set it down and reached for a black one. "How's this?"

"Much better, thank you."

She forced the cap on, situating it low over his brow. "Blends in with your hair, but it works."

Royce glanced into a tiny rectangular mirror, "You know this will go to charity when we get home."

"Seriously? You're not going to keep it as a memento?" Her eyes and mouth synchronized into a droopy pout.

"Don't make that face."

"You mean this one?" She wrestled for more eye contact, making him wish he could make love to her right there.

"Yes."

"Does it bother you?"

"Yes." Royce pulled her close, tipping the brim of the cap backwards. "Shall we continue this back at the apartment?"

"Is that a proposition?"

"Yes."

"Mmm, only if you agree to a selfie in our caps."

Royce reflected on the situation while counting the number of people that skimmed through the exact some ball caps, "Alright, but you're not posting that on social media."

"Agreed." Cordelia flipped the cap off his head and purchased both hats before he could change his mind.

They maneuvered past shoppers and those strolling through the busy streets, undecided on where to grab their next meal. Following the crowd, Cordelia paused at the pinnacle of the Rialto Bridge, placing the gondolier's hat on her head.

"Selfie time."

"If you insist."

"I do. Put it on." She was eager. "Now look excited, like you're having the best time of your life."

Royce hugged her waist and attempted an exaggerated expression: wide eyes, toothy smile, sideways ball cap.

She laughed, giving him the opportunity to snap a few loving, sportive photos. Her voice, her giggles, brought freshness into his life. It was as if she knew how to unlock his youthful spirit and expose it to the world.

They took approximately thirty photos, each more ridiculous than the last. Cordelia insisted on peace signs, then bunny ears, then something she called "duck lips" that made him question their entire relationship. A nearby pigeon remained on the bridge's railing throughout, a permanent member of their escapades. It even lingered and posed during their last photo.

Another bridge. Another kiss. He made note.

This time, she led them through the narrow streets, further exploring the San Marco district and doing her best to wander opposite the congestion. When they stumbled upon the Scala Contarini del Bolovo staircase, she insisted they take the tour. Halfway up, she began counting the remaining forty stairs and declared it the second-best workout. After the Eiffel Tower.

Others left as they arrived at the top, giving them a private escape from the noise below. He wrapped his arms around her waist, brushed her hair to one side, and kissed her cheek. The sun sparkled on the canal water, and the sky turned pale yellow. They stood embraced for fifteen minutes, each listening to the cooing birds on nearby buildings.

Cordelia rested her head on his shoulder. Their bodies molded together. Royce captured the moment on his phone. A black and white portrait. Their eyes fixed on one another. Nothing passionate, nothing heated. Just unspoken love.

"Tell me something no one else knows," he murmured against her hair.

"Like what?"

"A secret. A fear. Something you've never admitted."

She held the silence for so long he thought she must be fearless or withholding. But then she blurted out, "Swans. I'm terrified of swans."

He pulled back to see her face. "Swans? Those beautiful white birds?"

"Yes, those things."

"Are you joking?"

"Have you seen them? They're vicious. All that graceful stuff is a lie. They're just pretty geese with better PR." She shuddered. "One chased me when I was eight years old. I stopped at the park to feed them, and this angry bird bolted out of the water, nipping at my feet. I've never trusted them since."

"That's your deepest secret? Your biggest fear?"

"You expected something darker?"

"Actually, yes." Royce examined her expression. "You hid this from everyone, never telling a soul?"

"I swear, I never told anyone. I knew people would think I was overreacting, so I always pretended to like them, but I don't."

"Right." Royce contemplated the revelation as he pictured her interacting with the swans at Hayton Manor.

"Now your turn. What scares Lord Brownell the most?"

He considered several options before settling on one. "Irrelevance. Waking up at sixty and realizing I spent my life studying dead people, while the world around me lived."

A church bell interrupted the moment, and Cordelia turned to face him. "You'll never be irrelevant. Look at everything you've accomplished."

"Except the things that matter most. Shall we go?"

She kissed the palm of his hand and held it to her heart. Her rhythm vibrated against his skin. "I want to stay in this feeling forever."

"Who said it's ending?"

"I hope no one. I mean, look at this view," She motioned toward the city skyline. "I want to believe that this was put here just for us, waiting for this moment. I want to freeze this feeling."

His fingertips caressed her hair, "Which is?"

"I don't have the words to describe it." She turned to face him. "Appreciation...that's your area of expertise."

"Say what you're feeling."

Cordelia gave him a quick kiss and rested her forehead against his face, "I don't want this to end...and some gelato would be *amazing*."

She had a way of deflecting. By now, he recognized when it was becoming too much, but he hoped one day she'd find a way to fully trust herself with him—to expose the emotional side, including the raw, vulnerable notes. But he understood what she meant.

They ambled down the stairs, stopping to feel the cool texture against their fingertips. Royce shared with historical information he remembered about the palace, which he admitted wasn't much. Halfway down, Cordelia took a photo of their palms outstretched on the white stone. Their thumbs overlapped.

Back onto the streets they strolled, attempting to hold hands whenever possible. After visiting another church, they stopped for gelato. Royce decided immediately on the chocolate, but

Cordelia spent several minutes vacillating between amarena and fig, while ignoring the line forming behind them. She chose fig. Royce hoped she relished his touch as much as she savored the gelato.

Chapter Five

At seven AM, the apartment terrace upheld Venice's promise of heat, despite the awning and trailing vines. A water taxi churned below, its wake slapped against the palazzo's foundation. The morning bells began their call. St. Mark's Basilica rang first, followed by Santa Maria del Giglio.

Dressed for the day's outing, Royce arranged breakfast with the same focus he brought to his writing routine—four cornetti on hand-painted plates, espresso and tea cups on matching saucers, and a sugar bowl centered on the table, even though she never used sugar.

He had given up on sleep around six, leaving Cordelia tangled among the sheets after her restless night. Her laptop remained open on the nightstand, the cursor blinking against half-finished cookbook notes.

His phone buzzed against the marble table. Neville Pierson's email appeared: *Re: Estate Planning Adjustments - Confidential Review Required.* He heard Cordelia moving in the bedroom and quickly opened it, scanning the details from his financial planner.

As requested, I've compiled the necessary documentation for restructuring your portfolios to accommodate future beneficiary designations. The family trust modifications you mentioned will require your signature upon return. May I suggest we also discuss future insurance policy adjustments and a prenuptial agreement at that time?

The words "prenuptial agreement" jumped off the screen; words he'd never considered with anyone prior to Cordelia. Necessary, certainly. The family trust demanded it. But now that it was his heart on the line, how would he broach the practicalities with her, without reducing what they shared to a transaction?

"Perfect timing," Cordelia burst onto the terrace, her hair twisted into the usual messy bun she wore during late-night baking sessions at BL London. "Wow, you've been busy." Her laptop tote hung heavy on her shoulder, a swap for the slim bag she'd carried on prior days. "Earl Grey and coffee? You're so sweet."

She poured a cup of tea without sitting, gulping it while simultaneously checking her phone. "I hope I didn't keep you up too much last night?"

"Not at all."

Her blue capris hugged her hips yet hung loose and wrinkled.

"I thought you were sending your clothes out for pressing?"

"Huh, oh, no, I never did." She placed the teacup back onto the saucer. "Do I look okay?"

"You look tired," he said, reaching for her hand, "but beautiful."

"Oh, no." Cordelia pulled her hand back and scanned an email with both thumbs.

"How about lunch at that osteria near—"

"Damn it Jessica," Her eyes, usually bright with curiosity, drooped with exhaustion. "Sorry, Royce." She paused, letting her eyes dart side-to-side. "Yeah, I don't know, maybe."

"Everything alright?"

"Just Jessica being her old self." Cordelia snatched a cornetto and wrapped it in a napkin. "It depends on how fast I get through things. And now I've got to deal with Jessica's screw-up on top of that." She gulped one last cup of tea. "I'm sorry. I'd love to, but I'll have to let you know." She gave him a peck, barely resting her lips against his.

"Don't forget, the cocktail party starts at seven."

She paused in the doorway, offering a smile reminiscent of the Scala. "I haven't forgotten."

"It's important to me."

She patted her tote. "And so is this." She blew him a kiss. "Gotta run, love you." Cordelia didn't wait for his reply.

Her lipstick remained imprinted on the teacup. Royce stared at Neville's email, the words "beneficiary designations" blurred together. The words sank like a pebble in water. Nine months. Nine months of loving her. And long enough to imagine forever. How would he tell her, 'I love you but please sign this document protecting my ancestral fortune.' Without sounding like every calculating aristocrat before him?

He typed out a reply, "Thank you. I'll be in touch when I return to London, and I appreciate your continued discretion regarding the family trust." He closed the laptop, stood, and listened to pigeons cooing on a neighboring roof. In his novel, the Viking hero would've pursued his fleeing bride, reassuring her that only he could keep her safe. But this was the twenty-first century Venice, not the ninth-century warring landscape. Cordelia needed her freedom more than his reassurance or protection.

A pigeon in search of crumbs joined him on the terrace.

Royce finished his tea and tossed a crumb to the bird. "I won't tell if you don't."

11:47 AM - Biblioteca Marciana

Inside the windowless research room, Cordelia rattled her fingers across the laptop keyboard, eager to record her thoughts before they faded away. The room smelled of old paper and modern floor cleaner, an old fragrance that settled onto her clothes. After over three hours of staring at Italian and Latin, her eyes ached from exhaustion. It was at times like this that she appreciated high school typing class. Burning, she closed her eyes, confident her fingers would land on the right key, as she silently recited her thoughts.

Her phone buzzed. Thirty seconds later, it buzzed again. She peeked an eye open and looked at her phone. Royce.

The osteria closes at 2. Meet at 1?
Can't.

Before she could refocus on her typing, it buzzed again. *Doesn't he understand I'm working?*

Cordelia
Later
Cocktail party, 6 pm. Gown delivered.

She read it but didn't respond. *Got it.* He knew she knew. *Why did he keep bringing it up?* The guilt twisted, sharp and sudden. She'd promised herself she would change her habits—no twelve-hour workdays, no choosing a job over him or their relationship. Yet somehow it's exactly where her ambitious plans always led—alone with success.

Royce encouraged without question. He rarely complained, even when he ate dinner alone. And he usually overlooked her excuses. The least she could do was set her work aside for one night.

But then she might never get access again. *One more hour.* Just one more recipe to type up and then she'd make it up to him. A surprise. She looked at her phone locator. It pinned him at the apartment. *Perfect.* She owed him her time and attention.

Four more hours passed, and her phone stayed silent. Suddenly, she preferred his interruptions. But the screen remained dark, and that annoyed her worse than his gentle persistence.

Three hours later...

The historic palazzo glowed like a jewelry box turned inside out. Jasmine and cigarette smoke competed in the humid air, and spilled prosecco near the entrance left the marble a game of treachery. Waiters crouched around the puddle, dabbing rags into the mess.

Cordelia smoothed the bodice of her cream cocktail dress and adjusted the straps that tied in a bow at the base of her neck.

"Why are you fidgeting?" Royce asked, his hand cradled against the small of her back. "You're beautiful."

"I look like someone who snuck in through the service entrance."

"If you'd given yourself more time..."

Their eyes locked onto each other. The criticism, as mild as it was, stung. His assessment was correct. "I know. I'm sorry. I just—."

"Don't apologize. We're here, and I'm certain you'll still be the envy of the night." He snagged two glasses of prosecco from a passing tray. "Just keep the shoes hidden."

"Why? They're designer." She'd bought them on a shopping trip with Cassandra. Definitely an impulse buy, but she thought the pale blue leather provided a hint of personality to an otherwise neutral outfit. "And they're Ada Rose approved."

"Don't get me wrong, I love my niece, but you're taking fashion advice from a baby who can't see beyond black and white right now?" His dimples appeared, causing her to smile.

"I trust her judgment." Cordelia lifted the hem of her skirt and admired the five-inch heels that elevated her to Royce's eye level. "I think she has excellent taste."

His thumb caressed her back. "To hell with them, show your shoes off."

And she did. Women subtly glanced; men catalogued her ankles, and Royce joked her feet needed their own security guard. He volunteered.

The Venice Historical Preservation Society's cocktail reception drew an international crowd, a global who's who that made Cordelia wonder how a pastry chef ever landed among them.

"Lord Brownell." A silver-haired man materialized from the crowd, offering Royce a firm handshake. His narrow-set eyes squinted. "How wonderful you could join us. And this is..."

"Cordelia Dyer," Royce's hand pressed firmly against her back. "She's the executive pastry chef for Bastien Larue."

"How fascinating." He somehow turned the word into five syllables while turning the 's' into a 'z'. "I'm Giorgio Grasso, the society's treasurer. It's such a pleasure, Miss..."

"Ms."

"Ah, yes. Ms. Dyer, have you found anything noteworthy in Venice? Besides our Lord Brownell, of course." His laugh startled her, like a shot of lemon juice to the eye.

She took a sip of Prosecco. "I couldn't begin to list everything. Your city is mesmerizing."

"Yes, I would imagine more interesting than an oven full of soufflés, no?"

Royce wrapped his arm around Cordelia, pulling her closer. "Giorgio, tell me, are you making the architectural presentation tonight?"

"No, no. Guilia will unveil the restoration project this evening," he took Cordelia's hand, "Tell me, Ms. Dyer, or may I call you Cordelia?" He didn't wait for her reply, "Have you had the opportunity to tour our Doge palace?"

"I, we plan to do that next week, I think."

"Maybe I can give you both a private tour."

"We'd like that, thank you." She eased her hand from his grip and cupped her glass.

"Yes, of course, Lord Brownell is one of our favorite patrons." He held his hands together in front of his chest, possibly in gratitude for the large donations but more likely in prayer that it'll continue.

"If you'll excuse us, Giorgio," Royce said, "I see Dr. Morrison across the room."

After escaping Giorgio's lingering goodbyes they weaved

through clusters of people who all seemed to know each other from childhood. Or at least from boarding school. Cordelia couldn't help but stare at one group of women who collectively wore enough diamonds to fund a small nation.

Royce kept a guiding hand on her back, detouring behind a statue. "Well done, Ms. Dyer." He offered her an assuring kiss.

"Don't be deceived, it's the shoes."

"You could be barefoot and still charm these people."

"The night's young." She stole another kiss and wiped the lipstick from his mouth.

Dr. James Morrison turned out to be a rumpled academic who looked as uncomfortable as she felt. Within minutes, the conversation evolved into a dissertation on current manuscript preservation techniques. Royce managed to interrupt long enough to excuse himself to retrieve cold drinks for them; a need with the humid summer air.

"Double prosecco for me, please. It's going to be a long night," she whispered as he made his exit.

"Where did you attend university?" James asked her, letting his Texas accent slip through the cracks of his facade.

"I didn't, not unless you count the four years of culinary school."

She soon learned James enjoyed baking bread when he wasn't up to his elbows in artifacts. He shared his latest triumph, a beer fermented seeded rye with a Guérande salt crust.

"James, I thought you were wearing the black jacket tonight?" Evie Lin. Her British accent dripped like molasses. "Cordelia Dyer, right?" She showcased her petite figure in an off- the -shoulder black dress and a chignon perfectly held up with a pearlized clip. Her eyes catalogued both of them, but revealed nothing.

"Evie. I didn't know you would be here."

"Neither did I. James invited me." Her red manicured nails scraped across the prosecco glass. "Is Royce with you?"

Cordelia answered her questions, making small talk until Royce returned with two chilled prosecco glasses.

"Royce, you look dashing tonight," Evie said, resting her fingertips on his forearm. The gesture lasted two seconds. Cordelia counted. *Aren't you sneaky? Professional enough to deny, but intimate enough to imply something.*

"Thank you." He moved closer to Cordelia, reasserting his presence around her waist.

"Royce, remember when we were up near York doing that fieldwork? The Viking settlement."

"Sure."

"I remember it as if it were yesterday. What a fabulous summer," she laughed like shattered glass. "Sorry, I'm being nostalgic after seeing you at the library. I just can't believe you're so...settled."

The word landed like a slap disguised as a compliment. Settled. *I'd be happy to settle you into the lagoon.* Cordelia sipped her drink, realizing at her current consumption rate, she'd break her own record of polishing off a bottle.

"Cordelia, how's the research going? Is that where you two met?"

"Uh, no, we met in Paris." Her shoulders flared. She moistened her lips ready for further rebuttal, but Royce's fingers traced down her spine.

James nodded, raised his finger to speak, but Evie interrupted him.

"How romantic. Speaking of romance, did you ever publish your paper on the Viking lovers separated in death?"

"Yes, two years ago." Royce said, clearing his throat.

"I remember now, yes, such beautiful writing," she bobbed her shoulders. "How could I forget? You had such a weakness for tragic love stories." Her eyes flicked to Cordelia. "Those beautiful, tragic distractions."

"Evie." Royce snapped like dry wood in a fireplace.

"Oh, I'm embarrassing you." She pressed fingertips to her lips in a practiced giggle. "I'm sorry, Royce, you know I love a good joke."

"Actually, I don't."

Cordelia's gaze drifted across the room, seeking escape from Evie's barbs. A man leaned against a marble column, as if a Roman god watched with amusement. Dark-haired, bronze complexion, and elegant—the way someone stands who knows their innate appeal. When their eyes met, he raised his glass. His attention dropped to her shoes before returning to her face, a smile suggesting he'd found something worth pursuing.

She looked away, resisting any physical response. Heat crept up the back of her neck, and her lips curved into a faint smile. The startled pleasure of being admired after Evie's insults surprised her.

"Cordelia?" The edge in Royce's voice snapped her back into the conversation. Evie talked in the background, her voice like buzzing white noise.

Across the room, the stranger hadn't moved, still watching with a knowing smile.

"Do you know him?" Royce asked.

"A new friend?" Evie's voice elevated with interest, "An old one?"

The man pushed off the column and disappeared into the crowd. His presence lingered like expensive cologne, there and then gone—nothing but an impression.

"No. But he seems to know us." Her eyes met his, finding

comfort in those pools of warmth that softened into a smile. The heat at the back of her neck raced down her spine, sparking desire.

Royce's hand ran down her arm, "There's someone I'd like—."

An older woman with a sharp bob haircut, dripping in pearls interrupted, "Royce, darling, there you are. Giorgio said you were here, and it took me ages to find you."

"Lady Penley, how are you?" Royce said. She hugged him in a maternal embrace. "Mother didn't tell me you'd be here."

"A last-minute decision. The wet summer got to Lord Penley, so here we are." She made eye contact with each of them, indicating a fascinating backstory, which she withheld.

"Lady Penley, may I please introduce Cordelia Dyer. She's the executive pastry chef at BL London."

"Fabulous. How do you stay incredibly thin working there?"

Cordelia politely replied with a "thank you" and quickly handed the social graces back to Royce, who introduced Evie and James. The pleasantries took less than thirty seconds and hinged on Lady Penley, who didn't appreciate Evie mentioning her son's broken engagement and, apparently, social embarrassment.

"Evie. Dr. Lin, from London, correct?"

"You've heard of me?"

"Yes, my dear. Stones leave ripples in the water, therefore, it's best to throw them lightly."

Cordelia choked on her prosecco, looking away to hide her smile.

"Goodness. Don't worry, those bubbles get to me too, dear." Lady Penley softened her eyes and offered a tissue. "If you'll excuse us, Royce, the Contessa Capaldi is here and would like to meet you. She's known your parents for eons."

"Right. In a moment, Lady Penley, if that's alright."

"We shouldn't keep her waiting much longer."

"Go," Cordelia said. "I'll see you in a minute."

He left with Lady Penley, who steered him like her prized yacht.

Cordelia watched Evie eyeing him, noticing the microscopic tension around her crinkled nose. She squared herself to James and cleared her throat. "Tell me more about your baking? Are you self-taught?"

"Yes, yes, I am. I took a course last year in Brittany. Well, not exactly a course, more like a day of learning. I traveled France extensively before beginning my position here, and ran into a chef who taught French bread techniques, so I thought, why not..."

"James, I don't believe she wanted that many details."

"Did he have his own boulangerie?" Cordelia said.

"He does. Here let me send you the details." James pulled out his phone, typed in her number, and forwarded the bakery information.

"Perfect, thank you."

"Tell me about your cookbook, Cordelia." She angled her body, exposing her leg and six-inch heel through the dress' slit. She smirked when James coughed and held a five-second gaze on her slim thigh. "It must consume your time."

"No more than any other project."

"I remember my first one. Nothing else mattered." She tucked her hand under James' elbow. "Dr. Brownell was an excellent mentor. He taught me how to organize, to compart-mentalize my tasks, so I could have a life."

"How fortunate."

Morrison excused himself to the bar, asking Evie if she wanted another drink. She did—a vodka tonic with two lime twists.

"I should apologize," Evie said, stepping closer and squaring her body to Cordelia's. Fine-boned like a bird, her face appeared more fragile, features that made men want to protect her. "I'm being awful, aren't I? Dredging up old times with Dr. Brownell. It's just, seeing him here, after everything that happened at..."

She trailed off, letting the implication hang. Cordelia steadied herself, her ankles tired of holding one position.

"He seems very happy. He always needed someone practical to balance his drive, but all the others," she rolled her eyes and sighed, "So wrong for him."

"I didn't realize you were so close."

"Something like that." Evie's smile turned wistful. "We're very similar. Back then, when I was in my graduate program, we were two academics feeding each other's obsessions for the past. It was intense. Not healthy, really."

"Funny, I heard that about your relationship with Dr. Andrews."

Her almond eyes narrowed. "You're mistaken." Her small breasts puffed outward, like a peacock waiting to fight. "I can see why Royce settled with you—different passions. Less competition."

Every word perfectly chosen. Every one sliced.

"But like I said," Evie continued, "I'm very sorry if I've made you feel uncomfortable. We had such good times together, academically speaking."

"Right."

She touched Cordelia's arm, as if they were co-conspirators. "As you know, he has such a generous nature. Always trying to help, even when it costs him professionally."

"It's who he is."

"I hope he's learned to maintain better boundaries."

"And here we go." James reappeared with Royce a few steps behind carrying their reinforcement drinks.

"Lovely." Evie's social smile snapped back into place. She

clutched the drink harder than James' elbow. "Now listen, we must have coffee before you leave. I'm dying to hear how you and Royce met."

"Maybe on our next trip," Royce said. His arm snugged Cordelia into his side, grazing the top of her buttock before resting his hand on her waist. "Now, if you'll excuse us." He barely waited for acknowledgment, leading her away from the crowd.

In the fairy-lit terrace garden, whispers echoed off the walls.

"Are we hiding?" Cordelia said.

"Regrouping."

"How was the Contessa?"

"Rich and easily distracted, as advertised. What did Evie say?"

"Why do you ask?"

"Because I know her, and more importantly, I know you, and that expression tells me you're bothered."

"It's nothing." She took a large sip, bigger than advisable, especially at an event where leering eyes are always watching. "She said you fed each other's obsessions for the past."

His jaw tightened. "That was—."

"Years ago, I know. When you were passionate about teaching and found someone who understood." She heard the bitterness in her voice. She hated it. "I get it."

"Actually, I don't think you do." He set his glass on a stone bench situated between rows of manicured hedges. "Evie was a brilliant student with unhealthy attachments. And yes, I shared my passion for archeology with her, but I never crossed the line. She was my student, that's all."

"Okay."

"She has a tendency to revise history. To make things sound more intimate than they were. She did that with Gavin, until..." He caressed Cordelia's hand. "Evie is smart and determined.

But she's nothing more than a former student with grandiose memories."

Giorgio appeared as subtle as a foghorn, insisting everyone return inside for the presentation. Cordelia smiled, nodded, and socially engaged, but the dark waters stirred.

Royce maintained a soft pressure against her lower back, twice finding an opportunity to kiss her shoulder. By the time they escaped two hours later, her feet screamed and her cheeks ached from diplomatic smiling.

Their water taxi glided through the dark canal, its engine purring beneath them. They sat close, their shoulders touched, but the space between them felt vast. The driver hummed something operatic, oblivious that the lovers maintained controlled appearances. Reflections from palazzo windows offered a light show on the dark water—beauty she wanted to share with him. She held back. Her celebrated shoes had left a blister on her heel. She ignored it.

Royce removed his dinner jacket and folded it across his arm, never offering it to her as a buffer from the night air. A small wedge that felt larger in the silence.

Cordelia took his hand and apologized for missing lunch. He understood, he always did, but she promised herself it wouldn't happen again. As she had in Paris and London, she chose Royce, assuring him things would change. The words tasted familiar on her tongue. *I won't hurt him again.*

The taxi slowed and approached the dock. Royce placed his coat around her shoulders and kissed the back of her hand.

Chapter Six

The bedsheets rustled as Cordelia shifted away from him, subtle but deliberate. For the first time they'd made love with reserved passion—hesitated touch, aware of their surroundings rather than immersed in intimacy, and her desire felt unsatisfied. The distance between them left him staring at the ceiling wondering how she could sleep with their unresolved wedge.

Around them, the palazzo creaked, releasing centuries of lovers' quarrels absorbed into its bones. While outside, a water taxi's engines cut through the night's silence like whispered accusations.

After what seemed like an hour, she murmured, "You're thinking loudly."

"Sorry." He turned toward her, finding her profile in the dim canal light. "I thought you were asleep." Royce inched closer, feeling the curve of her hips. Her body relaxed into him.

"Just thinking. Your circle of friends are..."

"They're not my friends. They're a social circle that occasionally overlaps with my family's obligations." He reached for her hand under the covers, finding her receptive to the touch. "You'll get accustomed to them."

"Does that include Evie?"

There it was. The wedge.

"She's an exception."

"How? Like unusual, I'll never see her again at these functions or off-limits, I'm not allowed to discuss her?"

"It's unlikely you'll see Evie again. She was never one for public events."

"Are you sure about that? She seemed to love the attention."

Royce counted the number of times Evie touched his arm—six—four on the forearm and two on his bicep. Not unusual. She touched everyone, men and women, when she talked. Although, six seemed excessive. "I'll admit, she can sometimes be peculiar."

"Peculiar? Try obsessive," Cordelia rolled over, eyes open, searching his face. "And twenty-seven hours, Royce? That's not maintaining boundaries with a student. That's companionship."

"I prefer exhaustion and poor judgment. Perhaps we should continue this in the morning."

She propped up on an elbow. "It is morning. And anyway, I can't sleep."

He sighed, mirroring her position. "It was my third year lecturing. She was brilliant and eager, always staying after seminars with questions. I was flattered when she expressed an interest in my research."

"Of course."

"Then she started showing up at my office during off hours. Texting about non-academic matters. And eventually offering herself as an off-the-record research assistant on the weekends."

"And the alarm bells didn't go off?"

A knot of guilt wedged in his chest. "Looking back on

things, yes, but I was trying to mentor her. After that weekend I discussed it with Gavin, and that's when..."

"When their story began."

"Right. But I swear, the line was never crossed. Nothing ever happened between me and Evie."

"But twenty-seven hours, Royce. At some point in that marathon, didn't you realize it was inappropriate?"

"Of course I did. Then she started crying about her parents' expectations."

"And you stayed?"

"Yes. I thought I could relate and encourage her."

"You told her your father is an earl?"

"I wanted to help."

"You gave her a reason to obsess more."

Royce sat up and leaned against the headboard, running his fingers through Cordelia's hair as she cozied into his lap. "We returned to our research and didn't talk for several hours. Then I realized we'd finished off the pizza I'd ordered the night before, and it was Sunday morning. When I returned with coffee and bagels, she apologized for being emotional. Come to find out, she'd ended things with her boyfriend of three years...because he didn't understand her goals like I did."

"She said that, and you didn't get the hell out of there?"

"I tried to leave, packed everything up and told her we both needed sleep. But she has a way of keeping you engaged."

"You mean, you."

"Right, me." The admission, a pool of vinegar in his gut. "I thought I could handle the situation professionally. I had planned to encourage her brilliance but set better boundaries."

"Royce, if she says you get her better than her ex, the lines been crossed. There aren't boundaries."

"Lesson learned." The snap in his voice gave hesitation. "That's when I went to Gavin. I requested that he take her on as a graduate student, and then I told her there wouldn't be any more after-hours meetings or personal discussions."

"And? Is that when their affair began?"

"Not at first. I don't know exactly when it began."

Cordelia moved closer, exploring his eyes. "Did you love her?"

"No."

"Not even a bit?"

"Bloody hell, Cordelia, she was my student."

"Like that's ever stopped a professor before." She leaned back on her hands, and a yellow stream of light highlighted half of her face.

"Well, it stopped me."

"So, if she hadn't been a student then yes, you could've loved her?"

"Are you trying to bait me?"

"No. I just want you to admit you loved her."

"I cannot admit what isn't true."

"Okay." She swung her legs out of bed, grabbing her robe. "I think you need to be honest with yourself, about all of it, because, to me, it's more than a fleeting intellectual connection."

"I never loved her."

"Only because she was your student." The light illuminated Cordelia's back, casting a glow around her nakedness.

"Evie was never anything except a responsibility. One I handled poorly."

"Right." She tied the robe with sharp movements. "Just a brilliant, beautiful woman who understood your work and wanted to spend days on end in your company. And even tonight, she looked at you with those sappy, dewy-eyes. Nothing romantic about that."

Royce recognized the attitude—the brittle sarcasm that masked deeper hurt. Usually, it emerged when discussing her career or something related to Daniel. "Where are you going?"

"To get water...air...space. Distance from whatever hold she has on you." Cordelia stood at the foot of the bed. "One more thing, we've been together nine months. Nine months of real life, up-and-down shit versus one weekend of academic obsession. Why does she act like that trumps everything, and everyone else?"

He grabbed a pair of shorts draped over a chair. "Cordelia, I'm trying to tell you, there are no feelings, at all."

She paused at the door. "Fine. I'm not angry at you. I'm angry at the situation. I'm angry at her for playing games, and most of all at myself for letting her get to me."

"Then ignore her. She doesn't matter. Neither do her tactics."

"Easy for you to say. You're not the one being insulted, as if I'm some anchor dragging you down, holding you back."

"You know that's not how I feel." He walked over to her. "Come back to bed."

"Later." She left, closing the door with deliberate quiet, a sound that felt louder than a slam.

He stood, listening to her movement around the kitchen: glasses clinked, the fridge closed, a drawer slammed. He told himself to follow, to do a better job explaining the situation, to tell her *why* Evie can twist a knife and manipulate his guilt. But something held his feet to the bedroom floor—perhaps the recognition that his past had crept into their present. Uninvited. Like the Venetian fog that simply appears.

In the corner of the room, his phone lit up. Against better judgment, he checked it.

Evie: Lovely seeing you tonight. I hope Cordelia enjoyed herself.

He deleted it and turned his phone face down. Cordelia had sensed correctly. Evie had inserted herself back into his life. The devoted student who hung on his every word, who morphed into desperation. The broken figure in a hospital bed, apologizing while bandages covered self-inflicted wounds. *Was she always calculating?* The thought unsettled him more than her presence in Venice. Because if she were, what did that say about his judgment? And if she wasn't, if her manipulative nature was shaped at university, what did that say about his ability to help her heal?

Royce dropped his shorts to the floor and crawled back into bed. He listened as a boat created a wake that slapped against the wooden dock. The bedroom door swished open and closed.

Cordelia tip-toed to the bathroom, letting the water run for several minutes. The water stopped. The light switch clicked off. She slid under the covers without touching him. An ocean of cold sheets divided their bodies.

He sighed, "I'm sorry."

"For what? Having a past? I don't blame you."

"I do."

"Royce, don't. She's doing this for her own agenda. Don't blame yourself."

"But?"

"But whatever you both think you owe her, you don't."

"I at least owe her professional support. But nothing more."

"That's why she looks at you like she owns you."

"I promise you, she doesn't."

Yet, she'd bled on his hands. He'd held her when she sobbed, wanting to disappear. The memory returned: a towel pressed against her wrists, her voice raw, and the requests. Questions became promises, apologies became expectations, and when she left the hospital, she took his guilt as emotional debt.

"Cordelia…"

"Shhh…" She rolled toward him and nuzzled under his arm. "This is our future, right?" Her eyes glanced up, wide and communicating hope.

He bridged the gap between them, pulling her against his chest. "This matters. This is real."

"Even when I make us late?"

"Even then."

"And miss tennis dates?"

"Especially then."

She laughed, her chin pressing into his chest. "Liar."

"Only occasionally." He kissed her hair, smelling the lingering floral fragrance from her styling products.

They lay quietly. Cordelia's breathing softened. Her body still held tension as she folded her legs away from his. Royce counted her breaths and stared at the ceiling.

The next day, he'd speak to Evie, set clearer boundaries, and let her know that whatever she thought they shared no longer existed. It was time for those ghosts to be buried and put to rest.

By 6 AM she'd barely slept, but Cordelia eased out from beneath the covers and dressed for a run. Royce stirred but didn't wake, his breathing deep and even after their restless night.

Soft, hazy light filled the room, replacing the golden blaze that earlier had pierced the darkness.

For a moment she watched Royce, his eyes fluttered open as his hand ran across the empty, vast bed. She crawled toward him. "Going for a run."

"Mmm. Early." He moved closer, his hand reaching for her, fingers grazing across her wrist.

"Just restless. Need to move." She leaned down and kissed his forehead. "Go back to sleep."

The kitchen glowed with under-cabinet lighting, casting shadows onto the white marble surfaces. On the island, a bowl of oranges and lemons scented the air. Beside it, her water bottle and folded paper. Her name in his handwriting.

C—It's 4 am. You were in my dreams. When I woke, I found myself listening, thinking as you slept. Your warm body curled against me. Your breath, delicate and peaceful. For a second I wanted to wake you, to tell you what I failed to say last night. It's what I want to tell you every night from today onward.

Your essence drowns out the noise, and in a sea of people, I only see you. You are the one who lingers in my thoughts. And I have loved you since Paris. Yours, R

A watermelon of emotions lodged in her throat. She paused over each word in the note, debating whether to take her run after all. Her heart clamored for Royce. Her body wanted him. His vanilla scent lingered on the note. She breathed it in and re-read it. *How could I doubt him?*

She tucked the note into her running shorts, topped off her water bottle, and scrolled through Spotify. Final choice—Sofiane Pamart. Mentally she was ready to escape, to feel her body sweat out the toxins. Evie had gotten under her skin, but why? As a young pastry chef, she'd succeeded where others lagged behind. She'd achieved her goals and brilliantly dominated her industry. Now, love had conquered her, despite resistance.

Despite everything, she was terrified. Not of losing—she'd survived heartbreak before—but of not being worthy of keeping.

Cordelia skipped down the stairs and bolted from the palazzo, pausing long enough to appreciate the garden roses blooming in various shades of peach, yellow, and red. *Just like a Venetian sunrise.*

Her phone dinged. Jessica.

Hey boss! Have three meetings for your calendar. Two for Monday when you get back and one for Tuesday. And the team says hi.

She halted, walking in circles as she replied.

Cordelia: What? With who?

Jessica: Lady Rinde, an American couple, and a TV producer

Cordelia: What do they want? And why on my first day back??
Jessica: You're gone for two weeks. They're anxious.

Cordelia paced, waving at a man who peeled the tarp from his boat. The air smelled like the forest, only saltier.

Cordelia: Fine.
Did you get the orders placed in time? You got enough butter, right?
Jessica: Yes. Yes.
Back to micromanaging, Chef?

She knew how to push a reaction out of Cordelia, to prove her 'boss' status. *Someone else who likes to bait me.* Cordelia typed out a response, deleted it, and replied with a simple "No."

Jessica: You're on holiday. Have fun.

Cordelia: Then don't create fires that require my attention.

Jessica sent a meme of a cat fighting fires. Their professional and personal relationship had been built on frustrations. The list of grievances they held against each other was layered like a croissant, but now Cordelia considered them a team, a vital part of each other's successes.

She pocketed the phone and noticed a baker emerging from a side door of his shop. With flour-dusted hands he sipped coffee, enjoying the cat that purred at his feet. Two elderly women arm-in-arm strolled past, their conversation an indecipherable rapid melody.

Against the stone walkways, her feet pushed a burning sensation upward, sending newfound energy into her lungs. The air tingled. Over bridges and around corners, the sound of her sneakers hitting the stone streets echoed off narrow walls, creating a rhythm that competed with Sofiane's piano. Together they found a solid rhythm, an ebb-and-flow like the watery canals she ran alongside. Her ponytail whipped at her neck as she sped up past the fish market. Vendors arranged the morning's catch on beds of ice, while shiny red tomatoes tempted her palate.

A church bell rang, signaling a new hour. *Just a little longer.*

Images of the previous night became distractions, forcing her to push harder. She blew out an extended exhale. Her pounding heart attempted to outrun the thought of Evie's fingers on Royce's sleeve, those casual touches that lasted more than a second. She wanted to cut the thread that connected them—those promises in the hospital room. Could their nine months together sever Evie's hold?

A gondolier whistled, called out, and blew her a kiss. Cordelia smiled and pushed herself faster. Turning alongside a small canal, she noticed the water captured each stride, fragmenting her reflection.

By the time she circled back toward their neighborhood, her shirt was soaked. Her legs trembled, but the burn felt clean. If only love were as simple as a morning run—no illusions, only satisfaction.

Her pace slowed to a walk. Venice stirred like a cat from a long slumber, nuzzling at her for attention. Royce texted, wondering if she'd run to Rome. She paused, snapped a selfie, and sent it to him with the message, "And let you miss this face? I don't think so!"

A sweet fragrance grabbed her attention and lured her into a shop. On the counter, brioche buns glistened with butter and a lemon cream. Without hesitation, Cordelia ordered, knowing Royce might have breakfast waiting. *Research,* she told herself, watching the elderly woman select four plump ones and place them in a bag. She thanked her and hurried away, anxious to share the feast with Royce.

By the time she reached the palazzo door, the warm bag had seeped butter onto her hands. A reminder that simple things bring pleasure, especially when shared with someone you love. She boarded the elevator and gazed at her reflection. The edges of the note, pressed against her thigh, crackled. She patted it and whispered, "I only see you, too." The elevator dinged. *You're my North Star.*

Chapter Seven

The elevator doors opened, delivering Cordelia into the main foyer beside the living room. She heard Royce typing on his laptop as he mumbled the words in sync with his fingers. A familiar rapid-fire sound; a comforting pattern.

On the terrace, she found him exactly where she expected, still in his shorts, finger-combed hair sticking out at various angles, and an empty espresso cup resting precariously on the edge of the table.

"Wow, those Vikings really have your attention," she said, placing the paper bag on the table.

He didn't look up. "I see you made it back from Rome."

"I see you missed me." Cordelia poured herself a cup of coffee from a nearby table. She found it odd that they still hadn't seen a single housekeeper, yet the apartment always appeared refreshed.

"Good run?"

"Fantastic, actually." She reached for a brioche bun and waved it under his nose. "I even brought treasures."

"Mmm, you read my mind." His fingers never stopped

moving. "Just... need to finish this scene. Haldor's about to discover his wife isn't dead after all, and if I stop now..."

"I know, you'll lose the momentum." She bit into the brioche, letting out an exaggerated moan. "Oh, my God. This is incredible." She moaned again. "All this butter...and lemon cream." She took another bite. "I think there's a hint of orange zest."

"Mmmhmm." Royce continued mumbling as he typed.

"The pastry's flaky. And warm, just the way you like it." She licked cream from her finger, glaring at him. "You're really going to let me eat all four by myself?"

"You'd better leave one for me."

"Just one? Babe, these are breakfast gold."

He murmured.

She moved behind him, reading over his shoulder. "Is Haldor's wife the one who—"

"Cordelia." He caught her hand as it reached to hug him from behind. "Five more minutes, please."

"Fine." She grabbed the crumpled napkin to the left of his laptop and dusted her hands clean.

"Sorry love. This chapter's been fighting me for weeks and now—."

"And now, the woman you claim to adore is standing here sweaty and bearing pastries." She leaned against the table, blocking his full view of the screen.

"Cordelia..."

"What? Am I distracting you from your fictional friends?"

His eyes scanned her body and returned to the screen. "You're literally sitting on my notes."

"Am I?" She stood, removed her tank top, and reached in front of him for the brioche bag.

He sighed, saving his document. "You're determined to disrupt me, aren't you?"

"Me? Never." She bit into the brioche, licking a dollop of cream from her finger. "I'm just eating my breakfast. All alone. While my partner chooses imaginary people over…"

"What are doing?"

"I told you, eating my breakfast." She moved out of his way and sipped her coffee. "How long have you been out here?"

"I came out right after you left for your run."

"Royce, that was over an hour ago. Have you moved at all?"

"Yes, I got an espresso. And text you."

She laughed. "You're hopeless."

"Give me five minutes."

"One."

"Three."

"One." She dropped her running shorts to the floor. "Don't even think about touching that laptop."

"Or?"

"I'm hiding it for the rest of the day."

"You wouldn't dare."

"Try me, Lord Brownell."

He pushed back from the table, pulling her onto his lap. "You're a distraction."

"I know." She kissed his nose.

"I'll never get this book completed in time if you keep this up."

"Then maybe I should go shower, alone." She pretended to stand, knowing he'd pull her back.

"Alright, you've got my attention." He wrapped his arms around her waist, holding her steady. "Tell me again, how was your run?"

"Relaxing. Venice is magical at sunrise. There were a few of the locals out, but otherwise it's pretty quiet. One guy flirted with me."

"A Venetian flirted? That's rare. Should I be jealous?"

"Definitely. And..." She took a sip of coffee, intentionally making him wait. "He offered to show me a special canal."

"Did he?"

"I swear that's what he said." She repositioned herself on his lap. "I told him my partner is a Viking historian who abandons me for fictional warriors, so I might take him up on his offer."

"Who's abandoning whom? You left me alone in bed."

"I couldn't sleep. Besides, I need to maintain this body you claim to admire."

"I do admire it." His hand slid along her thigh. "Considerably."

"Prove it."

He studied her face, stood, and lifted her with him.

She squealed, wrapping her legs around his waist. "Channeling Haldor?"

"You challenged me." He carried her toward the living room and laid her on the sofa, caging her with his arms. "And I accepted."

"I need to be sure and thank your warrior guy." She arched beneath him, watching his eyes darken and playfully poked his ribs.

He yelped. She did it again, finding the ticklish spot she'd discovered on their third night together. Royce caught her hands, pinning them above her head. They wrestled, laughed, and tangled their bodies.

"Yield?"

"Never." She tried to look defiant but giggled. "Death before dishonor."

"Very dramatic." He leaned closer, his mouth inches from hers. "What would your staff say if they could see you now?"

"That their boss has excellent taste in authors?"

"Flattery, but it won't save you."

"From what? Show me." She held his gaze for several seconds, lost in the inner expanse within his eyes.

The kiss started softly but deepened, morning coffee, sweet pastry and an underlying heat that never quenched. Her hands pulled him closer, running through his messy hair. His body settled over her, comforting, satisfying. She felt the tingle of his fingers gliding down her side.

Outside, his laptop chimed with an incoming FaceTime call. They froze.

"Ignore it," she murmured against his mouth.

It chimed again.

"What if it's an emergency?" He hurried to the terrace. "It's Marcus."

"This early?"

"Something must be wrong." He answered it, greeting Marcus, Emma, and Ada Rose.

Cordelia jumped up and stealthily redressed, while Royce made small talk. She slid onto his lap, adjusting her hair.

Their faces filled the screen. Ada Rose sat on Emma's lap, banging a toy on Marcus' hand. She had an orange residue on her cheeks and happily babbled when Cordelia said hello to her.

"I'm glad we caught you," Marcus said.

Royce leaned around Cordelia's shoulder. "Is everything all right?"

"Oh, sure, yes. We just wanted to chat with you, both of you, before you headed out."

"Mama." Ada Rose babbled, waving her rubber giraffe toy.

"Are you conducting a band?" Cordelia leaned forward. "Hi." She waved at her.

"What's going on? What couldn't wait?" Royce's voice deepened as he emphasized each word.

"Right, well, you're both impossible to pin down in London,

and we weren't sure when everyone would be in a relaxed frame of mind—" Marcus tapped his finger against his tea mug.

"Relaxed for what?" Royce said.

"It's nothing, just hear me out."

"We're here, tell us, please?"

"Marcus and I have been updating our wills, and we need to name guardians for Ada Rose," Emma said.

"Oh." Cordelia sat up straight. Her spine tensed, and despite Royce's hand on her lower back, she felt ill. The word transported her to when her father called, wanting to discuss his will. She'd assured him there wasn't a need, that he'd survive, but he saw the future better than she did.

"Babababa." Ada Rose blew a raspberry that sent orange droplets flying.

"Oh." Marcus dabbed his black shirt with a monogrammed handkerchief.

"Wills? Why?" Royce asked.

"Oh, Royce, there's nothing to worry about, it's only in the..." Emma searched for the words while dabbing Ada Rose's face.

"In the event something happens to both of us, we need to have guardians listed. It's nothing serious, I assure you." Marcus moved his face closer to Ada Rose. "You're very charming, darling, but pappa doesn't want to share your breakfast."

"If you're willing," Emma said.

Their words reverberated. Cordelia felt Royce's arm tighten around her waist.

"I, uh, of course. You know I'll always be here for her, whatever you need," Royce said.

"As we expected, but specifically," Marcus faced the camera, "We mainly called to ask Cordelia—."

"We would love for you to be her guardian, if that's acceptable to you?" Emma eyed the screen, looking directly at

Cordelia. "We're finally having her christening next month, and we can't think of anyone we'd rather have than you and Royce."

Cordelia's throat closed. The honor, the trust—the formal inclusion into their family. But the weight of being chosen to help guide a precious little girl's life crashed directly into her chest.

"I..." She looked at Ada Rose, who gnawed on the giraffe and then whacked Emma on the arm. "Are you sure? I mean, I'm not, we're not—"

"Married?" Emma's expression softened. "Cordelia, forget Royce is here, sorry, love."

"Understood," Royce said, squeezing Cordelia's waist.

"Cordelia, you've been family since the moment Royce first said your name. He lights up."

"Don't embarrass me," he said.

"She's right, you're family, married or not," Marcus interjected. "Besides, Ada Rose made it clear it should be you."

Cordelia laughed, feeling watery pools in her eyes.

"Dadadada." Ada Rose shrieked, as if in agreement.

"See? She agrees," Emma said. "We're meeting with the lawyers next week to finalize everything. So you have time to think about it, but—"

"Yes," Cordelia said, surprising herself with the immediacy of her answer. "Yes, I'd love to."

"Really?" Emma's face lit up. "Oh, lovely. I had an entire speech prepared about why we wanted you to say—"

"She said yes, Em," Marcus interrupted gently. "Don't talk her out of it."

The tears threatened, turning into droplets on her cheek.

"Darling," Royce murmured, kissing her shoulder and dabbing the tear away. "You all right?"

She nodded, not trusting her voice.

"We should let you go," Emma said. "But thank you, both of you."

"Yes, thank you. And welcome to the madness," Marcus cut his eyes at Royce. "Speaking on her behalf, she couldn't ask for a better uncle."

"Mama." Ada Rose waved her hands, sending the giraffe flying offscreen.

They waved goodbye and disconnected. Cordelia, stunned, leaned back into Royce's lap. Godmother. Guardian. Life-altering, almost larger-than-life words; an official role she didn't even have with her own niece.

"You can say no," Royce said quietly. "If it's too much."

"It's not too much." She turned to face him. "It's everything, it's amazing. Your family is..."

"I think they'd all correct you to say, 'our family'."

She curled into his lap, feeling his arms wrap around her like a cocoon of safety. Somehow, he understood the weight of her emotions. Somehow he knew all she needed in that moment was to be held. To sit safe in his arms, and sort through the tangle of emotions—joy at being chosen, fear of the responsibility, and wonder at it all.

"Godmother," she whispered against his chest. "That's some serious shit."

"Mmm, it is." His hand stroked her back.

"She can do sleepovers with me, and I can teach her to bake cookies, and we'll watch Disney movies together."

"If she has time. I'm afraid Uncle Royce will be taking her on hikes in the north, and reading Tolstoy to her."

"Tolstoy, oh my God, you're going to depress the girl before she's a teen," Cordelia laughed and kissed his earlobe. "I think my idea's more fun. Plus, she can talk boys with me." She pulled back, waiting, examining his clamped mouth.

"That conversation will end before it begins."

"What? Why?"

"I know Marcus, she won't date until she's at university. Won't even be allowed to think about boys until then." Royce slid his hand down Cordelia's back, letting it rest under her thigh.

"She'll definitely change that rule." Cordelia repositioned herself, straddling his hips.

"We might have to wager that one." He kissed her, letting his teeth graze her lip. "And I'm sure I'll lose."

"Me too." She climbed out of his lap. "I guess I'll get ready for the library and let you get back to your research."

Royce closed his laptop. "I think we should celebrate."

"Okay? What do you want to do?"

"I'll give you a hint, it involves that very large, enormous shower in there, and significantly less clothing."

She backed into the doorway, pausing to drop her shorts. "That one? In there?"

Royce stood and followed her. "The very one." He removed his shirt.

She backed toward the bedroom, pulling him along. "Since I'm going that way...you might as well come along."

"Right, conserve the water." At the doorway, Royce pulled her close. "What I said in the note, I meant. Since Paris, it's only you."

"Since Paris." Cordelia grabbed the strings of his shorts and pulled him toward the bathroom.

Chapter Eight

Between families navigating strollers between vegetable stalls, tourists photographing their cappuccinos, and university students loitering around the trees, the square near Campo Santa Margherita hummed with activity. Royce hurried to the cafe, five minutes late for his lunch with James.

"Royce." James waved from the patio corner table, papers strewn across the top. He half-stood and pumped Royce's hand, squeezing firmly. "Perfect timing, I just ordered all of us espressos. I hope that's all right?"

"Yes, thank you." Royce settled into the black metal chair, noting there was a third seat at the table. "All of us, are we expecting someone else?"

"Ah, yes. Should have mentioned—Evie's joining us." James busied himself stacking papers, corners protruding at odd angles.

"Gentlemen, I'm so sorry I'm late."

"Not to worry at all," James said, standing to pull out her chair. "We weren't waiting long."

She situated into her seat, a lioness observing her prey. "Is Cordelia joining us?"

"No, she's at the library today." He looked at his phone, which sat beside his water glass. "And if I know her, doing some shopping afterwards." Royce excused himself, stepped inside the restaurant, and texted Cordelia.

Meet back at the apartment soon?

Maybe. I'm wrapping things up, but I need to get a dress for tonight.

Want company?

Cordelia responded with a heart and laughing face. He decided not to mention Evie's presence at lunch, and instead replied, "Love you, Ms. Dyer."

When he returned to the table, Evie jerked her hand off James' knee.

"Sorry about that. I forgot I had a scheduled call."

Evie accepted her espresso from the waiter, smiling at him with a flirtatious grin. James straightened in his chair. "You said Cordelia was doing some shopping, I'd be happy to be her tour guide."

"Thank you. I believe that by now she knows the boutiques better than most Venetians. Yesterday, she was giving gelato recommendations to an elderly couple who'd lived here fifty years."

"Speaking of recommendations," James leaned forward, "Evie was telling me she's been recommended for a consulting position with the Naval Museum."

"Yes, well, it's only a recommendation, but James is encouraging me to pursue it." She patted his arm. "You're such a good friend."

Royce watched how James' toothy grin brightened his face, but dissipated when Evie angled her body toward Royce.

"I read your novel." Evie shifted her chair closer, casual but deliberate.

"So you've said."

She stirred her espresso, clinking the spoon against the side of the cup. "You made the right choice, leaving academia."

"It's worked out well." Royce leaned back in his seat, tucking his fingertips into his pockets. "So, James—"

"But you're free, just like you wanted."

"That's one way of looking at it." Royce looked away. "James, tell me about your presentation for the conference."

"It's on synchrotron radiation and micro diffraction analysis of ancient textiles. I'm presenting alongside Dr. Mason from the University of Alberta."

"Are you attending this year?" Evie asked Royce. She bit the corner of her lip, reminding him of how she'd approach with questions after a lecture—pensive and engrossed, hanging onto his explanations.

"No, I'll be in Toronto and New York for engagements."

"Engagements? Are you speaking at a different conference?" Her voice squeaked at a hopeful pitch.

"Just appearances for my next book."

"Exciting. Is Cordelia joining you?"

Royce locked his jaw and stared at Evie. James cleared his throat, sipped his espresso, and fiddled with the papers in his satchel. The sounds around them intensified: chairs scraping against the ground, dishes rattling on trays, church bells ringing.

"Is anyone else ready to order lunch?" James asked, clearing his throat again.

"You look so serious, Royce. Did I upset you? You know I mean well." She rested her hand on his arm, letting her fingers curl against his skin. "I never meant to offend you, please forgive me."

He pulled his arm away from her, aware James looked in every direction except at him and Evie. "Perhaps we should talk sometime, but right now is not the appropriate time."

James took a gulp of his coffee and jumped up, holding his bag under his arm. "I should check on those concert tickets for tomorrow night. Evie, are you still coming?"

"If I can. You know how unpredictable my schedule is."

"Right. Of course. I'll be right back, if you don't mind me leaving my bag."

"James, wait. You stay and let me get the tickets...as a gift for the two of you."

After a debate between the two, James dashed off and Royce returned to his seat, shifting his chair further away from Evie.

"James is a good man," Royce said.

"I agree."

"My guess is, he's in love with you."

"Probably," her voice chilly at best. "It's sweet, but I James is..."

"Safe? Predictable?"

She traced the rim of her cup. "Is that how you describe Cordelia?"

"Leave her out of this."

"Do you honestly think James understands what it's like to hold someone's life in their hands, to share raw feelings with each other in that moment? I don't think he does. But you do. You and I know each other—."

"Drop it, Evie."

"Fine, Dr. Brownell. As a colleague, I'm asking for professional courtesy when I email you regarding my research findings."

"Professionally, I'm declining."

"Gavin always said you were obstinate and condescending. But I think you're just fearful."

"Evie, this isn't necessary," he leaned toward her. "This isn't you."

"I'm only asking for your professional assistance, and friendship." She moved closer to him, dropping her chin down while cutting her eyes up. Her voice softened to a plea. "Wouldn't you say you owe me...at least that?"

"Don't—." Royce snapped.

James returned with tickets in hand. "We're all set. And I was able to get seats on the front-left side, where you prefer the acoustics." He dropped into his chair and waved at the waiter.

"Always thinking of me, thank you." She gave him an air-kiss and stood. "I must run before tonight's dinner. James, pick me up at seven? Royce, I'll send that paper. Just give it a look. That's all I ask." Evie dashed away, ignoring both of their replies, leaving a swirl of linen perfume in her wake. With a sense of naked longing, James watched her disappear into the crowd.

"She's remarkable, you know?" James said, waving at the waiter again.

"Evie's smart, I'll give her that."

The waiter ambled over, sighed, and asked if they were ready for the bill. In Italian, James ordered pasta and clams with another espresso. "And you, sir?"

"Just a glass of sparkling water, thank you." Royce said. The waiter nodded and hurried inside the restaurant.

"I wish I understood her better. It's like I can't quite reach her. Have you noticed that?"

"Some people don't want to be reached."

"You think? Maybe she's lonely?"

Royce straightened his flatware. He sought an amiable response and stumbled over his words. James saw her as an exceptional, isolated woman. Yet, in his experience, she had twisted her brilliance into calculated touches, strategic vulnerability, and someone who wielded trauma like a key for unlocking guilt.

"Perhaps she prefers it that way," Royce said, "But, she's lucky to have you." His phone buzzed. Evie.

> Notes sent again. I'll anticipate your feedback soon. Like old times:)

He deleted the message and placed his phone on the table, upside down.

"Everything alright?"

"Yes, it's nothing important."

Classic Evie. Always the brightest in the room. Always outmaneuvering everyone else, like a rook on a chessboard. And he just got cornered.

Cordelia stared in the boutique window, admiring the Italian goods, in particular a camel-colored tote big enough to hold her laptop. She debated whether to go in, knowing she wouldn't walk out empty-handed. The smell of tanned leather seeped out through the glass door, like a temptress luring her subjects.

The foot traffic on the Calle near Piazza San Marco appeared heavier than normal. The mixture of locals and tourists seemed eager to get somewhere, anywhere other than that street where local artisans sold their goods alongside international designers.

"Cordelia? What a surprise."

She looked up. Evie Lin. *Really? Of all the people.* Weighing down her petite frame were two designer shopping bags: Zara and Cosabella. And even with her cracked leather tote slung over her shoulder, she looked like she'd stepped from a fashion magazine. Not even the Venetian humidity hampered her beauty.

"Evie." Cordelia straightened, bracing her shoulders back. "Hi."

"Royce said I might find you here."

"Did he?"

"I had lunch with him and James. He said you were researching today."

"Lunch? I—"

"Don't worry, you didn't miss much. All scholarly with those two."

"Sounds exciting." She searched Evie's stoic expression. Her upper lip curled into a smile, a hint of the warmth Royce and James insisted she possessed. "Well, I need to run."

"Actually, I'd hoped to chat."

"Oh, ummm, sure." Cordelia steadied herself as a woman bumped past her. "Maybe this isn't the best time."

"It won't take long. I promise." Evie stepped into an alley, avoiding a puddle of water. "I know things have been awkward between us. But for Royce's sake I thought we should connect, be friends." A group of tourists formed a single line and squeezed past them. They paused a few feet away, photographing floral window boxes on a second-story balcony.

Cordelia nodded and stepped closer to her, hoping to keep the conversation quiet and brief. She caught a glimpse of Evie's wrist, the flesh-tone diagonal scar peeked out beneath a gold bracelet. "I can appreciate where you're coming from, but..."

A delivery man wheeled boxes past. Evie stepped aside, leaning her shoulder against the building. Despite the foot traffic, her intensity created a bubble around them.

"I thought you should know, I admire what you're doing. A

historical cookbook is brilliant, combining scholarship with practical application."

"Thank you. I've enjoyed it."

"I imagine. Honestly, I envy people who can cook. After years in university, living on takeaway, I never learned." She laughed—modest, slightly timid. "Royce used to joke that I'd starve without him."

There it is, reminder number one. "He mentioned you occasionally worked together."

"Constantly." Her cheeks molded into a smile. "But you don't want to hear about that. Tell me about your cookbook. What's the most interesting recipe you've found?"

Conniving... She grinned and launched into a full description of the Morschella records. Cordelia enjoyed watching Evie glaze over in boredom, and yet maintain a frozen smile. The longer she smiled, the more Cordelia listed.

"Wow, you have a grasp on the historical significance. I never imagined." Evie paused, meeting eyes with a modelesque woman who towered above her. She folded her arms, letting the shopping bags bounce off her hips. "So many people think cooking is nothing more than a list of instructions, but obviously, you see the cultural context. Royce must love that about you. He always appreciates someone who has a fondness for history."

"It's more than that."

"Of course. I'd watch him though." Evie took a step closer. "He has a tendency to overwork himself."

"Really? I haven't noticed."

"Back at university, I had to literally drag him from the library. Once I found him asleep at his desk at three AM, still clutching his pen."

"He can get absorbed."

"Absorbed is an understatement. To be honest, I think he's the one who would've starved. We had a routine where I'd schedule office hours just to bring him a sandwich," her narrowed eyes nostalgic, resentful. "But nothing fancy—not like what you create. I'm sure he loves your cooking. I'm terrible at it."

There's number two...intimate caretaker. Cordelia noticed the time.

"I'm sorry, I'm keeping you. Clearly, you're shopping."

"Yeah, I need to get a few things before the dinner tonight."

"Right, of course. What I hope you know...I'm trying to be friends here. We're both concerned about Royce's well-being and—"

"Royce is fine."

"I assumed that would be your response, but hear me out. I'm concerned about him. At the reception he looked tired."

"He's very healthy, with lots of energy."

"Right. And I'm sure you take good care of him," Evie touched Cordelia's hand, a gesture of feminine solidarity. "It's hard not to worry. Especially after everything he sacrificed."

"Sacrificed? What are you implying?"

Evie's eyes widened. "He hasn't told you? Oh, I assumed...of course he wouldn't. He likes his secrets."

"Whatever it is that you want to say, just say it."

"No, I've said too much already. Royce would be mortified if he knew I'd mentioned—"

"Evie." Cordelia kept her voice soft despite the irritation crawling up her spine. "We're all adults. If there's something you want to share, then I'd appreciate you directly saying it."

"I really shouldn't. I mean, what happened, for both of us, was so painful. I'd, I had assumed, hoped he would've told you everything."

Cordelia studied the slight twitch in Evie's eyes, and the way her lips held an upward position. She pressed her tote against her ribs, ignoring the notebook jabbing into her chest.

"The night I...in the hallway outside his office." Evie began, her voice dropped to a whisper. "Royce...I was barely conscious, but I remember his voice. He said a lot of things to keep me awake."

Cordelia found herself leaning closer, noting Evie's version of the night.

"He applied pressure, called for medical, and talked." She stared at the ground, and when she looked up, a tear welled up in her eye. "He literally held my life in his hands. Do you understand what that means?"

"I'm sure it was traumatic for both of you."

"He's never said, but I believe it was. My parents were in Hong Kong and couldn't get to London until the next day. Royce talked me through the darkness. But he never made it about himself. I guess that's why I worry about him."

The tears spilled. Cordelia questioned if they were genuine, immediately feeling guilt for suspecting fakeness. But her instinct doubted, noticing how Evie dabbed at the tears, concerned about preserving her makeup. "Royce is very kind and caring." She patted Evie on the arm.

"Kind?" Evie cracked a laugh. "He saved my life, and he assured my parents he'd look after me while I finished my studies." She dabbed her cheeks. "I'm sorry, I should say anymore. Royce hasn't discussed it with you himself."

"I wouldn't say he hasn't talked about it."

"Well, you should know what a wonderful man he is, and I know he keeps things to himself."

"He's pretty open."

"Oh, how nice. We talked frequently during my recovery, when he'd stop by to visit me."

"At the hospital?"

"No, no, my flat."

A piece of the story Royce had obviously omitted. The

narrow alley closed in around Cordelia, as if it constricted her breathing. She wasn't jealous of Evie, or even angry at Royce. Hurt, yes, he'd consciously omitted details to what, protect her? To protect Evie?

"I see," Cordelia said.

Evie pulled out her phone and scrolled through photos. "This was taken at a faculty event, just before everything happened. This is Dr. Andrews."

The photo showed Royce and Gavin in academic robes, Evie between them in a cocktail dress. She stood close to both of them, comfortable, laughing at something off-camera. She clicked her phone off and dropped it into her bag.

"When I heard he'd met someone in Paris, I was happy for him. He deserves love, especially after everything he gave up."

"That's the second time you've implied he's sacrificed his career, and you're mistaken. Royce is doing well, and he's very happy."

"I hope you're correct, sometimes I wonder if everything he does now is a form of penance for what happened with Gavin."

"What?" Cordelia shifted her weight and checked her phone.

"I don't mean you were a charity case."

"Excuse me? Listen, I need to go. Is there a purpose to all of this?" She took a few steps toward the main Calle, throwing her hands into the air. "A piece of advice, move on. Royce has."

"Wait," Evie skipped after Cordelia, grabbing her wrist, "I've upset you. The last thing I want is to cause problems. It's only out of concern for him that I'm saying anything at all."

"I think you've said enough."

Evie gripped Cordelia's wrist tighter. "You need to know, Royce has a savior complex. He couldn't save me from Gavin, or prevent what happened. But he and I, he and Gavin...we all survived something together. That creates a bond, whether he wants to admit it or not."

"A trauma bond," Cordelia yanked her hand from Evie's grip, feeling the throb of her blood coursing through her veins. "Isn't the same thing as a genuine connection. Trust me, I know."

Evie's eyes narrowed. "You think this is a school girl crush, but it's not. I care about my former mentor, my friend. And I thought you did too."

Cordelia knew to walk away. Her stomach gripped, vibrating like a gasket about to explode. Instead, she took a step toward her. "You don't think I notice the casual mentions of late-night sessions, the photos, the implication that I'm some kind of rebound from your student-teacher deep connection? I do. And so does Royce."

"You're very direct."

"You gave me no choice." Cordelia adjusted her bag. "And here's some directness for you—Royce chose to leave that life. He chose to build something new for himself. Without you. Your trauma, your shared history is exactly that—history."

"Which has a way of repeating itself," Evie said softly. "Especially unresolved history."

"Then I suggest you work on resolving it. Alone." She walked away before Evie could respond, holding her composure until she turned the corner. As she merged into the crowded Calle, the revelations flooded like a checklist: his hospital vigil, his visits to her flat, the promises to her parents. Her disclosures left seeds of doubt, exactly her agenda.

Cordelia resisted the lingering questions birthed from Evie's manipulation. She had every reason to doubt her, and even more reasons to trust him.

Her phone buzzed. Royce.

Still shopping? Or did your mysterious gondolier whisk you away?

On my way. One stop left.

Hurry. Your Aperol spritz awaits.

She stared at the message, wondering if he had minimized or omitted things entirely. But why hide his sense of duty to a student?

What Evie revealed didn't change her feelings for him. Everyone had a history. Everyone had a narrow memory. Daniel taught her that lesson. The problem wasn't his past, the problem was how Evie interjected herself into the present, attempting to disrupt the future. The problem was him allowing it.

The sun settled behind the rooftops, splattering rose light onto the basilica. Two older men stood in a pizza shop doorway, passionately debating. One of them held a newspaper, smacking it as he stressed his point.

Cordelia dashed into a boutique, and ten minutes later exited with a shopping bag. As she walked back to the palazzo, Evie's words resurfaced.

Royce texted again.

Better hurry, the palazzo ghost is getting thirsty.

Give him a glass of water.

Her heart swelled, loving him for all the little things. Savior complex, maybe. Trauma bonded to Evie, doubtful.

Chapter Nine

The private dining room at the historic palazzo hotel glowed with old-money elegance. A crystal chandelier cast rainbow fragments across the silk wall coverings, and cherubs seemed to whisper from their elevated positions. Their expressions reflected a time when Venice dominated refinement and culture—proud and mocking.

Wall sconces and candles provided warm lighting, illuminating the name cards at the sixty seats surrounding the long table. The room smelled earthy with hints of citrus and spice, reminiscent of a Moroccan market than a palace.

Royce found himself seated between James and Lady Penley. Her husband, Lord Penley, portly with a thick head of silver hair sat beside her. An "unusual couple," his father would always say after returning from their dinner parties, "but delightfully entertaining."

Cordelia walked around the table, looking at each place card as she moved further away from Royce's seat. When she found her place, a hint of disappointment washed across her face. She pointed at a seat and mouthed one word at him,

"Evie." He nodded silent encouragement and watched as she took her seat across from Lord Penley.

After taking her seat, she greeted Lord and Lady Penley, making small talk about Venice. The pearl earrings he'd given her for her birthday dangled against her neck, a spot he longed to kiss. A spot that always made her melt.

He paused before taking his seat, admiring her ability to radiate such charm, while hiding the nervousness that settled between her shoulder blades. For years, he'd kept love at arm's length, always convincing himself it wouldn't work. But Cordelia had slipped past every defense, navigating his world, and loving him despite those walls. His heart felt like a tree on a cliff—rooted between the ordinary and the unknown.

Cordelia stunned in her emerald green dress. He looked forward to the end of the night, when he could run his fingers down the open back and untie the thin strings that held the dress close to her body.

James tapped Royce's shoulder, interrupting his thoughts. "Ah, here's Evie."

He followed James' gaze, noticing the man entering behind Evie—the stranger from the cocktail party who'd taken an interest in Cordelia. He approached, walked around their end of the table, and took the empty seat beside Cordelia.

"Lorenzo Benedetti," introducing himself to her. She half stood, shook his hand, and flickered a smile when he kissed both cheeks.

"Hi." There was a hesitation in the way her finger smoothed the edges of her lips, something Royce hadn't noticed before. A blush settled on her cheeks.

Around him, conversations continued, becoming muffled behind his thoughts. On both sides of the table, waiters served wine and chilled water.

"You were at the cocktail party the other night." Cordelia said.

"Yes, and you wore those extraordinary blue shoes." Lorenzo accepted the wine, sniffing it before taking a sip. "I hoped to see you this evening."

The blush on her face quickly receded into neutrality when she glanced at Royce and met his stare.

"Lorenzo is a famous composer from Florence," Evie said. "He's produced pieces for the London Symphony Orchestra." She stretched around to look at him. "You visit often, correct?"

"Yes." He stared at Cordelia, who focused more on the wine swirling in her glass than him. "I might consider it more if asked."

"I would think it's more meaningful to work with an Italian symphony, like the one here in Venice. Evie, you attend their performances a lot, correct?" Cordelia's eyes cut across the table at Royce, seeking his approval.

He resisted a smile, but offered her a raised eyebrow. She sipped her wine and mirrored him as a pinkish color returned to her cheeks.

"Actually, I do attend quite often. I find the box seats intimate. They add a personal touch to the performance. Perhaps, Lorenzo can reserve one for tomorrow night's concert."

"We'd like that, wouldn't we, Royce?" Cordelia said.

"I believe—."

Her attention shifted back to Lorenzo, who launched into a description of his latest composition, "a watery collection". She listened, appearing to hang on his words.

The first course arrived, a delicate crostini topped with a whipped salted cod. An orchestrated team of waiters placed the plates in front of guests, while two sommeliers followed, pouring prosecco into secondary wine glasses. Conversations softened under the delicate sounds of chamber music, coming from a three-member ensemble perfectly staged beside a white marble fireplace.

"This reminds me of that place near the university," Evie paused and smiled. "Remember the tiny restaurant across from the art gallery, with the funny little owner?"

Royce chuckled. "Yes. The chef who spent as much time in the dining room as he did in the kitchen."

"I thought I'd been banned, remember that night?" Evie laughed, the sound warm and understated.

"I do. But he forgave you, once you complimented his well-behaved children." Royce said, realizing he and Evie shared a smile, one that awkwardly lingered. Her warmth dissolved into sighs when Lady Penley interrupted, asking about his niece. He gushed and shared a photo.

Across the table, Cordelia blurted out in laughter. She tilted her head at Lorenzo, the same engaged expression Royce assumed she reserved for him. *Apparently not.* Her fingers played with the wine glass stem as Lorenzo gestured wildly, describing what appeared to be a conducting technique.

"Music is mathematics," Lorenzo said. "But cooking is pure emotion, yes?"

"I wouldn't say that, both require math and emotion, otherwise, the rhythm and results are off."

"Ah, but you forget the most important ingredient." Lorenzo leaned closer. "Passion. Without it, even perfect technique produces nothing worthwhile." Lorenzo's eyes softened. "You know, my brother is a chef in Florence. He speaks as if each meal holds a piece of his soul."

"Yes, exactly." Cordelia's whole body turned toward him. "People think it's just following recipes, but—"

"But it's alchemy, yes?"

Cordelia smiled at him. The one that made her eyes crinkle.

The one she'd given Royce that first night in Paris. The one she'd given him every day since. "So true!"

Royce watched the spark between them. Attraction? Perhaps. More a recognition. Something he knew well. He adjusted his dinner jacket, glancing from Cordelia, to Evie, and back. His sips of wine became longer and more frequent.

"She seems happy," Evie said, cutting her eyes at Cordelia and Lorenzo.

The second course arrived, a risotto with sea urchin. The salty flavors sparked a table conversation regarding Venice's fishing traditions. Lord Penley held firm in his beliefs regarding greater sustainability, a debate that caught Royce and Lady Penley in the middle.

Yet, the parallel conversation across the table seized his attention.

"Lorenzo, that's beautiful," Cordelia said. "I never thought of it that way." She dabbed the corner of her mouth with her napkin, letting the cloth graze her lower lip. He spoke softly while talking with his hands. His exuberance was meant only for her.

Lady Penley interrupted the debate between James and Lord Penley, forcing the men into a truce.

"Yes. Yes, you understand," Lorenzo's voice boomed.

Cordelia fiddled with her left earring, a tell about her nerves. The pearl caught the light and shimmered against her skin. The night he'd given them to her, they'd just returned home from Richard's house party—more tequila than he cared to remember. They showered, and afterwards, she wrapped herself in his shirt. Her skin glistened from the steam. He went to bed. She made a cup of tea, discovering the box on her pillow when she crawled in beside him.

"You're staring," Evie said, tasting the main course that had been placed in front of her moments before.

"Am I?"

"Like she might disappear." She held her water glass up, waiting for a waiter to bring more. "I remember that feeling."

The words nostalgic. Her tone bitter.

Across the table, Lorenzo sketched something into a notebook as Cordelia looked on. The ease between them sparked an unfamiliar sensation in Royce's gut. *Not jealousy.* Something different, but then he'd never felt anxious about any woman, ever. He'd let her in, shown her pieces of himself no one else had seen: the writer who doubted his creativity, the son who loved and resented his legacy. *Did she find Lorenzo's artistic soul appealing?*

"See? Here, the melody rises like the basilica dome." His pencil moved quickly. "And here, it descends into the canal's reflection."

"So, you compose visually?"

"I compose with my senses. Tomorrow, you must let me show you."

"Thank you, but I..." Cordelia caught Royce's eyes. Her mouth held the words on the tip of her tongue, as she smiled at him. She motioned toward the door and stood. "If you'll excuse me for a moment."

Three minutes after she left, Royce followed. Cordelia waited near the lounge, guiding him to a quiet spot in the corner of the piano bar.

"I miss you," she said, wrapping her arms around him.

"Have you?"

She tilted her head, exposing the soft dip below her earlobe. "Very much."

Royce leaned down, placing his lips against her skin. She tasted sweet, like honey. "You seem to be enjoying yourself this evening."

She pulled back. "What's that supposed to mean?"

"Only that you seem to be enjoying your dinner companion."

"I could say the same to you. You and Evie have been chummy all night."

Royce tugged her closer. "We're far from *chummy*. And you're not conversing with her."

"Because there's nothing to discuss." Cordelia stepped away from him. "This was a mistake."

"What was?"

"This, trying to have a moment alone with you."

Royce reached for her hand, dragging her back into his arms. "I disagree." His fingers traced her jaw, "I enjoy these moments."

"I do too, but..." Her words faded beneath their kiss.

The music stopped, and a lone man at the bar clapped, a reminder they'd been away too long. When Royce returned to the table, Cordelia had resumed her conversation with Lorenzo, and waiters served the dessert course.

"Strange," Evie said, waiting for coffee service to finish pouring, "how we can sit across from someone and feel miles apart."

"Time does that. Creates distance, both wanted and unwanted." Royce said, fidgeting with the spoon that sat beside his untouched dessert.

Evie stood, resting her clutch against her chest. She whispered something to James, took a few steps, and returned. Her fingers rested on Royce's arm, the touch casual yet calculated, "It looks like the decision's already been made for you."

He slid his arm out, retreating from her touch, but not before catching Cordelia's glance. *Shit*. He'd been trained in the art of polite distance, but suddenly he'd found himself trapped between guilt and vulnerability. His father would call it poor form, a miscalculation—the inability to manage simple dynamics while reducing complications.

As the space between them stretched. He watched her, waiting for eye contact. She rebuffed his efforts, laughing at Lorenzo's words.

Soon, the dessert plates were cleared. Royce wanted to rewind the day, return to the morning's intimacy, and skip social obligations. Lord Penley interrupted his thoughts, inviting them to the lounge for brandy. He declined, promising they'd visit before the masquerade ball.

Lady Penley air-kissed Royce good night. "She's wonderful, you're amazing, and this," she motioned toward Lorenzo, "Is nothing more than a summer shower, it dissipates, and you forget it happened."

Back at the apartment, the bathroom door clicked shut with merciful finality. Cordelia leaned against it, feeling the cool wood against her back. In the bedroom, Royce undressed: the whisper of his jacket being hung, the soft thud of shoes on the floor, the rhythmic footsteps as he placed them in the closet alongside his sneakers.

Her reflection stared back from the gold-rimmed mirror. Her cheeks still flushed from wine and conversation. Or was it the compounding annoyances between her and Royce? The ones that seemed to build like a brick wall.

She removed her pearl earrings, holding them in the palm of her hand. *So delicate and precious.* Her fingers closed around them, remembering the night they'd appeared on her pillow. Royce pretended to be asleep, making a god-awful grunting noise—his rendition of a snore. Tequila-induced lovemaking delayed her from trying them on until the following morning, a memory that still made her laugh.

Untying the dress herself, it landed in a silky, green pool at her feet. Hours earlier, it had made her feel beautiful, confident, and claiming her place in a room full of hierarchy. Now it felt more like a costume, a veil of confusion. She hung the dress on an ornate hook and put on a comforting nightshirt—one of his V-neck tees.

Hot water flowed from the faucet, creating a cloud of steam that rose to her face. *Was I flirting?* Royce casually mentioned it on the way back to the apartment. The cotton pad smeared makeup off her cheek. *I'd been polite, engaging—exactly what I'm supposed to do at these events.* How dare he accuse her of flirting when she behaved like everyone else?

She tossed a stack of makeup-stained pads into the trash. "Seriously," she whispered to her reflection. Did Royce really think she'd toss him to the side for some charming man who compared musical notes to pasta shapes?

The steam moistened her cheeks. The issue wasn't Lorenzo. It was Evie. She played games, life-altering games—ones she seemed hell-bent on playing with Royce again.

With a fresh face, she turned off the bathroom light, and tiptoed to bed. In the darkness, she made out his form, positioned on his side near her pillow. When she crawled under the sheets, he didn't move, but she knew he was awake. His breathing remained steady and controlled.

"I never thought I'd say this," she whispered, staring at the ceiling, "but I miss home."

"I do too."

She rolled toward him, finding his arms ready to embrace her. "I love you."

His lips pressed against her forehead. "And I love you." A

silence hummed, interrupted only by a boat passing in the canal. "Lorenzo seemed…"

"Lively?"

"That's one way of putting it." He held his breath, exhaled, and said, "Well, Evie was Evie tonight."

"I noticed." She repositioned herself, attempting to see his eyes. "When we get home, I want to go visit your family."

"You do?"

"Yes, have you forgotten, Ada Rose needs some chill time with her favorite godparent?"

Royce laughed, debated, and finally conceded the title to Cordelia.

Chapter Ten

The toy shop displayed a jungle of handcrafted wooden and porcelain animals, gondolas, and pinnochios. Against the back wall, animals were arranged by category: pet, birds, safari. Cordelia inspected a giraffe, admiring the way the craftsmanship.

"We really should be looking at stuffed animals. These'll end up in her mouth."

"Stuffed animals are trivial. What about this one?" Royce said, reaching around her for an elephant with movable legs.

"Maybe. I still say a stuffed animal is the safest bet." She set the giraffe back and selected a simple gondola on a string with wheels. "Remember Emma talking about Ada preferring a napkin and spoon to her rubber stacking toy?" She tucked the boat under her arm. "I'll get this one for my nephew, Casey. Five isn't too old for this, is it?"

Royce shrugged, "Shouldn't you know these things better than I?"

"What? Are you kidding? You don't want to go there."

"Oh, there's the fire." Royce took three steps backwards. "I meant you would know him better than me."

She studied his face. "Mm-hmm."

"I'm being honest." He walked to the far end of the wall and held up an intricately carved dragon. "This is incredible. Look at the carving details." His fingers ran across the rounded edges, noticing the angry expression on the dragon's face. "I suspect this one might traumatize her."

"Stuffed animals are still a viable option."

His phone buzzed in his jeans pocket. He glanced at it, raising his eyebrows. "It's Evie."

Cordelia faced the three shelves of dragons, folded her arms across her chest, and tapped her fingernails against the wooden boat. "What? Why?"

Royce took the call, pacing in circles. "Right. Let me ask her and get back to you shortly." He paused, noticing Cordelia's glare looked similar to the dragons. "Right, yes. Alright, I'll be in touch. Thanks."

"Apparently, she has a spa appointment this afternoon and her colleague canceled. She wondered if you'd like to join her." He waited for a reaction, but Cordelia stood silent, staring at the dragons. "She thought it might be a proper way to connect—a peace offering. Her treat."

"How generous." Her voice, stiff and reserved. A tone that usually meant unease.

"It is. She's obviously trying." He moved closer. "I know she can be intense. Maybe she just needs a friend."

"I'm sure she has friends." She moved to a nearby display. Her fingers trailed over the painted blocks.

"Academic colleagues aren't the same thing." His hand found her waist, turning her gently to face him. "She's not asking for much, just one afternoon."

"But why me?" She plopped her forehead against his shoulder. "I mean, better me than you, but still, why me?"

"Perhaps because you're kind," he kissed her cheek. "And caring," he kissed her lips.

"And?"

"You want more?"

"Of course."

"You're a good listener." He kissed her neck, pausing when a toddler with his nose pressed to the window watched them.

"Did she say what kind of spa treatment?"

He recalled the information, "A facial."

"Where?"

"The Aman."

"She has good taste."

"Is that a yes?"

"It interferes with our plans."

"We'll have the evening to ourselves, no interruptions." His thumb traced her jaw, "And by time you get back, I'll have my chapter finished."

"Dinner in?"

"Whatever you want."

"Fine. But if she starts in on another story about your marathon research session or the hospital—."

"Text me and I'll call with an excuse." He kissed her forehead. "I appreciate you giving her a chance to know you better."

"Why? So she'll stop fixating on you?"

"Yes." He pulled her closer, smelling the soft floral scent on her cheek.

"By the way, you owe me."

Royce leaned back. "Being in your debt, isn't as bad as you think."

"We'll see about that." She tapped him on the rear and walked toward the front of the shop. "I'm getting this boat for Casey."

"All right. I'll let Evie know." He texted her, and she immediately replied, thanking him for convincing Cordelia that she wasn't evil. Royce deleted the message, happy he'd found a solution to the Cordelia-Evie tension.

He took one last look at the dragons, but decided Cordelia was right, a stuffed lion was perfect for Ada Rose.

Two hours later, Cordelia approached the Aman hotel, winding through the narrow calle that led to the historic palazzo. She'd listened to a meditation podcast on her walk over, hoping it would relax her clenched stomach.

The spa cocooned them in creamy earth tones, a subtle luxury that transported Cordelia from Venetian opulence into an oasis scented in ginger and bergamot.

"This is divine," Evie said from the adjacent treatment bed as aestheticians prepared their faces for masks. "This is my monthly self-care routine. Although, usually I come alone."

Alone by choice or design? Cordelia closed her eyes, trying to surrender to the gentle cleansing routine. Despite her silence, Evie talked, sharing her knowledge of their products: ingredients, sourcing, and even the history of said ingredients.

After ten minutes, five of which were enjoyed in silence, the aesthetician misted Cordelia's cheeks in a gold-honey concoction. That was the second time Evie had used the word "divine."

"I hope last night wasn't too uncomfortable," Evie said as their faces were painted with masks. "I noticed Lorenzo monopolized your time."

"He was friendly."

"That was more than cordial. He ignored everyone else—the man couldn't take his eyes off of you." She paused, releasing a groaning sigh. "Royce noticed too."

Cordelia peeked over at Evie, a serene Renaissance painting, who didn't stare back, waiting to choose her next calculated move.

"Yes. And...?"

"It's only, I've never seen him quite like that, the way he watched you. Really tense. He tried to hide it, but after knowing him as long as I have, I recognized the tells."

"Tells?"

"Little things. How he held his wine glass. The way he adjusted his watch when confronted or uncomfortable." Evie sighed, almost longing for something. "I don't think he's used to competition."

"There's no competition. Lorenzo was just being chatty." The clay mask felt suffocating. *Did he give off signs?* She tried to remember, but the evening blurred together: Lorenzo's lesson on music, the wine, the piano bar.

"We both know that. But men see things differently, don't they? Especially someone like Royce, who's never had to work for attention."

Cordelia forced her breathing to remain steady. "That's not Royce. He's not—."

"Of course not. He's too sophisticated for blatant jealousy." Evie's treatment table shifted.

Cordelia looked over, meeting glances with her. She remained silent, listening to sound bowls drift in from a nearby room. A row of three black votive candles added to the room's ambiance.

"But uncertainty, that's different. That's about confidence, not possession, and you made him uncertain last night."

"Over what? He has no reason to feel uncertain," Cordelia laid back down. "I don't think we should talk about this anymore."

Evie settled onto her table. "I'm telling you, he does, and I never saw him this way with Mia, Julia, or Leigh. But then, you're different."

I really shouldn't ask, but... "How am I different?"

"He cares. That's why you made him feel uncertain last night."

Wait, Mia? Leigh? How does she... The names dropped like breadcrumbs, leading her down a risky path. "You were his student, so how do you know about his past relationships?"

"We worked a lot of hours together," her voice pitched higher, almost surprised or confused by the question. "I saw it all: the demands of work, his family expectations, and revolving dates. But I never saw him doubt himself until last night."

The aesthetician removed Cordelia's mask, chattering in Italian to the other woman who treated Evie.

"Maybe you read into things. Royce knows Lorenzo meant nothing," her heartbeat throbbed in her ears, and the aesthetician's description of the cleansing milk barely registered above a hum. *She doesn't know what she's talking about...she's just trying to get into my head.*

"Perhaps. But I've known him a while. He ended things with Mia after a month. She snapped at his housekeeper, and he told her to leave. And—."

"Evie, we shouldn't talk."

She cut her off abruptly, dismissing the aesthetician for a moment. "You wanted to know why I warned you, this is why. Royce doesn't play games. He doesn't doubt himself, and he doesn't get jealous. You think you know him, but you don't, not like I do."

Cordelia swung her legs over the table. "You *did* know him. But he's different." Her hand gripped the front of the robe; her knuckles turning white. "Now, I came here because Royce asked me to. He thought this was your peace offering. And no, I haven't told him about our conversation in the alley, yet. But I will. I'll add this to the list if you keep on." She plopped back down onto the table, situating her robe like a comforting blanket on a winter's morning.

Evie sat on the edge of her table, remnants of the mask streaked across her forehead. "I'm sorry, Cordelia. You're right, I'm being thoughtless." She reached her hand out, palm up, fingers outstretched, exposing the scars. Her visceral reminders of the lengths he went to, to rescue her from herself. "I want us to be friends...for Royce's sake."

Cordelia sighed, accepting her hand. *He may not play games, but you sure do.* There was a tremor in Evie's touch; energy coursed through her veins. Cordelia's eyes drifted past her disfigured wrist, and up to her face. Sorrow sat behind her glassy eyes, yet the soft lines around them lifted—hopeful, convincing. "Friends. For Royce's sake." *I still don't trust you.* Cordelia smiled and stared at the ceiling, doing her best to listen to the water chime sounds playing in the background.

A short time later, they relaxed in the spa lounge. Still in their robes, they sipped a floral green tea that had an earthy honey scent.

"Thank you for joining me. I mean it. I don't have many friends."

I wonder why.

"I guess that's why I value Royce and James. And at one time, Gavin." She touched her wrist. "They protect me, and I protect them."

Cordelia took a large gulp of her tea, burning the roof of her mouth. *Ugh. When is this going to end?*

"For what it's worth, I know you didn't seek Lorenzo's attention."

"I wasn't seeking anyone's attention."

"Oh, I know." Evie sipped her tea, released her hair clip,

and draped everything to one side. "I'm here if you ever need to talk."

Stop listening to her. Stop talking. Just leave. "Talk about what exactly? Royce?"

"Anything."

"Royce and I are good. As I told you yesterday, Royce is fine. We're fine. You need to stop worrying about him, and focus on yourself." She felt the angst knot in her stomach, knowing a part of her doubted the words.

"Do you want to know why Royce ended things with Leigh?"

"No, no, I don't." Cordelia gulped the last of her tea, feeling the burn as it trailed down her throat.

"He didn't tell you, did he? She was a lawyer, prominent political family. Pushed and controlled everyone, herself most of all. And she always demanded everyone's attention. That night at the hospital, he called her. Told her he wouldn't make dinner, that night or ever. They were together for three months."

She's playing you and you're a fool for listening. Cordelia stood, tightening the sash of her robe. "Thank you for the facial. Royce is at our apartment. We have dinner plans tonight, romantic dinner plans. See you at the ball." She turned and left, leaving Evie alone, sipping her tea.

"You're massacring that dough," Royce observed from the doorway.

The kitchen smelled like home—butter, vanilla, and lemon zest. Cordelia worked methodically; her muscle memory guiding her hands while her mind churned. The rhythm and smells usually soothed her. "I need to get it right, it's off here."

"At ten o'clock at night? In Venice?" He stepped into the

kitchen, surveying the controlled chaos. Flour dusted the cold stone, with two empty mixing bowls in the sink. "What are you making?"

"My Tudor cookies." She pressed the rolling pin forward, forcing the dough to spread thin.

"Why?"

"I needed to think."

"You were quiet at dinner."

"I know." She rotated the dough, slapping it onto the counter.

"Cordelia." He stepped to the other side of the island. "What happened at the spa?"

"Nothing. Girl time, like you wanted." She attacked the dough with the rolling pin, pushing and pulling. She didn't look at him.

"Right. Which is why you barely ate, hardly talked, and have spent more time with that dough than with me."

"It's not always about you. Why are you reading into this? I bake all the time at home."

"Darling, what happened? Was Evie difficult?"

Yes. No. Both. "She was fine. Chatty. Talked about you, Lorenzo..."

"What about him?"

"Evie said you were jealous, no what was the word...*uncertain*. I made you feel uncertain about us."

He tucked his hands into his shorts pockets. "I noticed he monopolized your attention, yes."

"Monopolized? I thought we already discussed this." She set the rolling pin down and met his eyes with dejection. "I was being polite, you know that. I made conversation, exactly like I'm supposed to do at these dinners. Nothing more, nothing less."

"I'm not saying you were anything other than charming."

"Your tone did." She returned to rolling. "And according to Evie, you kept adjusting your watch. Did you know you do that when you're uncomfortable? Apparently, Evie does."

"Cordelia—."

"She suggested I should be mindful of my actions or end up like Leigh."

"Obviously, my suggestion was a mistake," he raked his hair, dropping his hand onto the stone. "Don't you see what she's doing?"

"Yes, I do. But do you?"

"Quite clearly, I assure you." Royce approached her, respecting her space. "Cordelia, look at me. I wasn't jealous of Lorenzo, unless you count the fact that he got to sit beside you and spend three hours listening to your laugh."

She stopped rolling, cutting her eyes at him. "Were you ever uncomfortable or frustrated?"

"With Lorenzo, yes. With you, no." He brushed a row of flour into a pile. "I was more uncomfortable with Evie's manipulations."

Cordelia glided her hand across the dough, brushing off any excess. "Then why did you ask me to go today?"

Royce caught her flour-covered hand. "I thought...I hoped that if she got to know you, she'd stop playing her games." Her rigid fingers rested in his palm.

"Well, she didn't."

"Whatever she said, I'm sorry. I'll straighten everything out tomorrow, and that's the end."

She pulled her hand back. "I need to chill this dough."

"It's ten fifteen. Let the dough rest."

"No, it can't. I need to bake them off."

"Listen, you're covered in flour, beating up on innocent dough, because a woman who manipulates and exaggerates spent two hours picking at your confidence."

"Two hours and forty minutes."

"Fine. Let's call it three. She spent three hours distorting the truth and influencing your emotions. Don't you see, you're giving her what she wanted—division between us."

"Yes." She dusted her hands on a dry towel. "You know baking is my therapy."

"Maybe this time you're deflecting rather than relaxing." His hands settled on either side of her, holding her between himself and the counter. "This is what she wants. You doubting yourself, and the two of us doubting each other, rather than talking."

"Then next time don't push me to spend time with her."

The words hit like a cold shower. He'd tried to manage the situation like a chess match and lost. *Damn, just like Pop.* "I'm sorry, I won't, I put you in that position again."

"She made me feel like I don't know you at all, like I don't belong."

"That's ridiculous," leaning in to kiss her.

She turned her head. "Is it? Be honest with me."

"I swear on my..."

"Don't say your life, that never turns out well. "

"Okay."

"I'm serious. People swear on their lives, and bad things happen when they don't follow through."

"Alright, that's new to me. I swear," he looked around the room. "I swear on this dough that you are the one person I want beside me, day and night. Therefore, you belong." He placed his palm on the dough.

She rested her forehead against his. "Prove it."

"How?" He stared into her eyes, noticing a glint he hadn't seen all night.

"I'll let you decide." She turned in his arms and folded the dough in on itself. "Royce?"

"Yes?" He leaned into her, resting his chin on her shoulder.

"Do you really think I was inappropriate last night?"

"No."

"You suggested I flirted." She wrapped the dough in plastic, turned, and faced him. "Didn't you?"

He stepped away, running his hands through his hair. "I... yes, I hinted at it last night, but that's only because I was frustrated with Evie."

Cordelia yanked open the refrigerator and shoved the dough inside. "And you never told her I behaved inappropriately?"

"Never." He leaned his back against the sink counter, watching Cordelia wash the flour dust from her hands. "Yes, I watched you last night. Yes, I felt a little jealous—."

"Which she called uncertain, doubt."

Royce squared his body at her. "I watched the way you lit up when he talked, it reminded me of Paris."

"Oh, Royce." She flipped off the water, drying her hands with a paper towel.

"I kept thinking about the first night we shared a bottle of wine together. You get animated when something genuinely interests you."

"Why didn't you say anything when we were in the lounge?"

"I wanted to focus on us, not Lorenzo." For someone who crafted words for a living, he struggled to express himself. "I guess I realized that beautiful charm of yours," his finger traced her collarbone, "isn't reserved just for me. That someone else might offer fewer complications."

"Royce."

"And Evie played on it. I'll give her that, she read me well."

"I'm sorry. I let her get into my head."

He pulled his phone out of his pocket. "I should've done this months ago."

"What are you doing?"

"I'm calling her."

"It's late. Just call her tomorrow."

He sent her a text, telling her they needed to talk first thing in the morning. The guilt that had guided his actions for two years had crystallized into anger.

She replied, suggesting they meet at her classroom. When she asked what about, he told her, "Some changes." She quickly responded.

11 AM. We'll have privacy.

Royce didn't reply. She was a shark, and he was done being her bait. He placed his phone on the counter. "I will not let her poison us anymore, I promise."

She moved in to him, wrapping her arms around his waist. "I made a mess."

He looked around. "This? We can clean it." His lips found her forehead. "Later."

"I can't leave it like this."

He pulled back, touching, tracing her lips. "Yes, you can. There's something else that's even more important." His hand brushed past her breast, lifting her shirt, feeling her skin. She flinched when his hand slid underneath the lace underwear.

"You know, Lord Thornbury, we're in a kitchen."

He backed her against the island. "I'm aware." Her lips tasted of red wine—cherries, bold cherries. "And for the record, my name's not Lord Thornbury."

She hopped onto the island, wrapping her legs around his waist. "I'm aware." Her parted lips kissed him, letting her tongue slide against his. Against his lips she said, "Since Paris, Royce, since Paris."

He nodded and lifted her off the counter. "Come with me, Ms. Dyer." She followed, flipping off the kitchen light.

Chapter Eleven

The university courtyard, surrounded by terra cotta colored buildings, appeared like any other campus. Students mingled on the grassy lawn debating Dante, while others sketched the architecture.

Cordelia walked with purpose, maintaining a discreet distance behind Royce. He wore an olive-green shirt with black trousers, making it easy to spot him if he got too far ahead.

That morning they'd lingered in bed, almost making him late for his meeting with Evie. When he left, she texted Marnie, her thumbs racing to spill the news. She responded with a shocked emoji.

> He's really going to do it? Finally.
>
> Just left.
>
> And you didn't go? Are you INSANE? Follow him. You need to hear what she says.
>
> I need to let him handle it.
>
> That's what got you two into this mess. Go. NOW.

Impulsively, she threw her sneakers on, grabbed her tote, and raced downstairs. She'd caught up with him, following the route he'd shown her when they were out exploring the city. It was a maze, but she'd found her way there without him ever seeing her. She had no idea what she would've said if he'd spotted her. *Picking up coffee? Just shopping.* At least she didn't have to navigate that conversation.

She stood outside Evie's classroom, a lecture hall with massive palazzo windows, tons of natural light, and a view of the Grand Canal. Cordelia positioned herself close enough to hear them, but far enough to deny eavesdropping if discovered. Although, she had no idea how she'd justify getting coffee on a university campus.

Outside the wood door, Royce's voice echoed, a controlled tone where each word was emphasized. Nothing like the man whose whispers had left a trail of kisses on her skin only a few hours earlier.

"Evie, we've talked about this. You can't keep framing my resignation as some noble crusade," Royce said.

"But it was." Her footsteps tapped across the wooden floor. Her voice dropped to an intimate register, one Cordelia despised. "You gave up everything because of what happened to me. Isn't that noble?"

The hallway had emptied, leaving an unnatural silence behind. Cordelia heard her heartbeat alongside the footsteps of former residents. She struggled to focus on their voices.

Oh, the hell with it. She moved closer, peeking through the cracked door. Cordelia watched Royce's body language shift into a knotted pretzel left baking in the sun.

"I've told you, it wasn't about you. I left for my own personal reasons. Besides—."

"Don't," Evie's voice cracked. "Stop pretending that I don't matter. That night in the hospital, you said I was important. You held my hand and told me that."

"You are."

"Then stop lying to both of us about what happened that night."

"Nothing happened, Evie. You've taken my words out of context."

"Well, I disagree." She pulled something from her bag, a faded hospital bracelet. "See this. I kept it. This goes pretty much everywhere with me, to remind myself that someone, out there, thought I was valuable."

"Evie..." He adjusted his watch band and wrung his hands together.

Oh my God, he does do that. Cordelia watched the tension build in his body—the way his hands fought for composure.

"You're that someone." Evie dropped the bracelet into her purse.

"You've misunderstood my intentions." Royce tucked his hands into his pockets.

"Just hear me out before you say anything else. I know you're with Cordelia. I've tried to respect it. For godsakes, I like her, but," She sat on the edge of a wooden table at the front of the room.

Cordelia pressed her eye to the crack, trying to get a sharper view.

"You need to stop deluding yourself, and misleading her. What we have isn't going away."

Royce threw his hands in the air. "Evie. You're in denial. You're deceiving yourself, and quite frankly, delusional if you ever think I had any intentions with you outside of friendship." His words were a scalding hot faucet, scorching anyone who got close.

Ten seconds later, her watery eyes leaked. Somehow the

tears made her more beautiful, more fragile. Her porcelain skin radiated in suffering. Evie became a wounded bird.

Royce's expression changed—from certainty to exhaustion. Well aware that a caged animal doesn't stay passive for long.

Cordelia held her breath, noticing the hallway remained empty, and returned to spying.

"I didn't mean...all I'm saying is you're misguided in your beliefs about us, and for your sake, it needs to end."

"Misguided?" She wiped her cheeks and stepped closer to Royce. She touched his face. "Tell me you don't think about it. Tell me you don't remember holding me in that hallway, talking me through the darkest point of my life. Holding me in the hospital, at my apartment, helping me see myself through your eyes rather than Gavin's."

Seriously, Royce? Her apartment? Cordelia's neck tingled.

"Yes, I admit, it had a profound impact on me. But not in how you've imagined." His shoulders rounded and squared. He tugged his watchband.

How did I never see him do that? She tilted her head for a different view.

"I love you, Royce," Evie said. Her words rang like a Venetian church bell. "I've loved you for so long." She took another step towards him. He didn't walk away. He froze, massaging his temples.

What are you doing? Move away from her.

"And I think part of you loves me," Evie rested her fingertips on his arm.

Royce shifted his arm away.

Cordelia's lungs forgot how to work. *Royce, move. Say something. Stop this.* Through the crack, she watched Evie rise on her toes, frame Royce's face with her hands, and come within an inch of his mouth.

"We fit, Royce. Both of us shattered by that place, but

rebuilt into something new. That Cordelia can never understand."

What the fuck?

Royce didn't move. He just examined her face. His eyes narrowed, fixed on her. Cordelia wondered if they'd even notice if she interrupted them.

Evie's lips moved closer. Royce's hands hovered near her arms. Cordelia tilted her head, desperate to see. *Is he pulling her close? Pushing her away?* She couldn't tell. Time stretched like pulled sugar, brittle and ready to shatter. *Fuck. Dammit Royce.*

Cordelia backed away and fled. Her heart raced, her hands shook, she wanted to scream like a wounded Venetian ghost longing for relief.

Her sneakers carried her across the courtyard and into the maze of Venetian streets, hoping to lose herself in the city's grand illusions. But the image refused to fade: Evie's lips close to his, Royce frozen in a moment of indecision, and the intimate space of shared trauma that excluded everyone else, even Gavin.

Cordelia finally stopped running and walked. Every puddle that hid from the brilliant sun reflected her sadness. While beads of sweat gravitated down her cheeks as she sat in the shadows of the Basilica Santa Maria della Salute. Like strangers that passed by, her thoughts meandered—ghosts of the past resurfacing and haunting her heart.

The lecture hall door clicked shut with a finality that jolted Royce. The space suddenly felt too small, too quiet, too charged with her confession hanging between them.

She repeated the three words again. This time they echoed off the wood-paneled walls. He forced himself to breathe, to think, to find a definitive response. He wanted out. He gripped her arms, and pushed away. "This isn't happening. You've got to stop. Do you hear me?"

Her face crumpled. "This is her fault. She turned you against me."

"I don't love you, and I never will."

"You're lying."

He held her back as she advanced closer. Her desolate expression was devoid of understanding. "Listen to me. I care about you as a former student, as someone who survived something terrible. But that's all."

"I don't believe you. You came to my apartment. You held me, not Gavin, you."

"That night, when I found you, I was doing my job, what anyone else on campus would've done."

"Your job?" She laughed bitterly. "Your job was to let me bleed out, to walk away like he did."

"My job was to be a decent human being."

"Who's the delusional one now? You made promises to me in the hospital. You shared with me. That wasn't your job, that was your heart."

"And that's something I regret, but you're the one who's built it into something it wasn't."

"I saved you." Her voice shrilled. "I helped you leave, to see the truth about Leigh, and to follow your dreams. Don't you understand? I saved you from becoming like all of them. Like Andrews."

Royce tousled his hair and paced. "What are you saying? Evie, I'd already made those decisions. I shared them in a moment of weakness, with a student, that's all. That's my regret. The debt you think I owe you, doesn't exist."

"But that night...I told you to be free. We saved each other."

"No, you were sedated. Anything we said is inconsequential."

"That's a lie. You told me I was important." Evie sobbed, a reminder of when he held her hand as she cried over Gavin. He'd abused their working relationship, encouraging a sexual relationship in exchange for grade support. But somewhere along the way, their mutual agreement became a lover's affair, sweeping Evie's emotions into a raging river. She lost herself in him, in their actions.

Royce had watched it happen. The only things he owed her were comfort and time. But even that debt had an expiration date, which had long passed.

"Evie, you are important," Royce held her by her shoulders, "But not romantically."

She pulled away from his grip. Her arms flung in expressive motion. "I'll never believe you."

"Then don't, but I'm telling you, this is over. No more texts, no more manipulation, nothing." Royce raised his voice. "I don't owe you my guilt every time you want to use your actions as a weapon against me. Do you understand?"

"Yes, I understand. I understand you're scared of us, of what we could be?"

Royce rested against the table. "Evie, for Christ's sake, move on from the past."

She approached, boxing him in as she stood with her hands on her hips. "Just tell me I saved you. Give me that much."

"Why?" He shifted left; she mirrored him. Right; she followed.

"Because I need to hear you admit that it's me, not Cordelia, truly has your heart."

The lecture hall's generous space had somehow shrunk to this small battleground between podium and table. Royce pushed past her. "I'm done. Goodbye, Evie."

"Then why do you keep protecting me?" Her question stung. "For two years you wrote recommendations, you helped me finish my doctorate, why? Why do that if I meant nothing more than fulfilling your duty?"

He didn't turn around. "Regret." Royce looked over his shoulder. "Responsibility. I was caught up in my own stuff and didn't see the warning signs sooner. Guilt that I allowed it to happen." He faced her. "But guilt isn't love, Evie. It's a burden."

"Contrition. That's all I am to you?" She stalked him—coy and methodical.

"I came here to clear the air. Now, I stated my position, and I'm asking you to respect the professional friendship we've had. The emotional games are over. Finished."

She slapped him, leaving a slight sting on his cheek. "Do you know what I dream about when I recall that night?"

Royce turned toward the door, hands in his pockets.

"I dream about you holding my hand, telling me I matter. Every. Single. Night. You should've left me there. To hell with your duty."

"You don't mean that."

"Here's something else for you. While I'm here, free from that system, you're still trapped by it. Still playing by the rules, letting honor, and duty, and human decency dictate your choices."

Royce shoved the door open, refusing to look back.

The last thing she said as he stepped through the doorway, "I guess I was wrong about you. You weren't my hero, you were my undoing. A failure."

He left, deleting her number from his phone. Three flights of stairs, two courtyards, and one gate—he'd be free of the ghosts that had haunted him for two years. He was done being a character in her tragedy. *Maybe she had saved herself.* Funny how one revelation can rearrange everything, creating relief and uncertainty.

As she pushed the heavy palazzo door open, the sun disappeared behind her. The weight of the door had never felt so heavy. Cordelia stood in the doorway, key in hand, contorting her face into an agreeable, charming expression.

She'd walked for five hours, letting Venice swallow her in its maze of bridges and alleys. Twice she'd stood in front of the train station. Twice she'd almost bought a ticket. And once she'd stood outside a nondescript hotel, ready to book a room just to avoid seeing him.

But she changed her mind after watching an Italian couple argue with a fierceness that made the cats flee. Five minutes later, that passion revealed it had another face—both intense and intimate. Cordelia decided not to be her mother.

Upstairs, the apartment smelled like home, a mixture of old wood, canal dampness, and the cedar candle Royce always lit when writing.

"Cordelia?" His voice came from the living room. "Babe, I was starting to worry. You never answered your phone." He appeared in the doorway, wearing the same olive-green shirt from the morning.

"Sorry, I was at the library." She set her purse down on a side table, where the white floral arrangement had dropped a few petals. "Very focused." She hated lying to him. It got her nowhere the last time, but she couldn't tell him she'd wandered all day after seeing him with Evie. That would raise too many questions.

"Find anything useful?" He moved toward her, reaching for her hand. Her skin tingled at his touch.

"A few things." She hesitated. "How did it go with Evie?"

"Fair." Royce headed to the kitchen, very relaxed for a man who may or may not have let his guard down. "We talked, and I established new boundaries." She felt his heartbeat, a soft rhythm that intertwined with her own.

"Good." A stagnant sound in her throat. "That's good. She clearly knows how you feel?"

"I believe so." His voice carried the same rehearsed tone, the one Cordelia had used herself when keeping Daniel a secret. He reached for the wine glass, keeping his face shadowed. "She won't interfere anymore."

She wanted to ask more, what was said, how Evie reacted, why he hesitated when Evie leaned into him. *What the hell was he thinking?* But each question would reveal her fears.

"Well," she cleared her throat. "I'm glad it's done."

"Me too." He opened the Amarone, the cork releasing with a soft pop, and slid a glass toward her. Their fingers hesitated, nested together.

"To us," he said, raising his glass.

She touched her glass to his, the crystal sang. On her tongue, the wine tasted rich and complex, just like Royce. How could he be normal, romantic, when a few hours earlier Evie had declared her love?

"You must be tired," his thumb tracing her knuckles.

Cordelia sipped the wine, letting the warmth soothe her throat. Part of her wanted to step into his arms, to make love to him, and pretend she hadn't seen anything. But the image of Evie so close to him kept intruding. She swirled the wine and set the glass down. The soft clink against the marble seemed louder than normal, breaking the careful quiet between them.

"I'm going to take a bath."

"It's big enough for two." His eyes twinkled with a warmth that still ignited butterflies.

"Give me a few minutes. I need to clear my head." He still hadn't questioned why she'd supposedly gone to the library without her laptop and notebook. *He's always attentive, so why hadn't he noticed? Distracted?*

As she turned to go, he caught her hand and pulled her close. "Ms. Dyer, I love you."

"I love you too." Their kiss tasted exactly as it had that morning, minus the wine. And when his hand slid down her back, love shielded her, embraced her—just like that morning, he embodied home.

In the bathroom, she sank into the hot water, watching steam rise from the tub and fog the mirrors. She'd cracked the bathroom door, hoping he'd join her, almost testing him.

Twenty minutes later, he knocked, "Babe."

"Yeah, come in."

Royce entered, carrying a wood board covered with cheese, crackers, and soft, warm bread slices. "Be right back." He set it down, stepped out, and returned with wine glasses and cloth napkins draped across his arm. He'd changed into a pale blue tee and his favorite gray shorts, the soft ones he wore on lazy Sunday mornings—the ones that made her lose concentration. Despite everything, her eyes lingered a moment too long. *Blasted shorts.*

His bare feet padded on marble, offering her a glass of wine, "For you." He playfully bowed. "We have a selection of cheeses and spreads. Would madame like a sample?"

Cordelia found herself laughing for the first time in hours. Tears streaked down her cheeks, a release of stress. "Join me?"

"In a minute." Royce handed her a slice of bread with soft goat cheese and rose petal jam. He sat on the edge of the tub, snacking on a cracker smeared with spicy fruit jam and cheese. His fingers dragged through the water, brushing past her thigh.

"Don't you think it's odd?" She focused on the ripples in the water. "That people can share their lives, share their bodies, and still have parts of themselves that aren't shared?"

He finished the last of his cracker and sipped his wine, while gently caressing the water, as if he tried to capture it in his hand. "Cordelia, I—."

"I followed you today. I was outside the classroom."

"Why didn't you come in?"

"I didn't think it was right, but trust me, there was a point where I wanted to."

"And that was..."

"When she got too close for *my* comfort."

Royce smirked, setting down his wine glass. "And that was when..."

"You know exactly when. I don't need to recount it."

He nodded. "Ah. Did you see what happened next?"

Cordelia drew her knees up, creating small waves. "No. I left. I couldn't stand there and watch her inches from your face. And you allowed it."

"So, you didn't make your presence known, and you didn't wait to see how I would handle Evie?" His head dipped.

"No. Will you tell me?"

Royce silently undressed, slipped into the water and wrapped his body around her. "I froze. All I thought was, *Not again.* But she kept saying it over and over. I snapped, told her I'd helped out of decency, that I was doing my job."

"You did? What did she say?"

"She repeatedly called me a liar."

"But what about the kiss? Did you let her..."

"No. I promise nothing happened."

Cordelia reached up and touched the red bruise on his cheek. "She hit you?" Her wrinkled fingertip traced the mark.

"More of a slap. Right after I said that, guilt equaled a burden, not love."

"Ouch."

Royce studied her face, brushing back a damp strand of hair that draped onto her shoulder.

"I'm sorry I followed you," Cordelia said. "I know how it looks."

"Like you don't trust me?"

"I didn't trust her."

"Right. Well, the last time I checked, our relationship wasn't dependent on her. Ultimately, you didn't trust me."

She shifted, moving closer to him. "When you put it like that..." The water lapped against the tub's edge. "Mad at me?"

"No."

"Disappointed?"

"No."

"Not even a little?"

"Do you want me to be disappointed in you?"

"No." She shivered from the lukewarm water. "I just thought if you knew, then you'd get upset with me."

"Why? You knew I was meeting with her. So, you overheard part of the conversation, I don't care. What bothers me is that you doubted us, and then fled when things got uncomfortable."

"God, you really know how to phrase things. Remind me not to get into a serious argument with you."

"Stating the obvious. Care to talk about it?" He leaned over the side, grabbed his glass of wine, and took a sip.

"Really?"

"Sure."

Cordelia repositioned, leaning her back against his chest. They reclined and talked, adding more hot water into the bath until it was so full they had to pull the drain. By then, the city had lulled itself to sleep, and her skin had crinkled into ridges and valleys.

But the warm night air drew them outside under the terrace fairy lights. In time, they finished their wine and cheese board while playing checkers. Royce had won two games to her one. As she watched him reset the board, hope flooded her body, loosening a fear she'd held in her core. For once, Cordelia didn't need all the answers, nor did she demand resolution. Compromise offered satisfaction, like the moment a fever breaks: still weak, still recovering, but confident wellness will return.

Under the lights, she mentally traced the details of his face. The angle of his nose, the shape of his lips, the dimples that emerged as he smiled, realizing she was watching him. She reached for his hand, hesitated, and intertwined her fingers with his.

Chapter Twelve

The Rialto Market burst with color as the morning light reflected off the damp pavement, giving the air a golden haze. At nine-thirty in the morning, the Erberia vegetable stalls captivated the senses. Fishmongers from the nearby arcades called out to one another, conversing with tourists and locals alike. The aromas, an intoxicating bouquet: earthy, briney, sweet.

Cordelia waited by a stall lined with ruby-colored tomatoes, plump eggplant, and fresh radicchio. Her tote bag was already weighed down with lemons. Basil wrapped in paper protruded from the bag. A young woman speaking in Italian handed her a bag of vegetables and some coins.

"Grazie," Cordelia said, handing the bag to Royce. "Do you mind?"

"Not at all." Royce pocketed his phone, taking the load off her hands.

They headed for a distant stall where mountains of shelled and shucked scallops nestled in ice, alongside crabs straight out of the lagoon. After fifteen minutes of deliberation, Cordelia selected swordfish steaks and scallops, excited to spend an evening dining alfresco on their terrace. She'd gotten up early, planned the menu, and checked ingredients. The night would be perfect—perfectly romantic and drama-free.

After delivering everything back to their apartment, they returned to the bustling streets around the Rialto Bridge. They wove through the crowded lanes, past tourists photographing fruit like art installations, and beyond the jewelry vendors who'd maintained their presence for hundreds of years. Royce led her down a narrow calle as seagulls rang louder than the church bells, and traffic thinned to almost nonexistent.

The alley opened onto a small courtyard dominated by an ancient wisteria vine. Open windows with colorful floral boxes and matching shutters overlooked the quiet square. A well dominated the center, with three patio chairs haphazardly arranged around it. Beyond that, a table.

"Ping-pong?"

"If I recall, you owe me a rematch."

"How did you find this place?"

"Signora Benedetti. As it turns out, she lives here."

"This is amazing," she flung her arms around his neck, giving him a peck on the cheek. "And by the way, I owe you nothing. I won fair and square in Paris."

"There was nothing fair about that game. You distracted me the entire time."

"Distracted you? What are you talking about? I was nice."

"Are you joking? Every time that brilliant smile of yours emerged, I'd forget about the ball. Face it, you used it as tactical warfare against me."

She laughed, hugging him. "That's not cheating, that's strategy, baby." She patted his firm abs and giggled.

"Perfect, you are here." Signora Benedetti emerged from an arched alcove dressed casually in jeans, a T-shirt, and ballet flats. "I have your equipment, as requested."

They met her at the table, where she unloaded paddles and balls from a bag. She mentioned she'd also packed two Pelligrino waters, a stirato loaf, and some prosciutto. Cordelia and Royce thanked her, eager to get their game going. But before Signora Benedetti left, she explained how to reach her apartment, insisting she was available if they needed anything.

Once the signora disappeared past the arch, Royce handed Cordelia a paddle. Their fingers lingered. "Same rules as Paris?" Royce said.

"You mean when you lost?"

"No, when I let you win."

"You let me?" Cordelia set up, lobbing a soft serve across the net.

"I was taught ladies first." He tapped it back.

She exclaimed, "I was taught women can do anything a man can, and many times better." She smacked the ball into the corner of the table, sending it flying past him.

"Oh, that's how we're playing." Royce retrieved the ball.

"I assume we're playing first to eleven?"

"How about best of twenty-one?"

"Why, so you can...take more of a beating?"

Royce bit his lip and whizzed the ball past Cordelia. "What? I didn't quite hear you. Who's taking a beating?"

Cordelia scampered for the ball, tapped her paddle onto the table, and grounded her feet for the next play. "Alright, Lord Brownell, it's on."

She served, and he returned. Their game of volley, and words, continued for thirty more minutes. Their match, a playful rhythm, loaded with sweet, sharp competition. She remembered their first game in Paris, how he'd simultaneously entertained and enticed, driving her to greater curiosity. Then, he was a handsome man who rescued strangers with handkerchiefs. A year later, he'd become a partner—deep, complex, a haven. Somewhere in there, trust and love kept resurfacing, pushing her to choose him with every serve and return, teaching her to believe love is more than just a game.

"Did Richard teach you that backhand spin?" Royce asked.

"No. I taught him." She served, attempting to show off her technique.

"Then I guess there's no one to blame for that weak second serve, is there?"

"Stop psychoanalyzing my game." She smashed his return, grinning as he stretched to reach for the ball, tipping it onto the ground.

"It's not psychoanalysis, it's observation." Royce served, putting an intense spin on the ball. "Like aiming for the left corner when you're ready to end a rally."

"Or the way you like to distract me with conversation, especially when you're losing."

"I'm not losing."

"Are you sure?"

"I'm winning, 15-14." Royce set his paddle down, grabbing two Pelligrino from the bag tucked underneath the table. He opened Cordelia's and set it on her side of the net.

"No, I am."

"Sorry, love, I kept count, and you're losing."

Cordelia's eyes darted as she mumbled, recalling each play. "Oh, crap, you're right." She swigged her soda water. "That's unacceptable. I can't let you win, I'll never hear the end of it."

Royce guffawed.

"I'm serious. You'll tell Richard...you'll tell Cassandra." She set her soda aside, grabbed the ball, and positioned herself to serve. She won her point, making it 15 all. Royce served, and she somehow returned a wide corner shot, but lost on a soft lob.

"Focus, Ms. Dyer, focus."

"I'm entirely focused."

His gaze said otherwise. By the time they reached 20, they were both breathless. The sun, straight above left them hot and eager for shade.

"Match point," she said, bouncing the ball with deliberate slowness.

"No pressure."

"I thrive under pressure," serving with a light hand, hoping he'd anticipate differently and miss the point.

Royce returned. The ball landed just over the net, dropping in front of her as she leaped onto the table. Her elbow smashed underneath her. The ball rolled away. Despite his victory, he helped her off the table.

"Please don't tell Cassandra, I'll never hear the end," she said, rubbing her forearm.

"And deny her the satisfaction? I'm not sure—."

"Fine, what do I owe you in exchange for your silence?" Royce examined her arm.

He paused, rubbing his chin in thought. "Remember your victory dance in Paris?"

"Yes."

"I want a private performance tonight."

"I can do that... if I survive my injury."

They shook hands, and Royce wrapped his hands around her waist, caressing it with his thumb. "It'd be a tragedy if I missed out."

"I don't know, you might steal my moves. Maybe I should've countered."

He kissed her. The taste of lemon soda lingered on his lips. "Ready for lunch?"

"After a selfie."

"Here?"

"It's our tradition now." She pulled him closer and took

three quick photos of them with the table and courtyard in the background. On the last one, they kissed.

As they walked underneath the arch toward Signora Benedetti's apartment, Cordelia glanced back at the table where they'd just battled for victory. A game, a simple thing in life. But it felt like more, like each one was practice for the real match—knowing each other, challenging each other, choosing each despite all odds.

"Rematch tomorrow?" she asked.

"What makes you think you'll win?"

"I know I will."

"Why's that?"

She grinned. "Because I know you."

Later that afternoon they entered the perfumery-bookshop near the basilica and Doge Palace. The historic space felt like a Mayfair boutique, filled with books, stationery, and a perfumery. Upstairs, Royce joined Cordelia at a honey-colored table surrounded with shelves of glass bottles. A German couple shared photos of their two children with her, wondering if she had any of her own.

"No, but I have an adorable goddaughter and nephew," she said.

The fragrances filled the room with layered scents of citrus, amber, spice, and floral. Each breath provided a unique tangible experience, without sending the senses into overload. Soft music played, a classical sound.

A woman in her thirties with dark hair swept into an elegant ponytail shared the history of perfume, Venice's role, and the three notes within a fragrance. "A scent captures the essence of your partner. As you create their personal aroma, think about them, their essence. What emotions do they evoke? What memories?"

Cordelia and Royce looked at each other, holding a gaze.

"Now, close your eyes. How do you want to capture them in a fragrance?" the woman, Lucie, said.

Immediately, Cordelia drifted into Royce's mind. He envisioned the morning light resting on her chestnut hair with that lively smile that bordered on mischievous. He pictured her working, with dustings of flour on her cheek, with an energy that filled empty spaces. Soon his mind settled on her heart, the reason he loved her. *Warmth. She makes anywhere feel like home—a roaring fire, Scotch, memories.*

"When you know their essence, let your intuition guide you to the scents."

Royce moved to the wall of bottles and pulled Bergamot: for brightness, the way she expresses her passion. Cedar: for strength and authenticity. Orange Blossom: because she's delicate, resilient, and nostalgic.

On the far wall, Cordelia selected bottles. The grin hadn't left her face as she pulled each one from the shelf, breathed it in, and placed it on her tray.

"Remember, this is a journey, an expression. Don't look at each other's choices, not yet," Lucie said.

Cordelia returned to the table, keeping her bottles hidden from his view.

Royce worked methodically, as if he were back in the lab studying artifacts, uncovering a story. He tested combinations on strips, adjusting proportions. The technical aspect appealed to him, like finding the perfect synonym in a thesaurus. But behind his precision lay vulnerability. He wanted to capture her accurately, but in a way that expressed how she made him feel. He hoped he did her justice.

"How do you know when it's right?" Cordelia said, looking up at Lucie.

"You feel it, like recognizing someone's laughter in a crowd."

A few minutes later, Royce grabbed a few more bottles, adding a drop of sandalwood to his blend. Perfect, that's Cordelia. He smelled the fragrance several times, paying attention to the layered notes that created a complex but harmonious scent. Somehow, he'd crafted a perfume that was bright, grounded, and comforting while still mysterious. He cut his eyes at her. "I'm done."

"Really? I thought I'd finish before you." Cordelia said.

"Disappointed?" *What if I misjudged and got her completely wrong?*

She shook her head no. "But I'm curious." Her fingertips tapped together, eager to hold a representation of herself.

Lucie provided elegant bottles for their creations. "Please, enjoy." She glanced at the other couple, who'd already swapped test strips and deciphered their fragrances.

Cordelia and Royce exchanged bottles, both cautiously sniffing.

His first inhale brought a surprise. He smelled again, listing the aromas. With each one, she described the meaning. Sensual leather: traditional, enduring, comforting—a reminder of him in his favorite reading chair. Oak: strong, reliable, courageous—he was all those qualities summed up on their date to Old Harry Rocks. Black pepper: deep, complex—he challenges her to be the best version of herself.

"And lastly, the warm vanilla is because it reminds me of home. You're my home." She said.

"Cordelia." Words had been his companion, a tool for expression, but they fumbled out, "It's incredible."

"You really like it? Be honest."

"I do, thank you. Now, what do you think of your fragrance?"

With her eyes closed, she inhaled slowly. A smile played on her lips, growing wider with each breath.

"Oh, Royce," she opened her eyes. "You remembered the orange blossoms." A flower reminiscent of her father. "And cedar. I love that smell. But why cedar?"

"They're not native to England, but they're valued on every estate. And they're strong, like you."

She kissed him. "Thank you. I'll treasure it." Cordelia misted the fragrance on her wrists and capped the bottle. The scent warmed on her skin, leaving a lingering smell of honey and vanilla.

Lucie thanked both couples for attending the workshop and escorted them downstairs.

As they walked through St. Mark's Square, Royce reflected on the intimacy of the experience contrasted with the indifference of the nameless faces they passed. How many people had they encountered within one minute, five minutes where the connection was nothing more than a fleeting look—an interaction that lacked familiarity? He squeezed her hand tighter, feeling a sense of belonging in the crowd of detachment.

The workshop became a door, an invitation to deeper knowledge, through the simple act of mixing oils and essences. In two hours they'd created portraits of each other, revealing just as much about the creator as the subject.

Cordelia and Royce weaved along a canal where gondoliers clustered, mooring their boats tightly together. They browsed shop windows before returning to the apartment for a planned evening of domesticity.

Later that evening, Cordelia paced in front of the apartment's living room sofa. Her laptop sat open on the oversized marble coffee table. "No, Jessica, we need five pounds of chocolate, not fifty. Five. F.I.V.E."

"But I ordered our normal amount. You said, 'order chocolate', and I did."

"That's for the Ecuadorian nibs, not Madagascar. Did you read my message clearly?"

"Yeah, I thought so."

"Jessica, you've got to up your observation skills better."

She read over a piece of paper with handwritten notes. "Bugger. Got it, sorry, Chef." She rocked in the desk chair. "I'll give 'em a call."

Cordelia looked at her watch. "You can't, they're closed. Just do it in the morning, first thing."

"But you've got Philippe's mobile here. I'll call him."

"No. Let me handle it." She sat on the edge of the sofa, leaning over the laptop.

"Ya sure, I can fix it."

"I know, I just..." Cordelia imagined Bastien's reaction if the invoice went through.

"I'll call him. I promise it'll be fixed by morning."

Another damn mess for me to clean up. "Fine. I'm trusting you to handle this, Jessica."

"I will, I promise. And Cordelia, I'm sorry."

"I know you are. Just take care of it. Text me in the morning once you've gotten written receipt of the order change."

"Yes, chef."

"Make sure Philippe sends over a new invoice with proof of cancellation."

"I will."

"Okay, thanks. Anything else I need to know about?"

"No. Nothing that can't wait."

"Alright, and those two appointments are still on the books for next week?"

"Um," Jessica paused, looking at a calendar on Cordelia's desk, "Yep, still the same."

Cordelia wrapped up the call and closed her laptop. Sighing, she rested her back against the sofa.

Royce appeared from the kitchen, carrying two Aperol spritzers. "Work emergency?" The sunset orange cocktails induced a sense of relief in her.

"Jessica misread my instructions and ordered fifty pounds of Madagascar cocoa nibs instead of five. I know we agreed, no work today, but I can't imagine what Bastien would do if that order went through." She gratefully accepted the spritzer.

"Well, tragedy averted." He sat beside her, wrapping his arm around her shoulders. "Jessica is more capable than you give her credit for, just trust her to fix the situation."

"I do, but—."

"Cordelia, there's not a but. You've got to give her more opportunities to make mistakes and learn on her own."

"I am, *but* this one's big. And it affects me. I could lose my bonus over this one."

"That doesn't sound like Bastien."

She set her drink down and nestled her head into his lap, looking up at him. "Maybe you're right." Royce ran his fingers through her hair, massaging her head. "She's great at pastries. I just wish she'd apply those abilities to administration. If only... you really think I'm worried over nothing?"

"I didn't say nothing. I said, I doubt Bastien would withhold your bonus over a mistake Jessica made."

"I don't know. I'm the one who initiated the request for our limited edition bonbons."

"I thought that was Bastien's instructions."

"No, I'm the one who—." Cordelia's phone rang, causing her to jump up. "Crap, I've got to take this. Bonjour, Philippe."

Royce took a sip of his spritzer, placed it beside Cordelia's, and left the room.

"Right, right, I know...yes, I knew Jessica was calling." Cordelia paced. "Yes, I know it's eight-thirty, and I'm sorry she called you this late." She ran her hands through her hair, nodding while listening to Philippe. His voice shifted from objectivity to irritation. He clipped his words.

After a minute or two, Royce walked out of the kitchen and pointed toward the foyer. He mouthed, "Be right back," and hurried out.

Cordelia heard the elevator ding. *He's leaving? Where's he going?* His departure distracted her. She refocused on the call and took a large sip of her spritzer. "Yes, Philippe, I completely agree." She apologized again and assured him the staff would understand work boundaries better.

Their conversation returned to the friendly rapport they'd developed over the last year-and-a-half. Philippe said he'd adjust the order and send a new invoice in the morning. When they hung up, Cordelia stretched and twisted, releasing the tension from her back. She sent two text messages, one to Jessica and the other to Royce. He instantly replied.

Back shortly. Don't bother cooking.

What do you mean? I've already started. Grabbing her spritzer, she went into the kitchen and realized he'd put the food away. Even the cutting board had been washed.

She tore a piece of ciabatta and headed for the terrace. Standing two feet from the balcony's edge, Cordelia watched as Venice sparkled like a basket of jewels. Faint music played on the outdoor speakers, a reminder of the night they danced alongside the Seine. She closed her eyes and swayed. A breathy saxophone jazz ignited the air and oozed sensuality.

They'd had dinner with one of Royce's former mentors from the British Museum, Guy Simon. *Such a flirt.* The man, old enough to be her father, wore a classic suit and bow tie. He spoke with a sophisticated accent.

That was the first time Royce whispered, "Dance with me." That night, their arms held each other close. His hand had caressed her lower back, letting her feel his pulse against her chest. Under the spell of the saxophonist, they kissed. their mouths in tender exploration. Moist. Urgent. Lingering.

That was the night Cordelia envisioned herself in Royce's world—something beyond a holiday fling.

"Starting without me?" Royce asked.

Cordelia jumped, spilling her spritzer. "Oh, geez. What are you doing sneaking up on me like that?"

His body shook with laughter. "I brought pizza, will that make up for it?"

"Ooh, it's a start."

He placed the pizza box on the terrace table. The way he stood in the dim fairy light with hands tucked into his jeans pockets, head tilted to the side, evoked more memories of Paris.

"Dance with me," she said, extending her hand to him.

Royce accepted her hand and yanked Cordelia close. Her body tingled, a warm sensation that spread throughout, like a kiss to each cell. His hand wrapped around her waist, encouraging her to rest into him, to move as one. Closing her eyes, she felt the rhythm—crescendos of emotional tension and desire.

"I could've made dinner," she whispered.

"Shhh."

The song ended. They waited to separate until the next song began.

Before long they sat across from each other, sharing the pizza and a bottle of wine.

"This is nice," she said.

"Pizza on the terrace?"

"No, well, yes. I mean us. Having us back is nice."

Royce picked off a slice of eggplant and put it onto his plate.

"You don't want that?"

"I don't like eggplant."

"Since when?"

"I've never found it appealing."

"Then why did you get it on the pizza?"

"Because I know you enjoy it, and we're in Italy."

"But I bought eggplant today. You were right there, and you didn't say anything."

"That's different, you were cooking it."

"Okay. So you'll eat it to appease me, but you hate it."

"I didn't say hate. I said I don't find it appealing, there's a difference."

"Oh my God, Royce, I'm not going to make something you don't enjoy."

They debated whether she should buy a different vegetable for the next night's meal. He eventually backed down, conceding that as the chef she had the right to change the menu. After dinner, Cordelia undressed, dropping her clothes like breadcrumbs from the kitchen to the bedroom. Royce followed, flipping off lights along the way.

When she woke later that night and ambled to the kitchen for a glass of water, she noticed a lamp beside the sofa had been left on. A note lay on top of her laptop.

My darling, Ms. Dyer, Go back to bed. Love, R

Chapter Thirteen

Cordelia woke with a startle when the sunlight streamed across the bed and hit her in the face. Royce, still asleep, rested his arm around her waist. She reached for her phone. Her blurry eyes blinked, trying to focus.

"Crap." She bolted upright. "Royce!"

"Mmm? What?" He burrowed deeper into the pillows.

"It's nine-thirty. I'm supposed to be at the library in less than an hour. Alessandro's going to be waiting for me."

His eyes snapped open. "No, I set an alarm."

"For Tuesday." She scrambled out of bed. "Today's Wednesday."

"Buggers." He rolled out, nearly colliding with her as they rushed for the bathroom.

"You shower, I'll make the coffee," Royce said, pulling on a t-shirt. "How about breakfast before you go?"

Cordelia darted into the bathroom, calling back, "Just coffee! I don't have time."

"You need to eat." His voice scratched as he rubbed his eyes awake.

She showered in record time, rushing to find her clothes.

"Royce," she hurried into the kitchen wearing her short silk robe. "Have you seen my blue shirt?"

He handed her a cup of coffee. "Yes, it's in the bathroom. You left—."

"Not that one." She took a large sip and burnt her tongue. "Oww. The short sleeves, buttons one."

He plated a pastry for her. "Look in the closet."

"I did, but couldn't find it." She grabbed the pastry off the plate and scurried away with her coffee. "I love you, by the way, thanks for breakfast."

"Love you too," Royce shouted.

Cordelia searched the closet and found her shirt hanging among Royce's. *How did that get there?* She slipped into it along with a pair of white trousers, and colorful sneakers. *What else?* She bolted for the bathroom, finishing up in less than five minutes.

Royce lounged in the living room, drinking coffee and scrolling on his phone. "Do you have everything?"

"Yes." She kissed him, leaving a dab of pink gloss on his cheek. "Sorry," she said, wiping it off. "Have you seen my bag?"

"By the door where you left it. Don't forget we have Lorenzo's concert tonight."

She paused, fidgeting with her clothes. "I thought you didn't want to go."

"James went to the trouble of getting tickets. And the Penleys will be there."

"Gotcha. Does that mean we're sitting with James and Evie?" She took a huge bite of her pastry, racing to leave it and her coffee mug in the kitchen.

"No. They attended last night," Royce shouted from the living room.

"What time?" She dashed into the living room and took up residence on his lap.

"Eight. Do you want to cook an early dinner or dine out?"

"I'll cook. Meet you here at one? Maybe we can do some shopping beforehand?"

"Sounds perfect. Do you need anything else from the market? I can pick it up this morning."

"Not unless you want something other than eggplant."

Royce pulled her closer. "I'll give it a shot, only because you're the chef." He scanned her face.

"Do I look okay?"

"Beautiful. You'd better go before I decide to hold you hostage here." He kissed her cheek.

"Tempting." She kissed him back, looking around as she resisted his lips pecking her neck. "I better go. Where's my bag?"

"By the door." He escorted her to the elevator. "Try not to get too lost in those recipes."

"Try not to kill off too many Vikings," she peeled herself away. "God, I hope Alessandro isn't upset."

"He'll understand, he's Italian, remember?"

"True." Cordelia stepped onto the elevator and pushed the button. "I love you."

"Love you, see you here at one, sharp."

The door closed, and the elevator made a grinding noise, jolted, and descended.

It stopped.

She checked the panel and pressed the ground-floor button. Nothing. She jabbed at the door-open button. Still nothing. The polished brass walls reflected distorted images of her, reminders of the palazzo's forgotten former residents. Her panic intensified.

"No, no, no..." Her chest tightened, realizing she was trapped between floors. The walls shrank, feeling like an elegant vice. She hit the call button. Three times.

"Pronto?" A crackled voice answered in Italian.

"I'm stuck! Can you help me?" Her voice squeeked.

A stream of Italian followed. She understood only three words: yes, name, soon—everything in between made no sense.

"English? Do you speak English?"

"Si, un momento."

The speaker went dead. Cordelia's hands trembled as she fumbled for her phone. The narrow space pressed against her lungs. *Not now. Not when I'm already late.*

She called Royce. Her palm gripped the brass rail, slick with sudden perspiration.

"Miss me already?" His teasing voice answered on the second ring.

"I'm stuck." The words tumbled out. "The elevator stopped, and they don't speak English, and the walls are closing in."

"Breathe."

"I am, but it's not working." She leaned against the back wall, one hand gripping the rail.

"Let me call Signora Benedetti."

"No! Don't hang up."

"Alright. Then we'll breathe together." She heard him suck in air and exhale.

She tried, but the air grew thicker. "What if it drops? What if—."

"It won't. You're safe. Close your eyes and pretend you're looking at me." His voice dropped to a soothing sound, the voice he used when she spiraled over work. "Remember the London Eye?"

"Yes."

"Remember counting the buildings and boats, until you forgot and enjoyed the view?"

"This is different." She heard a soft sound from him. "I can hear you smiling."

"Good. When you're ready, open your eyes and count the floor tiles."

"I think I'd rather stay in my dreams with you."

"We can do that. Tell me about the recipe you and Alessandro are transcribing today."

Cordelia described the Torliani journals, where she found a cake recipe that contained grains of paradise, saffron, cinnamon, and a brown sugar-wine syrup. Royce asked questions, she talked. Her breathing slowed. She had more faith in the reliability of exactly measured ingredients than elevator cables.

The elevator lurched. Cordelia yelled.

"You're okay. I'm here," Royce said. "They're fixing it."

Within seconds, the elevator shifted and resumed its descent. When the door opened, Royce stood in the ornate lobby alongside Signora Benedetti and a maintenance worker. The two of them spoke rapid Italian to each other.

"Royce," she breathed into the phone, smiling at him. "Oh my God, you're the most beautiful sight I could ever hope for." Her body collapsed into his, wrapping her arms around his neck. Her legs still felt shaky, despite being on solid ground. "I love you."

"You're safe," he whispered, pulling back to look her in the eyes. "Always."

The exterior of the Scuola Grande San Teodoro softened to a yellowish-cream in the evening light. Concertgoers gathered outside the venue, creating an echo within the Campo San Salvador.

Cordelia's sapphire wrap dress drew out the slivers of blue in her eyes, and draped her like a gift waiting to be discovered. Royce rested his hand on her lower back, resisting the urge to sweep her into an alley and kiss the sweet spot of her neck.

"You're staring," she mumbled as they found their seats.

"Admiring. There's a difference."

"Really? Enlighten me."

"Staring is idle. Admiring is active appreciation." He helped her with the cream pashmina wrap, trailing his fingers across her shoulders. "I'm definitely admiring."

The glimmer in her eyes with a pursed smile promised later rewards, but the lights dimmed before she responded. The small orchestra took their positions, and then Lorenzo appeared.

After the dinner, Royce took it upon himself to research the charming Italian. Thirty-eight, Florentine, celebrated for his compositions that blended classical structure with modern emotions. Critics described him as innovative and sensual.

No wife. No known children. No partner.

But a revolving door of beautiful women was always featured in his public appearances.

Walking onstage, Lorenzo moved with fluid confidence, scanning the crowd and flashing a devilish grin. He positioned himself at a piano-keyboard combination and played a piece that sounded like a babbling stream.

"He's shorter than I remember," Cordelia said. "But just as impressive."

"How so?"

"I don't know, striking I guess...for a smaller man."

"Should I be worried?" Royce joked, keeping his tone light.

She elbowed him. "No."

Lorenzo's eyes swept across the audience. He paused and admired Cordelia, creating a momentary ache in Royce's chest.

The first piece flowed into a string-filled melody that captured the essence of Venice's lively, romantic past. Lorenzo conducted with his entire body, drawing passion from every sound.

"It's beautiful," Cordelia said. "It's like magic."

Royce nodded, dropped his arm around her shoulder, and pulled her closer.

The second piece began slower, more intimate. A solo violin emerged—a longing that had been birthed into sound. Royce's hand slid down her back when she leaned forward, absorbed by the music. He remembered she'd responded the same way at the symphony in London. On those nights, the music held her attention, but she'd never stopped sharing the experience with him.

As she listened to the violin, the stage consumed her focus. Lorenzo and his musicians became her center point.

During the third piece, Lorenzo's gaze found Cordelia again, lingering a second too long before returning to his keyboard. One time, a chance look. A second, it's intentional. The third time, a craving. Royce had excused the looks and given him the benefit of the doubt, but with every look a knot developed in his stomach.

"You're tense," Cordelia whispered, removing her hand from his grip, and resting it on his thigh.

Royce's jaw clenched, and a muscle ticked. His back rigid against the seat. "Just absorbed," he said, attempting to relax his neck and shoulders. Therapeutically, he caressed the soft strands of hair that spiraled down from the base of her neck.

During the final piece, Lorenzo's newest composition, the strings moaned, gradually building into a frenzied, over-whelming wave of sound. The piece was beautiful, like controlled destruction—an orgasm—where one is dismantled and reborn in a single moment.

As the music crescendoed, Cordelia's hand tightened around his thigh. Her wet eyes stared at the musicians, as if she drew them close, needing more of what they had to offer. But was it the music or the creator she desired? Royce rested his hand on top of hers. His fingers stiffened, as if his knuckles resisted a loving touch. She looked at him and smiled.

The audience erupted in cheers when the last note faded into serene silence. Cordelia rose, applauding enthusiastically. Royce followed, clapping with appreciation while sensing a coldness settling in his stomach.

"That was incredible." Her eyes brightened with joy, a particular happiness brought on from experiencing art.

"Yes, it was." He wrapped his fingers around hers, comforted as she pressed her palm into his. "Shall we skip the reception? Perhaps a checkers rematch?"

"We should at least say hello. It would be rude to leave without thanking him."

Rude, maybe. Ideal, yes. Royce watched Lorenzo circulating among the two hundred guests, accepting congratulations with a pretentious smile and nod, slowly working his way toward them. She was his aim. He molded his face into a socially acceptable grin, waiting for Lorenzo to pounce on her.

"Ah, you are here," Lorenzo said, taking Cordelia's hand with a continental friendliness. "Tonight you are even more radiant." He kissed the back of her hand. "Did you enjoy the performance?"

"It was amazing," she said, blushing and pulling her hand back. "The Venetian water song was..."

"Orgasmic," Royce said.

Cordelia's mouth dropped open, and she shot her eyes at him. Over her uncomfortable laugh, she stumbled for words. "Royce. I, I wouldn't..."

"Yes, you understand, my friend." Lorenzo's face appeared pleasantly surprised. "Yes, you hear the beauty in the annihilation of control. Water is passion. It's as you say, orgasmic."

"Royce has a way with words," she said, her wide eyes staring.

A middle-aged woman in sequins tapped Lorenzo on the shoulder, thanked him, and passed a note to him. He slipped it into his pocket and chatted with her.

"You're staring," he whispered to her.

"Do you blame me?"

"Come on," Royce rested his hands on her hips. "It was funny."

"It was shocking, especially coming from you."

"Excuse me," Lorenzo rejoined them. "She is an old friend." He placed his hand on Cordelia's arm. "As I was saying, water is passion, it's—."

"Right," Royce said.

Lorenzo leaned back and examined Cordelia as if he were about to paint her. "Mr. Brownell, you must be the luckiest man in Venice."

"Yes, I am," Royce said. "And we've monopolized your time long enough."

"Si, si. I have patrons to speak to. Can I invite both of you to lunch tomorrow?"

The word *lunch* hit—an intimate opportunity for him to spend time with her, even if he was there. Royce's jaw tightened as images flashed: Lorenzo's hand brushing Cordelia's at dinner, the way he'd leaned into her during dessert, and that overly confident smile. His chest constricted, a primal urge pounded.

"Thank you, but she has plans...we have plans tomorrow. Maybe another time," Royce said, wrapping his arm around Cordelia's waist and nesting her under his arm. *She has plans?*

Bloody hell? The words escaped before his brain caught up. An uncomfortable revelation that matched his sweaty palms.

"Then maybe a coffee? We can continue our conversation." Lorenzo looked at Cordelia.

She glanced at Royce, waiting for to reply. Her raised eyebrow silently challenged him.

"As I said, we're booked solid. But thank you for your offer, it's very generous." Royce's fingers slid forward on her hip, resting on her lower abs.

"Of course, a man guarding his treasure." Lorenzo's words ended with an edge, a dare to his tone.

"Oh, It's not about guarding. He didn't mean it the way it sounded." She elbowed Royce.

"Si, si. Forgive me."

"No, Lorenzo. We'd love to have coffee with you before we leave."

Royce and Lorenzo engaged in a visual standoff before he bowed his head and said, "Thank you for coming this evening. Perhaps our paths will cross in London."

Cordelia reached for him, placing a kiss on each of his cheeks. "It was incredible. Thank you."

Lorenzo nodded at Royce and walked away, immediately absorbed by a crowd of admirers.

"Shall we go?" Royce said.

Cordelia kept her back to him. "Yes."

They walked several blocks before either spoke.

"She has plans? You're answering for me now?"

"Well, we do."

"No, at first you said, 'She has plans'."

Royce stopped beneath a streetlight and faced her. "I used those words because of the way he looked at you."

She rolled her eyes. "And how was that?"

"Like you were a composition he wanted to master."

She guffawed, "You make me sound like a piece of meat. He was being friendly."

"He was being Italian. There's a difference."

"How very British of you."

"Now you're insulting me, when I was protecting you?"

"Oh my God, Royce. We're not in the 1800s. I don't need rescuing."

"Forget it." He walked away.

She grabbed his arm and pulled him backwards. "Why are you acting this way?"

"Which is?"

"Haughty." Cordelia cupped his face. "What's going on?"

"You're a beautiful woman, and he already has a collection of them. He doesn't need you too. Did you see the one who passed him the note?"

"She was an old friend."

"Italian men like him, don't just have female friends. They have lovers."

"Oh, are you sure?" Her hands rested on his chest.

"Yes. He wasn't just being polite. He was testing boundaries."

"By inviting us for coffee?"

"Inviting you for coffee. I was an afterthought."

She stared off into the dark canal. Puzzled.

"Darling, you're not naïve. You know when a man's interested."

"Sometimes." She cut her eyes at him. "And even if he was, that doesn't mean I was interested."

"Are you sure?"

The question dared her to defend herself. She pushed off of him, standing a foot away. "Are you serious right now?"

"Cordelia, just admit you were completely absorbed, hanging on every note—."

"It was beautiful music. What was I supposed to do, sit there like a rock?"

"You could've remembered I was there, beside you." The words escaped before he could stop them—too revealing, too selfish.

Her mouth opened and then closed. "I held your hand for most of the performance."

"While staring at him."

"While listening to the music." She pulled her wrap tighter. "Royce, you have no competition, none." She reached for his hand. "Why are you acting like a jealous teen? You know I love you."

"I'm not jealous. I'm protective."

She slipped her arm around his and started walking. "Of what? My virtue? Do you know how many times women approach you at events and get closer than I'd like?"

"That's different."

"How?"

"They're not Italian. And they don't have his charm or looks."

"Wow." She rested her head on his shoulder. "This is a new side of you."

He nodded in agreement. He'd never been the jealous type—an emotion overrated and overplayed by television. Yet, a subtle question lingered: despite loving him, was the brightness in her eyes for Lorenzo or the music?

They walked in silence for a bit, before she said, "Since we're being honest, I did find one man riveting tonight?"

"Don't tell me, the short guy in seersucker shorts who fell asleep."

"Nope, but give him twenty years and he'll be smokin', I mean with parents that look like that."

They laughed, and agreed the little boy's parents lacked visible flaws, apparently chiseled into perfection.

"No, the hottest guy there was that historian who used words like orgasmic at a social event to tell a composer his work was impressive." She bumped his ribs. "Lorenzo's still probably trying to figure out if you were complimenting or insulting him."

"Let him wonder." Royce kissed the top of her head. The tension had eased, but remnants lingered between his shoulder blades, a nuisance that radiated into his lower back. He kissed her, feeling the softness of her mouth, but a flash of Lorenzo's gaze into her eyes disrupted the moment. Something irritated him, like an itch he couldn't scratch—foreign and unsettling.

The palazzo's wooden garden gate groaned and clicked shut behind them. Cordelia paused and faced him. "Remember what you said to me this morning when I was freed from the elevator?"

"You're safe."

"The same goes for you, Lord Brownell. Now, if you'll excuse me, there's a very sexy historian waiting for me upstairs." Cordelia slipped off her heels and bolted for the apartment.

Chapter Fourteen

The romantic fish dinner Cordelia had prepared the night before became a rushed mess as they hurried to make the concert on time. Somehow the chaos followed them to the concert, and the best thing about that day had been sleep.

But mornings not only brought fresh light, they offered a new perspective. Cordelia woke—stale breath, mascara remnants, and a messy knob of hair, yet Royce made love to her like that night at Hayton Manor. But just like then, she sensed they each held something back. Questions? Fears? *What am I afraid of? What's he not telling me?* With only a few days left in Venice, she decided to spend the day baking and cooking. Her plan: dinner, heart-to-heart and getting back to where they'd been, physically and emotionally.

In her bag, Cordelia carried porcini mushrooms, squash blossoms, and greens, purchased at the Rialto Market. For dessert, she'd decided to make a favorite of Royce's—peppercorn-prosecco chocolate mousse with a lemon-honey whipped cream.

She stood outside a historic butcher shop in the Cannaregio

district, scanning her ingredients list. Only one item remained unchecked on the list ; a satisfying shopping day. She checked the time, glancing at her watch. *Grab the sausages and get back.* She needed to check in with Jessica before cooking consumed her focus.

"Looks like someone's planning a romantic dinner." Evie tapped the prosecco bottle protruding from Cordelia's bag.

She froze. *You. Why?* When she spun around, Evie stood behind her, looking polished in her red trousers and white silk blouse. "Evie." Cordelia popped her head sideways, hoping the exaggerated smirk wouldn't be lost on her. "What are you doing in this neighborhood?"

"Heading to see James."

"He's not around. He met Royce at the Hotel Monaco for breakfast."

"Oh, I know. They're done, so I'm meeting him over here." She shifted her stance. "Is that a problem?"

Cordelia adjusted the items in her bag. "Not at all. It was nice—."

"Wait. I need to talk to you." Evie blocked Cordelia's path and removed her sunglasses.

Cordelia's stomach clenched. Her morning's peaceful outing suddenly felt far away. She shifted her weight, aware that the vegetables warmed in her bag.

Evie's bloodshot, puffy eyes looked as if she hadn't slept. "Please. Just two minutes."

"I don't think—" Cordelia said.

"He doesn't return my texts." Evie rubbed the back of her neck. "Doesn't answer my calls."

Cordelia stiffened her posture. "Do you blame him?"

"I know…I know I haven't treated you fairly, and I wouldn't blame you if you said no, but I need your help. I need you to…to talk to him for me."

She sighed, *This is a bad idea*. Cordelia pulled Evie away from the shop, avoiding high-traffic areas. "Why?"

"To apologize. I want to say I'm sorry." The words sounded rehearsed. She twirled the sunglasses in her fingers, then paused, and held them to her chest.

Could she actually be sincere? Or is it calculated?

Evie placed the sunglasses on her head—a perfectly timed performance.

"Alright. Anything else?" Cordelia folded her arms, partly from distrust but mainly self-preservation. She should walk away. Every instinct screamed—run. But isn't that what Royce would tell her to do? *Manage the situation, protect yourself.*

Maybe facing her directly would prove she wasn't the fragile thing everyone seemed to think she was, especially when her face was an inch from Royce's. An image Cordelia couldn't shake. She swallowed hard, pressing her lips together. She stayed. She listened, ignoring Royce's way of handling Evie.

"Would you tell him I understand that it was never, that he never intended..." Evie's voice cracked and she slipped on her sunglasses. "I jumped ahead, and he wasn't there yet."

Yet. The word lodged in Cordelia's chest. Her breathing quickened. Anger burned low in her belly, the same feeling she'd had the morning she discovered Daniel's lies. "Yet?" Cordelia's hands began moving well before the words came out. "This, is a mistake. I'll tell him I ran into you, and you apologized. But where you're going with this, I don't want to know." She scooted around Evie.

"You don't understand what it's like." Her tone was that of a threatened tiger making itself heard.

There's the Evie I know. The midday air carried the scent of fresh bread from a nearby bakery. The hominess of it clashed with her acidic tone.

"He's the one good thing that came out of that situation. I owe him everything."

Cordelia paused. *Don't stop. Just walk away.* "That's not true." The words escaped before she could stop them. *Damn.* She'd engaged and given Evie exactly what she wanted—more attention, a reaction, proof that her words were heard.

"I wouldn't have my career if he hadn't helped me."

"Evie..." *Fuck, I can't deal with this.* Against better judgment, she turned and faced her. "I told you the other day, Royce told you, it's time to move on."

"But I couldn't."

"Because you couldn't accept his boundaries. He didn't want you." She cringed, realizing it sounded harsher than intended.

Evie laughed with a note of bitterness. "Boundaries?" She tucked her hands into her trouser pockets. "Royce's boundaries. Do they even exist?"

"You know, I should've walked away five minutes ago. And now I'm going to." Cordelia offered her hand to Evie. "Nice to meet you, goodbye."

Evie accepted. She gripped it tight. "Boundaries. Nonexistent with Julia, Mia..."

Cordelia yanked her hand away. "God, you never give up. You fucking never stop."

"You shouldn't speak about what you don't know. Because you're next on the long list that thinks they're permanently inside his world, and then the boundaries change."

Her hands clenched into fists. *Walk away. Dammit.* "You know what, he doesn't want your message. He doesn't want you, at all."

Evie's voice dropped to a deep, methodical tone. "But he wants you because you're different. You're his muse, the one who finally made the untouchable Royce Brownell believe he'd found love."

Her fingernails dug into the palms of her hands. Why did she stay when Evie played on her fears? Why did she listen?

"This is your last warning. In case you hadn't noticed, he collects broken things, it's a challenge. And then he moves on. What do you think Katherine was?"

"God, you're a liar."

"Am I? Then why are you still standing here?"

"I don't know what you're trying to accomplish—."

"I'm preparing you, because soon, you'll be stronger, and just when you think you can let him go, he lets you go."

Cordelia massaged her forehead. "We're done."

"What was it that broke you? Parents? An ex?"

She stepped within inches of Evie, staring down into her eyes. "You're pathetic. You twist people into knots. You lie. He should've left you there."

Cordelia darted toward the shop, refusing to give Evie an opportunity to speak. Her hands trembled as she pushed through the crowd. The same hands that had confidently guided Royce's at their pasta-making class. She'd told him, "Trust me." Her voice soft and loving.

In weakness, her words echoed an unforgivable cruelty. She'd become someone she didn't recognize, someone who'd wish harm on another person. She'd lost self-respect.

Her throat burned with shame. *Was this what Royce feared? That one day I'd say something irreparable? And disappoint him?*

Maybe Evie was right. Maybe there were parts of him she didn't understand, or couldn't. This is how secrets are born—in shame. She texted Cassandra.

Need to talk. E ambushed me AGAIN. More crap about R.

After putting her phone away, she scanned the hordes of faces around her. Strangers with masked lives breezed past. She recalled something desparate behind Evie's tear-stained concealer—a hollowness, a fear. Whatever hold she thought she had on Royce, she was losing it.

She needed sausages, but her voice would crack if she tried to speak. Cordelia stood outside the shop, stabilizing her doubts that spread like spilled wine. *I try to be nice, and this is what it gets me.* Her heart settled. Anger liberated. *Just get the sausage and go.*

"Cordelia? It is you." With his outstretched arms, he hugged her.

"Lorenzo."

"This is fate." He kissed both her cheeks. "I thought you were busy today. Where is Royce?"

"He...he's meeting a colleague. I'm getting groceries." She rubbed her forehead.

"You look upset. Everything fine?"

"Yeah."

"This sad face is not because of me last night?" He tucked his hand under her chin, looking into her eyes.

The intimate gesture surprised her, causing a quick jerk backwards. "No. No, no, everything's fine with Royce. I'm fine."

"Something is upsetting you." He held his chin, studied her, and took her hand in his. "Come. We get coffee, and you tell the truth."

"I can't. Cordelia said.

"Yes, I saw." Lorenzo's voice gentled. "The woman in red. She upset you."

Her cheeks burned. *Great, he witnessed that disaster.* "It's nothing."

"Nothing doesn't make strong women cry." He dropped his eyes closer, studying her face.

"I'm not that strong." His fingertips felt rough against her palm. She slid her hand away from him and adjusted her bag. "I have dinner to prepare."

"No, no. Now come. One espresso. Besides, you cannot cook with those shaky hands."

She glanced down. Her fingers still trembled. *Royce would hate this. And definitely not understand.* But he'd kept Julia and Katherine to himself. One coffee wouldn't hurt anything. And just until her hands steadied. *It'll only compound the guilt.* She rocked on her heels with indecision.

"So, Cordelia, shall we bring that beautiful smile back to your face?" He reached for her bag.

She conceded, letting him take the bag. Instantly, her back felt lighter, free from the day's burdens.

Royce stepped out of an artisan jewelry store holding a small shopping bag, proud of his achievement. He'd discovered the shop during an after-dinner stroll with Cordelia and had mentally made a note to return.

That morning when he woke, the sunlight illuminated Cordelia's resting face. Crumbs of mascara dotted her cheek, just begging for him to brush them aside. And loose strands of hair escaped from her updo—wispy and delicate waves that curled around her neck. The neck he wanted to kiss. So he did.

He started beneath her ear, letting his tongue glide down her neck, and stop at the base of her throat. She moaned. Making love to her felt like it had in Paris. He sensed a renewed hunger between them—a deeper understanding and a desire to elevate their commitment.

After breakfast with James, he'd taken a detour to the jewelers in the Cannaregio district. It was near the Rialto Bridge and his favorite wine shop. The necklace he'd selected reminded him of her complexion that morning as the light danced on her skin. Made of Murano glass, the disc had peach tones with a single sapphire dot in the center.

Near the bridge, the crowds crew. He paused, orienting himself in relation to the wine shop. That's when he saw them.

Cordelia sat across from Lorenzo at a caffe table. She smiled, watching and listening as he spoke with wild, animated gestures. The image struck Royce like a blow to the stomach. A quiet, devastating ache.

Royce walked a few feet and stopped, frozen by the sight. His heart pounded, and sweat beaded on his palms. People pushed past, insisting he move out of the way. Yet, his feet were blocks weighing him down.

She dabbed her face with a napkin. *Is she crying? What did he say to upset her?*

He charged forward. His mouth opened, her name half-formed on his lips. But the words died. *Not here.* Not surrounded by strangers who'd turn his pain into public gossip. He pressed himself back against the wall, choosing to become a shadow.

Wait. What the...bloody hell? Lorenzo reached across the table and rested his hand on top of hers. Royce counted. The gesture lasted three seconds. She'd allowed it. *Three seconds.* The same amount of time she'd hesitated before taking his hand at dinner in Paris. Her gesture of trust.

His Cordelia, who rolled her eyes at overt flattery. *His Cordelia,* who hid when she longed to shine. What had changed? What had he missed? He glanced down at the shopping bag, the weight of a fool's mask dangled from his fingers.

She removed her hand and glanced at her phone, placing it

back on the table. But her actions weren't those of someone maintaining boundaries. Quite the opposite. Cordelia tucked a strand of hair behind her ear. A nervous tell, but about what—being touched or liking it?

Royce moved into a shadowed doorway. *This isn't...she wouldn't cheat on me.*

Lorenzo leaned across the table and said something. Cordelia nodded, wiped her face, and put on her sunglasses. *What are they discussing? I should confront them.*

He stuck his head out, hoping she wouldn't spot him. A waiter delivered two espresso cups and a pastry. Lorenzo pushed the cornetto to the center of the table, motioning for her to have some. She tore off a piece and nibbled with the same restraint she'd maintained at their first formal dinner together.

It was an act of familiarity and closeness, something he and Cordelia had done countless times. Earlier in the morning she'd eaten half of his biscotti, after he'd dipped it into his black tea. She apologized for consuming his breakfast cookie, offering a kiss as payment. Chocolate lingered on her lips.

He repositioned and studied the interplay between them. Royce noted their body language, observing the repetitive touches Lorenzo gave and her slow reaction to repel them. It crossed boundaries. His, to be precise.

Royce pulled back and contemplated his options. His back tensed against the wall. A pounding in his chest. An ache.

He turned. The shopping bag weighed heavily in his hand. A gift of love and a promise of hope—for what?

He needed answers. Royce stepped out of the shadows ready to confront them, to hear Cordelia's reasoning and to set clearer boundaries with Lorenzo. There had to be a logical explanation.

She didn't notice him moving through the crowded street.

She didn't look at him. She didn't sense him. Behind the sunglasses, her focus appeared to be solely on Lorenzo.

Royce paused, realizing she was crying. A tear ran down her cheek. But why? Why would she turn to him for comfort? He no longer trusted himself to remain calm or reasonable. He walked away. Words could wait. Everything could wait. He needed time to think, to process what he'd seen without the Venice heat and the weight of the shopping bag clouding his judgment. Whatever the explanation, it could wait.

As he navigated his way back to the palazzo, the gift bag bumped against his leg with each step. A memory, a realization cut through his anger for just a moment. She wore the same yellow sundress she'd worn to their cooking class. "Trust me," she'd said as she guided his hands around the wet dough. He crossed a bridge and paused, watching a gondola drift underneath.

When had she lost sight of him? A thought that settled like a shard of glass in his chest.

Chapter Fifteen

Afternoon light streamed through the vast living room windows. Royce sat on the sofa, balancing a teacup on his knee. He gazed off, staring but absent, as if he didn't hear her come in.

"Wow, it's crazy out there." Cordelia kicked off her sneakers, beads of sweat from the summer heat settled across her forehead. She rested the market bag beside her feet. "You got back sooner than I expected. Have a good breakfast?" She wiped her brow with the back of her hand.

He cut his eyes at her. "How was your shopping?" His eyes returned to the stream of light where dust particles danced and shimmered.

"Good," her voice cracked. "Crowded." She picked up the bag. "Pretty uneventful."

Royce sat motionless, almost statuesque—an uncomfortable stillness that made her grip the bag handle.

"You okay?" she said. "You seem upset or distracted." She slung the bag over her shoulder.

"Yes, I'm fine. Did you get everything you needed for dinner?"

"I did." She moved toward the kitchen. "I think you'll—."

"And Lorenzo? How was he?"

She stopped. "Lorenzo?"

"Yes, the Italian composer you met for coffee."

The bag slipped from her shoulder as she turned. She caught it, set it on the floor, and moved near the sofa. "How did you—?" The air in the room felt warmer.

"I saw you," a staccato tone to his voice. The teacup clanked when he placed it on the coffee table. "At the café. He seemed to be consoling you."

She fought to hide the heat that flooded her face. "But... were you spying?"

"No. I was walking back from the jeweler's, where I'd just purchased a gift for you." He stood, sliding his hands into his pockets. "Imagine my surprise, seeing you two there."

"It's not what you think. I was over at the butcher, and Lorenzo saw me upset, so he offered to buy me a coffee. That's all."

"That's all?" He rubbed his eyebrow and then rapidly blinked—a stressful gesture he'd never displayed before. "He held your hand, Cordelia. And you let him, for three seconds. I counted."

"You counted?" Her pulse throbbed, making it hard to swallow. "My God, Royce, he was just being nice, and kind."

"Kind."

"Stop repeating everything I say, and actually have a conversation, please."

Royce moved toward the window, keeping his back to her. "Men like Lorenzo have expectations, they're not kind out of generosity."

Cordelia snatched the bag off the floor and carried it to the kitchen. "Men like Lorenzo?" She dropped it onto the counter with a thud. "That's rude." She returned to the living room and stood with her hands on her hips. "What are you getting at?"

"You know exactly what I'm suggesting."

"For godsake, Royce, can we just discuss this rather than talking in circles? It's an easy misunderstanding."

He turned and faced her: arms crossed, nostrils flared, squinty eyes. An unfamiliar expression. Even he looked uncomfortable projecting it. Yet, there it was—raw jealousy. "He desires you, Cordelia. Ever since the cocktail party."

Cordelia chuckled, seeing the irony after her morning encounter with Evie. "So what? He might want me. Other women certainly want you. But it doesn't mean we feel the same way or act on it."

"You were crying, upset. About what? And why him?"

The question hit, lodging any response in her throat. How could she tell him about Evie's cruelty without admitting her own vicious response? He'd never look at her the same. Cordelia swallowed hard, folding her arms across her chest. "I wasn't crying. And it doesn't matter."

"Doesn't it? The woman I love, the woman I bought jewelry for, sought comfort from another man, and that doesn't matter?"

"Sought comfort?" Her voice rose. "I had coffee with him. Fully clothed. In public. That's it." She stormed into the kitchen and pulled groceries from the bag.

He followed. "You let him hold your hand. What else did he—."

"Stop." She pressed her palms against the counter. "Just stop. You're letting your imagination get away from you."

"Really?"

"Okay, you want to accuse me of having a lack of boundaries just because I let someone, in an act of kindness, touch my hand when I was upset? Then let's talk about Evie."

His jaw tightened. "What about her? We settled that issue already."

"Think again, mister. It's not a dead issue for her."

"What are you—?"

"She cornered me today, and told me all about Julia. And Katherine. She used it like a weapon, filling me in on every former project—."

"My project?"

"Your women. Your pattern. You collect broken women, including her. And me," her voice broke. "Apparently you try to fix them, but when they disappoint you, they're discarded. So, tell me, Royce, since we're discussing boundaries, am I your latest conquest—the American with an absentee mother and trust issues?"

"This is ridiculous. Evie's planted shit in your head. Utter nonsense."

"Is it? According to her, you have an impressive history with a revolving door."

"Come on, Cordelia, don't play stupid, it doesn't suit you well."

She glared at him, tossed the sausage into the fridge, and walked out.

He followed, "Cordelia...Cor—stop."

She whipped around. Her mouth parched. Her voice strained. "You're deflecting." She inhaled and loudly exhaled as he took a step closer. "Yes, I knew you had a large roster of women in your past. That's not the issue. It's your attraction to them...broken, incapable of commitment, flawed..."

"And that's how you see yourself?"

She clenched her jaw, desperate for honesty, even if it was Evie's truth. "Were you attracted to me for those reasons?"

"Do you see what Evie's accomplished by filling your head with lies?"

"Okay, let me rephrase it. Were Julia, Leigh, or Katherine distractions? Broken toys?"

"They were women I dated. Is that a crime? Obviously, in Evie's mind, it was."

"Deflecting."

"You think I'm going to rearrange my entire life and plan a future with someone who I believe is broken?" His voice deepened. "I fell in love with you, because—."

"Don't, not right now. I don't know what to think." Her hands flew up in frustration. "Evie's right, you keep things from me." Her fingertips tingled, aching to throw something, anything to release the building pressure.

"That's irrational, they're exes, not secrets. No different from Daniel."

"Irrational? I'm being irrational? Who's the one freaking out because I had one coffee with Lorenzo?"

"That's not what I meant. And I'm not freaking out. I'm questioning the rationale of it."

"There it is. You see me as flawed, just like Evie said. Obviously she knows you better than me." Cordelia marched past him, storming into the kitchen for a bottle of cold water.

Royce didn't follow.

As she scurried past, heading for the sofa, he massaged his temples and stared at the floor. She plopped down, speaking in a softer tone. "Royce, my boundaries weren't crossed today, no more than yours have been with Evie on this entire trip."

He nodded and sat on the arm of a chair. "Fair enough, but that doesn't change the facts. You let him hold your hand and comfort you, knowing his intentions."

"Do I need to remind you what happened in the lecture hall the other day?" She smirked and looked away. In her periphery, she noticed his foot tapping the floor, his gaze toward the window.

Sounds of lapping water smacking against the buildings mingled with pedestrian laughter. Royce went over, closed a far window, and returned to the chair. She counted the ticks from her father's watch. The sound reminded her of something he'd always say, *Cori, the strongest bridges only appear rigid. In reality, they're flexible.* She covered her hand with a throw pillow, deadening the noise.

"Why am I here, Royce?"

"Because I love you. Isn't that enough?"

"I don't know. Evie says I'm a rescued project just like her."

"Rescued?" His pompous laugh contradicted his confused face. "You think I rescued you? You were doing fine without me, exceptional some might say. Evie played you."

A knocking sound came from the kitchen.

"What was that?" Cordelia said.

"I have no idea. The fridge." He leaned back in the chair. "Cordelia, when it was me, you demanded I set boundaries for your comfort, and I'm asking you to do the same."

"I didn't do anything. I can't control what Lorenzo does."

"Yes, you did. Any stranger walking past would've thought you were a couple. It was intimate."

"Why? Because he touched my hand for three seconds and bought me a coffee? How dare he."

"Don't mock me." His fingers rapped against his crossed leg. "And certainly don't minimize your intelligence. You know what he wants."

"At least he's honest about it." The words left her mouth dry, the subtle taste of betrayal lingered.

"I've been honest with you...since Hayton, I've been honest."

"Really? So far you've managed information regarding Evie, tried to protect me from her ugly truth, and why? Because I'm fragile?"

"You're taking everything out of context, simply because of Evie's comments. Now can we get back to the issue at hand, which is Lorenzo?"

"There's no issue, and that's my point. You want to create one because you see me as flawed, and you either want to fix me or dispose of me."

He stood, pacing behind the chair. His eyes narrowed. "I bloody love you, Cordelia Dyer. I'm rearranging my life for you, and you would rather believe something Evie said in passing over trusting me. I guess I'm the fool. And you're the stubborn one."

"Well, I've rearranged my life for you too." Her heart pounded, creating a shaky feeling in her gut.

"Why did you turn to him for comfort?"

"If you cared, then why didn't you say something instead of retreating back here to over analyze it?"

"Should I have made a scene? How very American."

"Rude." She grabbed her water bottle, to a sip, and jumped up. "If what I did was wrong, you should've come over." She paused. Sarcasm streamed across the landscape of her mind like a ticker-tape parade. "But Lord Brownell doesn't do public displays. He comes home and prepares his case."

"Don't make this about my title."

"Why not? It's always there, isn't it? The weight of it. Nagging at you." Cordelia knew she was being cruel, but her mouth rambled before she could stop. "Maybe that's why you choose women like me."

"Women like you? I've never met anyone like you, so please, enlighten me about my pattern of broken women."

"I don't have to spell it out."

"Because you can't. So, I'll enlighten you. No, you're not British, you're not noble, you don't play social games, and you wouldn't know how to curtsey if the King himself stood in front of you right now. But you are brilliant, talented, and driven."

"That proves Evie's point, you'll move on to someone who is all those things and more."

"Listen to yourself. You're doing exactly what she did, looking for a reason to run before they leave you. You're just like —." His voice sounded like glass breaking into a million pieces.

"Say it. I'm just like my mother." The room became a vacuum, a cold, dark space despite the Venetian summer.

"That's not what I meant."

"Yes, it is."

"No. No, I meant, is this what she did, create problems where none existed?"

"You're the one who started this."

He placed his hands on the back of the chair, dropping his head as if he conceded defeat. "You have one foot out the door, Cordelia, not me."

"Just go away."

The silence collapsed around her. She couldn't scream. She couldn't move. She couldn't cry.

"I need you to go." She wanted to collapse, to erase the words as if they were chalk on a board.

"Cordelia." He approached.

She moved away, walking to the bedroom. "I can't look at you right now."

"I should not have said that. I'm sorry."

"Just go take a walk...just go." Cordelia shuffled back, grabbed her water bottle, and moved toward the bedroom. Outside, a gondolier broke into song. The irony tasted like burnt sugar.

He didn't move. There was a sorrow, a pity in his eyes. He knew how to use words to wound. Now she knew how Evie felt.

"Cordelia."

"Go!" The word ripped an unhealed scab. Her body trembled, a shockwave that radiated from her core.

"For the record, when you're replaying this conversation, you're nothing like her."

"Please."

The door closed with quiet finality.

Cordelia stood in the silence, hugging herself. The afternoon sun painted reddish-gold hues on the floor where they'd stood confronting each other with truths neither was ready to hear.

Defeated and wanting to crawl into a hole, she slumped onto the bed. She found a dent in his pillow and pressed her face into it, fitting perfectly into the space he'd left behind. His scent lingered on the cotton, a layered mix of spice and skin that had quickly become an aroma of safety. With each breath, an empty ache pressed against her ribs. She sobbed.

He'd compared her to her mother. The one wound she avoided, yet he found it with surgical precision. Was he right? Tears gushed and her body shook as she hugged his pillow.

When the tears subsided, she lay exhausted, listening to gondoliers shouting to each other. Venice hustled outside, and all she wanted to do was sleep. She breathed in his scent again, wiping a stray tear from the corner of her eye.

Her phone buzzed. She ignored it. Then another. And another. Three texts from Cassandra:

You alright, love?...Hello?...If you don't answer in 10 mins I'm calling Royce

I'm ok. I just need to think.

Darling, call if you need me

Cordelia stared at the screen, unable to find words. What would she say, Love isn't always enough? That sometimes the one who sees the deepest parts of you is also the one who knows exactly where to strike?

She turned the phone face down and curled back into his pillow. She pictured him wandering the streets, lost in analytical thought; he'd assess every word with regret, determined to rectify the situation.

But right now, she needed to rest, to figure out if the person she saw in his accusations was really her—or the woman she was afraid of becoming.

She dozed, but woke when she heard the apartment door shut. She sat up, listening to his footsteps. They seemed to go in circles, tapping and tiptoeing across the wood. The heavy guest bedroom door rattled shut.

The space between their rooms felt like an ocean. She pulled his pillow closer, wondering if they'd just shattered something that Venice herself couldn't repair.

Royce sat at a narrow desk by an open window. Rare Venetian nighttime sounds from the side canal drifted in: a boat collecting garbage bags, a street sweeper brushing the dock, a couple laughing on the small bridge.

He wrote on stationery with the initials RGB embossed at the top. A half-drunk cup of tea that had long turned cold sat within reach. Behind him, a blanket tumbled off a brocade floral sofa. The bed remained untouched.

Three crumpled notes littered the floor, evidence of his failed attempts to express sorrow and heartache. His fingers cramped around the pen. Email would've been simpler, less tiring on his hand, but it couldn't carry the weight of his regret. And she deserved the intimacy of handwriting, the vulnerability of scratched-out words rather than a delete key.

Cordelia,

My darling, sleep feels impossible without you curled up beside me. This room echoes reminders of the words I said. I know what I said was cruel. Unforgivable perhaps. You asked for space and I'm honoring that, but I need you to know, I'm sorry.

I'm here when you're ready.
~~Love—R~~ *All my love, Royce*

He paused, his eyes blurred as he read the note aloud to himself. *Too much? Not enough?* The words seemed inadequate, but he hoped his small gesture would begin to mend their relationship. He folded it, wrote her name on the outside, and walked out of the room.

As he passed through the dark living room, lit only by a single kitchen light, he swore the palazzo ghosts hovered in the shadows, holding their breaths and refusing to interfere.

Royce paused outside the bedroom door and listened. The thick wood masked the comforting sound of her rhythmic breathing. When he tucked the note between the frame and door, it creaked. *Perhaps I should slide it under the door.* The current location seemed more secure, more likely for her to see it when she woke.

Inside the bedroom, the sheets rustle, and Cordelia sleepily exhaled. A monotone moan he'd heard her make every time she stretched awake. She'd raise her arms above her head, roll her hips side-to-side, and smack her mouth. Soon after he'd find her pressed against him, falling asleep on his chest.

After grabbing a water bottle from the kitchen, Royce returned to the guest room and listened to distant church bells toll four times. He'd reached the mark where it was neither night nor day—a moment when the past and future lingered together.

The room felt colder, and exhaustion took hold. Grabbing the blanket, he crawled onto the bed, flipped off the lamp, and closed his eyes. Cordelia's floral scent lingered on the blanket, a reminder of the night they played checkers on the terrace. The memory carried him to sleep.

Chapter Sixteen

Cordelia woke to grey light pushing its way through the drapes. As she stretched, she listened to the peaceful sound of rain pattering against glass. But then the emptiness beside her brought the memories crashing back. His pillow held the stains where she'd cried herself to sleep.

She checked her phone. 7:23 AM. Another text from Cassandra, curious yet caring. Still a bit of a surprise to Cordelia, considering how their friendship began. But she valued her honesty, even if it sometimes came across as snobby. *Later, I'll call her later.* The masquerade ball gown fitting was at nine, and she questioned whether to cancel. She'd been excited about the ball: the glitz, the intrigue, and them dancing like Venetians. Would they attend together, fractured with an uncertain future? Would she go alone and lose herself in the mystery and forget reality? *Well, I can't lay here all day, fitting or the market?*

After listening to the rain for a few more minutes, Cordelia rolled out of bed with barely enough time to shower. She realized the biggest obstacle to making it on time wouldn't be the maze of bridges, but hiding the dark, puffy bags under her eyes.

A month earlier, she'd pulled an all-night baking session at BL London. The entire team, headed by Bastien himself, worked tirelessly making hundreds of pastries and desserts for the royal Windsor party. An event she later attended with Royce and his family. On that day, the circles under her eyes looked like unexplored caverns, but she'd managed to de-puff and conceal using a heavy dose of gel, cream, and makeup. She pulled the bottles from her travel bag and got to work.

The sound of his morning ritual drifted into the bedroom—feet shuffling across the floor, a cabinet opening and closing, and then the kettle's whistle. She caught a faint smile in her reflection, one she reined in and forced into a tight-lipped line. Dabbing on her lip balm, the scent of cardamom spiced coffee that seeped into the bedroom. A delight he'd discovered at the cafe on day two of their trip. She pictured him measuring each spice with precision, making sure the teaspoon was level. Her reflection softened around the eyes and then faded into a frown. *No, no, no. Don't do that.* Her stomach clenched.

Cordelia dressed quickly, putting on her dark jeans, a white tee, and red ballet flats. The rain tapped at the window, a bit heavier than when she woke. *There's no hope for my hair today.* She rummaged through her clothes, looking for a shirt jacket to keep her dry. *Nothing. How could I forget...* That's when she spotted Royce's faded blue jean shirt hanging on the back of a chair. *It's only for a few hours. He won't miss it.* She convinced herself the soapy smell of his skin on the shirt didn't affect her. She lied. Her heart ached and fluttered. But she kept it on.

Out of time, Cordelia grabbed her tote and flung the bedroom door open, cursing the tempting coffee smell. Something white dropped to the floor. *Royce.* She recognized the stationery and his crease pattern. *Leave it. Just leave it.* But her traitorous hands unfolded the paper, feeling his embossed monogram. The paper felt heavy, weighted.

His handwriting, messier than normal, revealed skips in the ink, where his pen had hesitated.

This room echoes reminders of the words I said.

Her throat tightened as the room's air dissipated. Cordelia held the letter to her chest, wanting to run into the kitchen, wrap her arms around his neck, and reconcile. But she remembered the comparison: to Evie, to her mother. He'd accused her of running. She loved him. He opened his heart within the lines of the notes, a willingness to risk rejection. Yet, her feet didn't move toward the kitchen. *I'm not ready.*

Outside, the rain intensified, streaming down the windows like the tears lingering behind her eyes.

She folded the letter, tucked it into her jewelry box between her father's watch and the pearl earrings Royce had given her. The gold bracelet engraved with *We met in Paris...* glistened underneath the watch. Her eyes rested on it for a second. She closed the box, opened it, and slipped on the bracelet.

As she hurried through the living room, the toaster popped in the kitchen. Another familiar sound that carried memories of him back in London, making his version of cheese toast—a double-toasted slice with sharp white cheddar shaved on top and arugula placed on top. Cordelia froze, counting her heartbeats.

Just like his note said, he gave her space. He was letting her choose the next move. *Damn him.*

The elevator doors closed, blocking the smell of cardamom, coffee, and cheesy toast. The notes' words echoed as she stepped into the rain-soaked garden.

Sleep feels impossible without you...unforgivable perhaps.

Perhaps he'd gone beyond absolution. Perhaps a life without him in it was more unforgivable than the words he'd said. Perhaps became loaded with questions.

Cordelia arrived twelve minutes late. Her soaked shoes squeaked with every step, leaving footprints on the floor. An obvious irritation for Signora Rissi, who complained or lectured in Italian—maybe both.

As a seamstress, Signora Rissi maintained the best reputation in Venice for designing ball gowns, but her organization seemed lacking. Rolls of fabric spilled from the back of the shop, into the windowed front. She had them stacked on shelves with no color coding, no fabric coding, just random rolls piled high with a small space for entering and retrieval. The back contained the bulk of her fabrics, along with two partial cluttered wooden tables, and three sewing machines. In a far corner, two gold-rimmed mirrors hung on the wall beside a draped changing area. The most pristine spot in the entire spot.

Royce had selected her, having been referred to her by Cassandra, Lady Penley, and his mother. Three influential opinions, all he considered the most knowledgeable when it came to Venetian fashion. Cordelia hoped the gown lived up to his expectations, even if he never saw it on her.

Signora Rissi retrieved the midnight blue gown, a billowing design of tulle with hints of silk and gold beading. Cordelia gasped when she saw it.

"Si, si. Please, put it on, and let me see you."

Moments later, Cordelia admired herself in the mirrors,

atop a fitting platform. Signora Rossi circled her with a cushion of pins, adjusting the gown that transformed her into a refined, mysterious image.

"Bellissima," Signora Rissi murmured, tightening the bodice and pushing Cordelia's breast upward. "Now you are ready for the ball. Happy?"

"It's incredible, yes."

"Yes, the color brings out your eyes. Your lovers will lose their breaths."

"Lovers? Oh, no, I don't have..." *My only lover spent the night sleeping in another room because I'm too much like my mother.* The thought hit like a bucket of ice water to the face. He pegged her right. She'd created distance because of Evie, she'd built walls, and even though she made it to the final dress fitting, she planned to skip the ball. Exactly what her mother would've done. Run. Protect. Destroy.

For a tiny woman, Signora Rissi had a boisterous laugh. "Si. He's a good lover, no?"

"Yes." Cordelia forced a smile. *The best.*

As Signora Rissi reviewed her hemming pins, Cordelia mentally strayed into Royce's touch, the sensation his fingertips created as they brushed across her skin, and the way his voice tickled her ear when he whispered, "I love you." His voice, his presence made her feel safe, but it also had the power to wound, to make her question herself.

"Hold still, please. I am almost done."

Cordelia stared at her reflection as the seamstress knelt and tugged at the gown. It was exquisite—layers of tulle that moved like water over strips of silk with delicate floral patterns hiding beneath the surface, while strategically placed gold beading caught the light like stars dangling above the lagoon. She felt like a starlet, a painted beauty who knew how to captivate a lover's heart while socially navigating ballrooms and bloodlines. Royce said she didn't need a gown to achieve that goal. But after the fiasco with Evie, she doubted herself.

"Umm..." She tugged at the thin straps that draped tulle onto her shoulders. She couldn't breathe. She looked like someone who belonged at Royce's side, someone very different from her mother.

"Something wrong?"

"No, no...I just. I guess I should've eaten breakfast."

"Ah, si, it's important."

From her vantage point, she noticed water pooling in the street. People trudged past, holding packages at chest level, while city workers lined the calle with elevated metal walkways.

"Signora, should we be concerned?" Cordelia asked, pointing toward the window.

"Pah!" Signora Rissi waved dismissively. "Is nothing. We have seen worse."

But the water continued to rise. What began as puddles when she left the apartment had become a stream outside the shop, pressing against the front door. A shopkeeper across the way placed a metal barrier across his threshold and paddled the water downstream. Meanwhile, tourists and locals alike walked the plank-like passerelle as if the flooding were an everyday occurrence. Instinctively, they composed a dance with the ancient lagoon.

"Maybe we should—"

"Fini. Perfectto." Signora Rissi pushed herself off the floor and fluffed the gown. "You will be the most beautiful at the ball. And Signor Brownell's love be very passionate."

"Signora," Cordelia felt a warm sensation travel down her spine, "You Italians don't hold anything back."

"Of course not, what is there to restrain? Passion is beautiful. It means you are alive."

Can't argue with that. She stared at her reflection, admiring the hourglass shape of her curves.

"Is good, no? The dress makes you happy?"

"Oh yes, It's perfect." Cordelia ran her hand across the bodice beading. "Mind if I take a photo?"

"Si, si," she motioned and walked to the front of the shop.

Cordelia hopped down and grabbed her phone. There were four messages from Royce.

Sorry I didn't see you this morning. Are you at the fitting?

Hope it goes well. Heading to pick up the masks. Love, R

Be cautious, the streets are flooding.

Cordelia? Please let me know you're safe.

There was a familiarity in his communication, an avoidance of the truth. But what was their truth, their joint reality? Words dropped in, and she felt each one land in her stomach, like little pebbles dropping into a pond. They'd become an intimate, vulnerable microcosm, merging two worlds and filling it with laughter, secrets, miscommunication, and love. *Dammit Royce. You're not making this easy.*

Her father's advice emerged from her memory: "*Cordelia, stubbornness might keep you standing, but it won't move you forward—better to bend before you break.*" She'd lost count of how many times he'd shared his wise phrases when teaching her life lessons.

She texted Royce back, telling him, "I'm safe. At the seamstress."

When she emerged from the dressing room, back in her regular clothes. Signora Rissi was on the phone, ranting in rapid Italian and gesturing at the flooded street. Water streamed in from the bottom of the front door, now blocked by two layers of sandbags. "We have a problem," she announced, hanging up. "The sirens, you hear, yes? They did not sound them early enough, and now, water rises all over the city. So, we wait here."

"Wait? I can't get on that elevated sidewalk and go back to my apartment?"

"No. Here is safer than the streets. Look." She pointed to a group of tourists who walked the sidewalk planks and laughed as their shoes sloshed through the water. "It's no good. You stay, have an espresso, and I finish your dress." She walked past Cordelia, patting her on the arm. "Don't worry, you will make it to your grand ball tonight. This," she flung her hand in the air, "This will be gone. Trust me." A phrase Cordelia had heard a lot lately. *Trust me.* It's as if the world highlighted a core issue for her—doubt.

She sank into a velvet chair, listened to the sewing machine whirl and tap, and watched a progression of rubber boots navigate the high waters. Her phone buzzed. Royce.

Have the masks. See you soon?
Cordelia: Stuck here but I'm fine. Maybe later.
Do you want me to come get you?
Cordelia: No.

Three dots appeared and lingered for what felt like a minute, but he finally replied, "I'm here when you're ready."

She didn't respond. Her thumb hovered over the keyboard. What if he got tired of waiting? What if her indecision exhausted his patience? What if he left? Panic thumped and fluttered in her chest, a caged animal fighting to be free. But he got jealous over Lorenzo. He overreacted, not her. It was her who'd been patient while he worked things out with Evie. *Royce had indecision too, and I was patient.*

A church bell rang, another hour had passed, yet the waters of Venice and her heartache hadn't receded. The rain had lightened up, and brought more people into the street. They rushed past, rattling the wood boards as they scurried by.

Cordelia scrolled through recent photos—an ache between love and preservation. *This is torture. What am I doing?*

"It is done. Your gown is ready." Signora Rissi stood, stretched her back, and hung the dress on a rack. She covered it with two waterproof dress bags. "Come, we get an espresso and celebrate."

"What are we celebrating?"

"Love, of course. A man doesn't do this, if he isn't in love."

Cordelia tucked her phone into her bag and joined Signora Rissi at a mini coffee bar setup, offering to assist.

"No, no. You are my guest, please sit." The signora made their drinks, as meticulous as she'd been with sewing. She ground, packed, and brewed the espressos, serving them in glossy red cups with a gold crescent moon.

"Tell me, why the sad face?" Signora Rissi settled into the other velvet chair, propping her feet onto an oversized footstool. "You are happy with the gown, yes?"

Cordelia balanced the espresso cup in her palm, tracing the rim with her finger. "Very. It's gorgeous." Cordelia hesitated, searching for the words, but her numb mind couldn't concentrate. "I'm just not sure if I'll get a chance to wear it."

"What? No. Did I miss something?"

"I might not go. I don't know. Can I ask you something?"

"Of course."

"Are you married? Have you ever been married?"

"Si, thirty-eight years."

Cordelia opened up to Signora Rissi, sharing every detail she recalled about Evie, Lorenzo, the argument, and her feelings. She ignored text messages from Cassandra and Emma. She disregarded the sun and receding waters.

Signora Rissi sipped and listened, and after an excruciating but thoughtful pause, said, "Love is complicated, my dear, but not the same as broken."

I pour my heart out and that's it? Cordelia opened her mouth to speak, but she realized the question wasn't "How do you know the difference?" but "How do you fix it when it's fractured?" Being with Daniel for eight years should've taught her the answer to both questions, but the second one remained a mystery. She knew when things broke with him—when she no longer craved his touch or longed to share good news with him first. The complications with Daniel weren't born out of love, but out of complacency. "Did your husband ever say something that made you think it was broken? Something so hurtful that you didn't know if you could forgive him?"

She roared with laughter. "My dear, if I remembered every time my husband spoke wrong, I'd need a palazzo to store my anger at him. But I will tell you, sometimes I want to hit him with a dish or two." Signora Rissi motioned with her hand. "Do you know, once I packed a bag. Sat at the train station for two hours." She shrugged. "Then I remembered I liked our bed better than my mother's." She chuckled and finished her espresso. "You speak of endings, but what about him? What does he want?"

"Reconciliation." Cordelia realized the time. "We have a dance lesson soon. I should go." Her sigh dragged with indecision and fear—attending would convey he was justified in his words.

"The rain has gone. Go, go to him." She leaned closer and said, "If you remember every hurt, you'll forget how to love."

Signora Rissi stood, retrieved Cordelia's dress, and escorted her to the door. "My dear, there is only one side in love, and that is love." She tapped Cordelia's heart. "Go dance with him. Let yourself enjoy. And know, any man who worries like Signor Brownell, during a little flood, is a man who stays during the storms."

"Thank you. Have you thought about writing a book?"

"On what?"

"Your advice. You're a goldmine of wisdom."

She took Cordelia's hand between her own. "Who has the time? I'm too busy making dresses." She chuckled, "And taking care of Signor Rissi. Una manciata!"

With the dressbag held above her head, Cordelia ventured into the calle, where water swirled and streamed, soaking her shoes as it made its way to the canal. The air smelled damp, with hints of roasted garlic from a nearby restaurant.

As she approached the dance studio, her nerves sizzled with anxiety. *I could just tell him I'm not feeling well.* That would buy her a few hours before facing him. It would give her time to decide about the ball. Or she could go and pretend the previous night hadn't happened, letting him hold her close. She could look into his eyes, and lessen the storm between them.

She pushed on the carved wooden door, awed by the ornate chandelier and spiraling staircase. Muffled voices filtered down from several floors above, yet the foyer echoed with a stillness, an invitation into a forgotten realm. A fresco displayed Greek couples from passion to tenderness—a depiction of love evolving like the seasons of nature. Cordelia paused and held her breath. The nearest couple stood with barely an inch between them, not touching but connected by something invisible. The way she and Royce had been before. Their painted eyes held a quiet knowing, a secret. *Could that be us?*

Signora Rissi's words soothed a resistance that rooted in her stomach. *There's only one side in love, and that is love.* Maybe she was right. Maybe complicated and broken were different.

Cordelia texted Royce, letting him know she was on her way. Her finger hovered over the send button, wondering if he was already there—wondering if he stopped to admire the fresco too. She sent the text and climbed two flights of stairs.

Chapter Seventeen

The dance school, located near the train station, catered mainly to locals, but Signora Benedetti had described Abbati Accademia as "an experience for the senses", sparking Royce's curiosity. On the outside, the yellow building blended in with its surroundings, but the foyer revealed a storied past with a palatial staircase and brass-inlaid flooring. The converted palazzo, owned by the Abbati family, smelled of pepper—a smoky, floral fragrance left behind from their years of trading.

Before ascending the stairs to the second floor, Royce stopped to admire a fresco, cataloguing the details. The third couple from the left appeared to be spring, the birth of wanting. The man's hand rested on the woman's waist, his fingertips barely touching her skin. She leaned into him but maintained her space, her center of gravity. They appeared to be in a state of trust without surrendering themselves; they desired without possessing.

His jaw clenched and flexed, remembering Lorenzo's fingers on Cordelia's hand. Three seconds. Three seconds of yielding herself to him, relying on his comfort. Much like the painted lovers. *Could she feel his breath?*

As his eyes followed the progression, the last couple caught his attention. They stood apart, perhaps a foot between them, but their eyes held a gaze on one another. Their hands gestured, open but not touching. It was as if they had a secret, a knowing, and the viewer needed to seek it for themselves. Beautifully, the artist had captured something indefinable—connection doesn't always require proximity. *Now I'm taking relationship advice from a Renaissance fresco. What next? Stray cats?*

Royce jogged up the stairs to the second floor and met Adriana Abbati, the palazzo owner and instructor. She met him on the landing, greeting him with a partial handshake. Her voice, harsher than her appearance, caught him off guard. He had expected someone soft-spoken and delicate, considering her stature. "Where is your beautiful partner?" She asked, escorting him to the ballroom large enough for fifty couples.

"She's delayed by the floods, but she's coming." He blurted out the words, hiding his feelings of uncertainty. *I hope.* After comparing Cordelia to her mother, which he knew cut deep at her core, the question lingered—would she forgive him?

"Si, si. May I offer you a bottle of water?"

"Yes, thank you."

"One for your partner?"

"Si, grazie."

As a ballerina, she seemed to glide across the floor, disappearing through a tall white door. It clicked shut and reverberated off the walls.

The rectangular ballroom had a polished crimson and cream flooring. It reflected in a wall of mirrors that stood opposite the ceiling-height windows, where geometric patterns shifted with the dissipating clouds. The high ceilings and flooring created a natural cooling system, a reprieve from the heat outside. The room smelled of soap and old wood, with an underlying scent of rain. It reminded him of Hayton Manor after a storm. An open window at the far end of the room carried the faint sound of an accordion from the street below. It blended into a melodic sound with the splash of oars cutting through water.

Royce paced. His black dress shoes clicked and echoed against the ballroom's frescoed ceiling with its cherubs that watched over the dancers. He'd arrived twenty minutes early, partly out of habit but mostly because of nerves. His hands stayed in motion, pressing and twisting, palms generating friction. His mouth had gone dry, and his pulse matched his scattered thoughts.

His phone dinged. Cordelia.

There in a sec.

He didn't take the time to reply, inspecting his outfit and hair one last time. Royce fretted over his outfit more than normal, changing several times before leaving the palazzo. The black T-shirt and black trousers he'd initially selected made him look like a man in mourning. So he changed into a pale yellow linen shirt with rolled-up sleeves and jeans. Just the message he wanted to convey, confident and relaxed. Although his stomach felt anything but calm. It fluttered as if it were their second date; the night they walked along the Seine. The night she made his heart fall in love.

At the window, he watched boats putter down the canal. A delivery boat navigated too close to a gondola, resulting in elaborate hand gestures and shouts. An older couple clung to each other, bracing for impact.

His phone buzzed. James.

Still on for drinks before the ball? Harry's?

Yes. 7:30?

James agreed to the time, mentioning Evie wasn't interested in Harry's *again* and would meet him at the ball. Even she had an exit strategy, an excuse to avoid confrontations. The last time he'd avoided difficult conversations, Cordelia followed him to Paris. Maybe this time, he needed to pursue her.

"Your partner has arrived," Adrina said, returning with two glass bottles of water.

Royce's pulse jumped. He faced the window and composed himself. The man who'd written that 3 AM letter retreated. That humble man needed her, but until he knew the fate of their future, he hid his raw heart behind a face of detachment.

Her footsteps on the marble stairs echoed. She hesitated, a pause became silence. *She changed her mind.* But the door opened.

Even with his back turned, he felt her presence like a drop in atmospheric pressure. The air shifted, charged with all their unspoken words. He counted two breaths and turned. Adrina greeted Cordelia with a warm Italian gesture. The edges of her rough voice faded into a cheerful presence, an animated character guiding them together.

That's a positive sign. Royce fought to suppress a smile, watching Cordelia hang the bagged ball gown on a gargoyle-faced hook by the door.

She wore the red Hermès flats she'd purchased in Paris after winning the baking competition against her number one rival, Paulette. The soaked leather bulged around her feet.

"Oh, you need shoes," Adriana said. "What is your size?"

"Eight."

"Eight? What size is this?"

"Right. Thirty-eight or thirty-nine."

"Si. Big feet, no?"

Cordelia glanced at her feet and blushed. "Not to me."

"Phhh," Adriana walked off, leaving Cordelia and Royce alone.

He took five steps forward, waiting to see how she'd respond. "Cordelia." He catalogued the shadows under her eyes—mirrors of his own.

"Royce," she said, pulling her hair into a messy poof, and walking over. "How are you?" Her eyes searched his face, skimming past his eyes.

"I'm well. And you?" He flinched at the coldness in his voice. To keep his hands still, he shoved them into his pockets.

"Fine...okay. I—."

Adriana interrupted them, scurrying over with a pair of dancer heels. "These are all I have in your size. Will they do?"

Cordelia's round eyes popped. He chuckled, knowing she would've probably said, "What the hell?" if she weren't trying to remain gracious.

"Umm, those are like six inches high?"

"Yes, can you not wear heels?"

"No, I can, I do, but..."

"Good. They will do." Adriana handed Cordelia the shoes. "Once they're on, we can begin."

Cordelia silently walked to a chair, strapped them on, and centered herself on the heels.

Adriana directed them together with instructions about frame and flexibility, partnership and trust. *There's that word again. Trust. If she only knew the relevance.*

Cordelia moved closer. Royce raised his hand. She wrapped her fingers around his palm.

"Closer, you must trust your partner, not resist them," Adriana said.

Her fingers rested in his, a familiar touch, as natural as

breathing. His palm found the delicate curve of her back. She arched toward him, placing the weight of her hand on his shoulder.

"More closer. As one. You must move together."

As she moved into him, her scent aroused his senses: floral, vanilla, and spice. The warmth of their palms together sent a current up his arm. Her fingers tapped the back of his hand, keeping time with the music. And their bodies seemed to respond to each other instinctively. Royce remembered each time they'd danced together in Venice, he'd cataloged them all in his memory. Yet this time he recognized something different, a stiffness in her frame.

As they spun, her scent teased him. *I know that smell. Where did she...?* Suddenly, he recognized the spicy aroma that blended with her usual floral fragrance. His cologne. *Did she... how did she...does that...?* He remembered seeing one of his T-shirts tossed at the foot of the bed. And his pillow had been scrunched, as if she'd held it during the night.

With the heels, their eyes met at an equal level. He studied them. She didn't look away. Her gaze softened. Hope rose.

Adriana clicked a remote, and the music began. A romantic waltz filled with graceful, light beats.

Their feet moved, following patterns, a routine he'd known since childhood, but his mind drifted. *What did it all mean?* If she had worn the shirt, then why did she avoid breakfast together? All she had to do was communicate with him, text him, and he would've comforted her. He would've listened more and reacted less.

"Better, but you resist. You must trust him, Cordelia. Royce, let her trust your lead."

Again with the one word that had been the source of every conflict between them. Trust—his title, her famous ex, Evie, Lorenzo. They both had been guilty of omission, and overreaction. His hand tensed against her back, encouraging her to lean into him, to let him carry her.

She stiffened and squared her shoulders. A defensive position she took when ready to run, but Cordelia gripped his hand and stayed. The resistance traveled through their fingers like a discordant note.

"No, no." Adriana stopped the music, repositioning them with a physical insistence to change their form. "Feel each other and breathe together. The waltz, she requires surrender."

Surrender. A simple task in the past.

Adriana clicked the remote, and their waltz continued. The space between them shifted, and her body molded into his lead. Golden chandelier light skimmed her hair and reflected in their mirrored image. Spinning her across the floor, he noticed their emotional distance dissipated. She smiled.

"Yes, this is what I want to see. Now you move together."

They responded to each other's moves with the same spark that had brought them together in Paris, and sustained them in London. The one that existed before they'd learned how to hurt each other.

Royce pulled her closer. Cordelia's lips parted. Her eyes held a rebellious mix of desire and defiance. She was close enough to kiss, one crucial inch away. The space between them buzzed with possibility. That inch lessened, and he tasted the sweetness of her breath—probably the sablé cookies she stress-eats. His body leaned closer, every cell remembering the thousands of kisses they'd shared. He craved her, but then the memories hit. Evie's manipulation, Lorenzo's assumptions, and her sharp voice, as both of them, were wounded by perceived betrayal.

Her words replayed: *"You just stood there. You did nothing when she declared her love, and practically kissed you. So, how long, Royce? How long would you have let her into your space?"*

His defensive cruelty deflected back to Lorenzo. *Why?* They'd circled each other like wounded animals. *For what, pride?*

He stepped on her foot. They separated, the moment lost.

Cordelia squealed, "What the hell, Royce?"

He fumbled an apology, offering to help her walk. But she refused. The defensives had returned, and she rejected any help from him as she hobbled to a chair near the door.

"See what happens when you lose focus? Try again." Adriana said.

"No, I'm done. I think we know what to do." Cordelia replied, rubbing her left foot.

Royce thanked Adriana, eager to stop Cordelia before she disappeared.

"Let me help you back to the apartment."

"No, I've got it." Her lips and eyes narrowed, their spark had faded behind her walls.

"At least let me carry your gown."

"I said I've got it." She kept her eyes down, only looking up after Adriana exited the room. Her voice, barely above a whisper, reverberated and caused hesitation. "Look, I'm trying here. But you're making it very difficult to think clearly."

"What is there...how long do you need?"

"I don't know." She cringed, slipping the red shoe onto her sore foot. "I just can't get it out of my head. What you said hurt."

"Cordelia...I'm sorry."

"I want to forget, I really do. But I don't know if I can."

He watched her gather her things, standing between worlds —embrace and release. Royce shoved his hands in his pockets, mainly to keep himself from going after her. "Cordelia, we'll find a way back."

"I hope so. I need to go."

"Will you be there tonight?"

"Yes, I just..." She stood close enough for a kiss. Or slap him. "Why did you say what you did?"

"It was an argument. No one is nice when fighting. But it doesn't mean—."

"I get it. What you said was fucking mean. And wrong." Her tone growled.

"I know."

She pulled back, looking up into his eyes. Her sigh drifted across his skin. "Someone told me that there's only one side in love, that two perspectives don't matter, only the sight of love. I want to see it that way, I really do."

Royce rested his fingertips on her arm, testing to see how far she'd let him in. The moment lasted longer than expected, at least three seconds. *There's hope.* His heart thumped as he inched closer to her mouth. She closed her eyes, welcoming his touch. Their lips brushed together, only for an instant, but Cordelia pulled away.

"I have to go." She rushed for the door, stopped, and looked back. "Thank you for the note. It means more than you know." Her eyes became pools.

"I love you."

She nodded, "me too. I..."

Adriana interrupted, "Signor Brownell, are you ready to go again?"

His hand reached for hers, but she was already turning away. Another opportunity stolen by circumstance. "Thank you, but no." He kept his eyes locked onto Cordelia. "We need to be going."

"Very well. Another time?"

Royce listened to Cordelia tottle down the stairs. "Ah, we'll see. Thank you."

When he reached the street, she'd disappeared, a ghost in the middle of a Venetian crowd. The water had completely receded, leaving little evidence of the morning flood. As he walked back to the palazzo, he meandered along a quiet residential canal, far from the hustle. Above the sidewalk, hanging laundry provided shade from the sun's rays. Music, ranging from American pop to Italian rap, spilled out the windows and immersed the neighborhood in a multicultural vibe. A single kayak guided a couple in a tandem boat.

Royce stopped at the top of a bridge to watch them pass underneath. When they cleared the bridge, he moved to the other side and continued watching as they paddled past a tree-lined grassy spot. He followed the sidewalk, kept pace with them, and met them at the shore when they landed under the trees. "Excuse me, do you give tours?"

"Si, si. One moment." The instructor helped drag the tandem boat further onto the grass, returned, and gave Royce his contact information.

"Are you free tomorrow?" Royce said.

"Si, tomorrow afternoon."

"Perfect. I'll call you in the morning to schedule a tandem."

"Si, yes. Thank you."

"No, thank you." He had an idea, a crazy idea. If she needed to find a way back to them, kayaking was ideal—she couldn't run away when things became challenging. "Talk tomorrow." Royce pocketed his phone and headed for the palazzo. His feet felt lighter, more optimistic than they had in twenty-four hours.

Chapter Eighteen

Cordelia shuffled along the busy calle, juggling the gown bag as she dodged masses of selfie-takers. Her left foot throbbed with each step, a sharp reminder of Royce's rare clumsy moments. *And it just had to happen on my foot.* The bag slid down her arm, the fabric slick with humidity.

A strand of hair had escaped her ponytail and fell across one eye. It clung to her nose. *Not now.* She swatted at it, almost dropping her gown. *I should've accepted Royce's help. Stubborn Cordelia, just stubborn.* A pair of French tourists abruptly stopped to photograph a cat in a window, forcing her to pivot on her sore foot. She winced in pain.

She pushed her way to a side alley, a spot where she could readjust the load and free her hand from the excruciating hangers. Her phone rang. *What now?* It turned out to be Cassandra, who had left another message. The second of the day.

I gotta sit down first. The first empty one she spotted was crammed against a window, its metal surface sticky with spilled aperitifs. She collapsed into a red metal chair and propped her foot up. The caffe buzzed with mid-afternoon energy, a visual smorgasbord: a trio of businessmen arguing over espresso, a mother bribing her toddler with gelato, a barista yelling inside at the bar. His Italian sounded like music with a steady beat.

Across the calle, a small bridge spanned a narrow canal where a gondola drifted past. A fashion photographer instructed a model on the bridge. Willowy, with high cheekbones, the woman, draped in a flowing wedding gown and diamonds struck a pose, to the amusement of gawking tourists.

Cordelia's stomach growled, a reminder she'd skipped breakfast and lunch, sustaining her energy with caffeine. While scanning the menu, she returned the call. Yet, nothing and everything appealed, leaving her in a state of indecision and hunger.

"Well, there she is, the hardest woman on the planet to reach. How are you, darling?" Cassandra's high-pitched voice offered a familiar comfort—home, where life seemed predictable and safe.

"Do you want the truth or glossy?" She nodded at the waiter, who placed an espresso and sugar packets on the table. "Hold on, Cass," she stopped the waiter. "Can I get some biscotti too, please?" He acknowledged with a slight nod and walked off. "I'm back. Seriously, it's been incredible but also a nightmare. I don't understand how it can go from perfect to disaster in a matter of hours." She dumped an entire sugar packet into her cup and stirred. The spoon clinked as it moved in a counterclockwise motion.

"Start from the beginning. Minus the sex. We've established that it's fantastic. And hearing you describe all that satisfaction will only make me jealous, so, start from nightmare."

"There's actually two, Evie and Lorenzo."

"What? Who's Lorenzo? Wait, start with Evie?"

Cordelia did her best to recall everything Evie had said about Royce in the past week, intentionally holding the almost-kiss for the end.

"No. He just stood there? You know I'll stand by Royce until my dying breath, but he knows better. Did he defend himself?"

"At first he made excuses—."

"He did not apologize?" Her tone dropped, emphasizing the lack of humility.

"He has, but it gets worse. What can you tell me about the women he's dated, like Katherine?"

"Oh. Umm, not much. Nice, intelligent, stunning, and I mean, gorgeous. Driven, like everyone Royce has dated. Mmmm, social climber, manipulative when needed to be a social climber. Why?"

"What about Julia?" The waiter returned, placing two plated biscotti and a napkin in the center of the table. Cordelia nodded and dunked one into her espresso.

"Oh, God. She was four, maybe five years ago. They dated for two or three months. No different from Katherine, but nowhere near as pretty. Katherine by far has been the prettiest he's dated...except you, you're the most attractive—."

Cordelia cracked a smile. "I got it. Thank you. Even though you're lying."

"No, I'm not. You're shoulders above them all."

"So, what you're saying is, he's had a string of beautiful, smart, driven, and agreeable women in his life?"

"Yes, that's what I'm saying...and it's been a string, until you. Which is the most important thing to take from this conversation."

"Right. Well, I guess I'm a fool. I did something that made all of Evie's crap worse. And we argued."

"How bad?"

"Bad. I made him sleep in the guest room." She crunched on the softened biscotti, tasting hints of lemon layered with almond.

"Oh. I see."

Cordelia opened up and shared about Lorenzo, the argument, and Royce's insult that landed him in the other bedroom. Over time, her napkin became small shards of paper piled beside her empty espresso cup. She paused whenever Cassandra gasped or grunted, waiting for her opinion to spill out like water from a broken dam.

"Well, it's a predicament."

"And?"

"You know I didn't like you at first."

"No, really?" Cordelia said, "Yeah, I'd say it was mutual."

"Darling, I'm trying to say, I didn't like you because you were different. And he adored you, which I'm sure he still does, but you made him care. You changed him into someone who feels, and expresses it, which is not typical for an Englishman. They don't like it, it's complicated."

"Right."

"See, you won me over. You showed me who you are, and who Royce truly is. He loves you, and if he said something totally shitty, then I know he regrets it."

"I know. I'm just not sure I can get past it."

"Darling, a cheating partner, you don't ignore. Saying something in an argument, you move past."

"Yeah, but—."

"No, he said something painful, I'll give you that. And he shouldn't have been that rude. But we both know that's not like him. Clearly, he's jealous of this Lorenzo. Which he wouldn't have been if you had ignored Evie *and* Lorenzo."

"Cassandra, you didn't hear the way he said it. It was a side of him I'd never seen before."

"Could he say the same about you?"

"No." Her voice pitched and squeeked. "I tried to stay rational, but he was so jealous and questioned me. I felt like a child."

"Right. He can get bossy. And so can you."

"Me?"

"Yes, you. Darling, I love you, but you're a leader, not a follower. Accept it."

"Your point?" She motioned to the waiter, requesting another espresso and two more biscotti.

"I'm trying to tell you to forgive him for saying you're like your mother. I understand how that might hurt, but could he, maybe just a tad, be correct?"

Cordelia dramatically exhaled. "I don't know."

"Well, I do. As your friend, a friend who has gone from despising you to adoring you, I'll support your decision. But let me just say, if you choose not to let this go, then you'll regret it. And the only way free from a lifetime of regret, will be a lobotomy."

"That's dramatic."

"Fits the situation, wouldn't you agree?"

"No."

"Darling, I must run to a meeting. My advice, let it go. I mean, he wrote an apology letter, not many men do that. Royce is a gem."

"I know you're right."

"Then stop being pouty, put your gown on, and be with him. You're in Venice, afteall."

"Okay."

"And remember, he's not Daniel. There is no reason to run from Royce."

They said goodbye, and suddenly Cordelia felt alone, as if she were drowning in a vast sea. The faces surrounding her held varying levels of joy and detachment. People strolled, they rushed, they moved in their own bubble, oblivious to her problems. She sipped the last of her second espresso, realizing her hands trembled as the caffeine surged. Cassandra's words stuck with her. *Am I being pouty?*

Daniel would've disappeared for days after a fight, blaming her and letting feelings remain unsettled, unresolved. *I've become Daniel.* Royce was the complete opposite. He'd written a letter, danced with her, tried to carry her dress, and offered a kiss even after she'd banished him. She fiddled with the paper strips, tearing them into smaller pieces. *Royce isn't Daniel.* His single moment of cruelty, his weakness in the face of jealousy, wasn't equivalent to Daniel's indifference. *I'm such a fool.*

Absentmindedly, she bit an undunked biscotti. *Ow!* She stared into the empty cup, swirling foam remnants and watching the patterns they made. One looked like a sailboat ready for an unknown adventure.

She held the biscotti between her teeth, but didn't chomp down. Her gown bag, draped over a chair, caught her attention. *Maybe it's best.* She dropped the cookie into the cup, dusted the crumbs off her hands, and scooched the shredded paper onto the plate. *After all this, that gown better still fit.* Cordelia lingered a bit longer, watching the photographer push back tourists who wanted to capture their photos for social media. A male model had joined the shoot. He tossed his curls to the side and brushed them back with his fingers. She smiled. *Royce does that.* Her heart sank. The thought of letting him go versus letting his words go created a sadness.

According to the time, Royce would soon be heading to the barber for a shave. The fashion shoot relocated, and the models draped themselves at the back of a boat that moored just past the bride. The photographer shouted instructions, switching between English and Italian.

Suddenly, soft, warm fur rubbed against her ankle. A grey cat wound around her leg and purred.

"Ciao, bella," she murmured, reaching down. The cat arched into her touch, shameless in its demand for affection.

A police boat roared past, its sirens wailing and scattering pigeons, but the cat didn't flinch. After a few minutes of affection, the cat stretched out at her feet, still purring like a small motor.

Cordelia leaned back in the chair, letting her fingers trace over the words engraved on her bracelet: "We met in Paris..." The rest had been unwritten—only whispered between them *and together created love.*

She pulled out her phone and began typing, sharing a photo of the cat with him. But then she stopped. What she missed most about him, besides the great sex, were the random moments shared. The cat meowed, jumped into her lap, and rubbed its face against her phone.

"You're right," she said, rubbing its chin. "We all need love."

After paying the bill, she placed the cat on the ground and gathered her things. She had a ball to prepare for—no ghosts, only magic.

Chapter Nineteen

The water taxi's engine purred and cut through the dark waters of the Grand Canal, distorting the shimmering palazzo reflections. Gentle waves circled past, lapping against the side as they puttered past. Jazz musicians played for diners at a canal-side restaurant; the smooth saxophone sound floated and followed them as they passed.

Cordelia sat at the far edge of the burgundy leather seat. Her gown pooled like liquid sapphire around the stilettos—the right one pinching her bruised toe. She clutched a gold Colombina mask decorated with pearls and white feathers as her fingers twisted the black ribbons. The boat cut through the water and turned, causing her body to sway closer to Royce.

She'd spent two hours and twenty minutes getting ready, thinking and planning everything she wanted to say to him, beginning and ending with *I love you*. But it was the middle part that made her jumpy—admitting he was right. She'd behaved like her mother, who'd found escaping easier than communicating, a level of honesty that knotted in her belly.

Royce maintained a balance of distance and availability. He

sat a foot away, yet close enough for her to feel the brush of his tuxedo on her arm whenever the boat shifted. At times, it could've been an ocean between them. At times, she wanted to reach for his hand.

They'd dressed in separate rooms, revealing their outfits to each other on the terrace. His eyes darkened when he saw her, a gaze that traveled from her face to the slit that exposed a portion of her thigh. "You look..." he said, pausing and offering a formal nod instead. For a moment, she felt her body lean towards him, aching to close the distance between them. She wanted to run her hands down his chest, slip them underneath his white shirt, and touch the warmth of his skin. But she broke the gaze between them—afraid of what she might do, or what he might not do—and looked out over the canal. When she looked back, he'd already tucked his hands into his pockets. He said, "We'd better go." The first opportunity of the night had vanished.

As the boat veered wide around a gondola, Cordelia studied Royce in her peripheral vision. His Phantom-style mask already in place, shadowed his face in white and gold. The mask shrouded him in elegant mystery, a revealing choice for the man who hid behind title and image. And his hands rested on his thighs, but she noticed a tension in the fingers. They pressed against the wool of his trousers, a single finger tapping like a clock keeping time. Those hands knew every inch of her body, every spot to caress, yet they seemed uncertain of their place. Or impatience to end the night.

The driver, a cheerful Venetian in his sixties, gestured at palazzos glowing with lamplight. "A beautiful night for romance, no? Is like fairy tale."

They both mumbled in agreement. Cordelia fingered the mask pearls, a nervous habit Royce had teased her about numerous times. She caught him looking at her. The corner of his mouth lifted. It felt like days since she'd seen his dimples. *God, I love those.*

"How long have you been married?" the driver said, oblivious to the arctic chill that surrounded them.

Royce drew a sharp breath and said, "Darling, would you like to answer this one?"

"Oh, we're—," she shifted to face him. "Royce, honey, I'll let you share it."

"Alright, honey. Nine months," Royce said with a blend of British reserve and quiet authority. "We've been together for thirteen memorable months." He patted her on the back. "Haven't we, darling?" His smirk revealed a tense pleasure in continuing to place the spotlight on her.

"Yes, yes, it's been memorable." She shifted the weight of her body toward him while resisting physical contact—to maintain appearances of togetherness. *Not married, but together. And in love.* The distinction hung between them, as if he challenged her. Nine months since meeting on that quaint, dusty street in Paris. Nine months of building something she thought would last. Nine months of feeling at home in his arms.

The driver beamed, looking back at them. "Ah, honeymooners. My wife and I, married thirty-six years. Every morning she wake like Medusa." He gestured wild hands above his head and scrunched his face into a scowl. "But to me, she is beautiful. She makes my heart sing."

Cordelia's lips twitched. She giggled. On their third night together, Royce snored: soft, rhythmic, endearing. A month later, it had become louder, disruptive, but a comfort. After two months, she recorded it on her phone and played it for him over breakfast. He'd been mortified and insisted she erase it. He chased her through the apartment, threatening to steal her phone. She let him catch her. *Your snoring drives me insane, but it's you. It's my solace*, she told him as he pinned her to the sofa and teased her body with his mouth. He'd used his tongue as a weapon, coaxing her to delete the recording.

She caught him looking at her.

"Well, Ms. Dyer, thirty-six years. Will that be us?" His posture remained controlled and stiff—legs crossed, hands clasped in his lap—clearly an internal battle raged between politeness and discomfort. A stance she'd seen him hold many times when dealing with family obligations that required facade over authenticity.

The boat rounded a corner, revealing an illuminated palazzo where Venice's elite gathered alongside a select group of international supporters and historians, all hidden behind masks and centuries of tradition. The building rose from the water like a vision, four stories of Gothic arches and Byzantine details. Every window blazed with candlelight, and chamber music spilled onto the light-strung dock. Valets lined the water entrance, dressed in ornate red costumes with plain gold Colombina masks.

Cordelia leaned toward him and whispered, "You tell me, Lord Thornbury. Will I be sitting across from you at Sunday dinners in thirty-five years and eleven months?" Her stomach fluttered.

"Nice deflection, Cordelia, but I believe it's your turn to serve." He re-positioned himself, resting his arms on the back of the seat, like a peacock flexing its confidence.

"Then love-all."

The driver pulled alongside the dock and tossed a rope to a valet. "Eccolo. You enjoy, yes?" He swayed his hips side-to-side, humming along with the music. "Dance like lovers."

Royce stood, "Si, si. Grazie."

The boat rocked as Cordelia stood, causing her to reach for

Royce's arm. She felt the weight of her body press into the sore toe.

"The dock's wet, be careful." He held her elbow and offered his other hand to help her out of the boat.

"I'll try." She looked at his open palm, a hand willing to provide help even after she'd rejected him. It was the same hand that traced her breasts every time they'd made love. The one that had written her love notes. That hand had brushed tears from her cheeks when she'd been gripped with self-doubt. And it was the generous hand that had handed her a handkerchief in Paris.

"Cordelia." He whispered her name, prayer-like. "Did you forget something?"

"No, sorry. I just thought of something."

"Is everything all right?"

"Yes...yes, everything's fine." She placed her hand in his, feeling the calluses from years of tennis and archeological digs. His fingers closed around hers, helping to navigate the gap between the boat and the dock.

"I've got you," he said, just as her heel caught in a gap between wood boards on the dock. Instantly, his hand wrapped around her waist, steadying her, and drawing her against his chest.

She smelled the earthy, black pepper fragrance she'd created for him. *My God, he smells good.* It was the first time she'd smelled the scent blended with his natural aroma. Cordelia wobbled, leaned a bit closer, and inhaled the scent off his neck, clinging to her breath as long as possible. "Thank you." *Thank you for being here.* Her body froze, hoping his hands would notice her rapid heartbeat—hoping his eyes would sense the apology she longed to whisper.

Around them, Venice sparkled as their driver departed with

a quick wave goodbye. The sound of laughter and clinking glasses drifted from the palazzo's open doors.

"Shall we?" Royce said as more boats arrived.

"Sure. But do you mind?" She asked, holding out her mask.

"I'd be happy to." He tied the black ribbon around her head, letting his fingers brush the base of her neck. Royce extended his arm, a gentleman's gesture he'd offered fifty times before, and every time the crook of his elbow provided security.

She accepted, tucking her fingers into their usual spot, and stroked the fabric of his jacket.

The entrance defined grandeur with a chandelier the size of a small car, cornice doorways flanked by ornate mirrors, and a sweeping marble staircase that guided party-goers to the ball-room. Every surface caught and reflected light. A wonderland for the senses. Four costumed figures, with their skin covered in gold, posed on pedestals, while masked guests swirled past in a riot of color and texture.

"It's beautiful," she said, forgetting their troubles.

"Stunning."

When she glanced at Royce, she realized he wasn't looking at the décor, his eyes were fixed on her. A flush hit and she fanned herself. "It's warm in here." She felt for her necklace.

His smile emerged from behind the mask. "We don't have to stay long," he said, letting his breath settle against her earlobe. "If you're uncomfortable we can make our appearance and then—."

"Are you kidding? Look at me. Do you think I did all of this just to make an appearance?"

"You have a point."

"Besides, if we go back, then what? Separate bedrooms?"

His jaw tightened. "Maybe we should discuss this later."

She turned to face him. "Royce, I don't want to go back. I'd rather stay here and pretend than be alone."

"I was going to suggest we talk. I think we could use an honest conversation."

"I do too."

For a moment, the world fell away. They reconnected in an unexpected, magical place, and it was just them—together. But then someone jostled past, bumping her and breaking the spell. They climbed the palazzo steps while keeping an emotional distance. Each step in unison—without communication or eye contact.

The ballroom erupted in splendor. A sensory feast that surprised even Royce, who'd attended societal events at grand venues throughout Europe, but the artistry gave him reason to pause. Strings of lights, shaped like tiny candles, created a starry night pattern dangling above the three crystal chandeliers. The glow turned the ornate ballroom into a magical realm, a world where even ghosts and fairies would want to dance.

On the walls, frescoes of mythological lovers: Psyche and Cupid, Orpheus and Eurydice, Paris and Helen, were frozen in moments of passion or loss. *Love tested by the gods. Sums up our week.*

Jewel-toned gowns swirled past, captivating Cordelia, but his attention rested on her as she turned in every direction, taking in the exquisite room. Her face, lit by the glow of lights, beamed with delight. Peeking out from her shoulder strap was the dandelion tattoo he'd touched many times with his lips, a spot that made her shiver. But it was the slit of her gown that played a game of allurement—taunting, reminding him of what had been—what might be again.

"Champagne?" he asked, already knowing the answer.

"Please."

He squeezed her hand, a test to see how she'd react. She didn't flinch. She didn't pull away. A warm wave of relief flooded him. "Be right back." He brought her hand to his mouth, stopped short when he realized she might not be open to a kiss, and then released it. "Let me get us that champagne."

"Royce..."

"No worries. Be right back." At the bar, the line queued through a burgundy-colored rope. With five men ahead of him, he checked his phone, noticing a text from Marcus.

Everything is set for Ada Rose. You and Cordelia are officially her godparents. Let's grab lunch when you're back.

Fantastic. I'll call to arrange.

"Champagne, sir?" A server appeared at his elbow with a silver tray holding chilled glasses.

"Thank you." He accepted two glasses and left the queue, soon discovering Cordelia near the Paris and Helen fresco. She also held two glasses. As he got closer, the crowd seemed to part for him, but in reality the magnetic pull toward her made everything else fade.

"Guess we're thirsty." Her lips curved upward. She took a sip from one. "Maybe we should..."

"Right." Although they were together, the awkward tension lingered. Royce felt nervous, first-date schoolboy jitters. He set the glasses on a nearby cocktail table and accepted one from her.

"Royce, I..." The ribbon tangled in her pearl earrings, distracting her from finishing the sentence. She reached up and tried to free it without dropping her champagne. "I..."

"Allow me."

She froze, bringing them closer than they'd been since dancing earlier in the day. He gently unwrapped the ribbon, looking into her green eyes that peered through the mask. They reflected the gold that shimmered around them. Her perfume, mixed with the sweetness of her skin, held notes of orange blossom, cardamom, and sugar. The fragrance stimulated a burn in his core. The heat radiated through his chest.

His fingers freed the earring, letting the ribbon drape down her back. "There." He should've stepped back and restored distance, but his hand lingered. The curve of her jaw brushed underneath his thumb.

Her breath strayed across his wrist, and she leaned into him. "Thank you," she whispered in a tone normally reserved for intimacy. "Your mask is slipping," she said, reaching up to adjust the gold edge where it had shifted. Her fingertips grazed his neck.

"Royce. I wasn't sure I'd see you here when I left Harry's." Dr. Morrison materialized like an unwelcomed ghost. "Glad to see both of you."

Bloody hell. Royce stepped away from her, taking a proper social distance. He placed his hand on the small of Cordelia's back. A spot that had become an anchor in the world of pretense. "James, lovely to see you again."

They moved through the crowd, effectively greeting museum directors, restoration experts, and other patrons. Cordelia proved as adept as his mother at working a room. She laughed at appropriate moments and deflected unwanted attention with diplomatic grace. A few times, when someone presumed too much, her fingers clutched his hand, and gradually she inched closer.

The bulk of the evening's networking centered around seven cocktail tables located closest to the bar, which is where the biggest donors refilled their Macallans and Cognacs.

"I need some fresh air, if that's all right," Cordelia said, resting her hand on his arm.

"Actually, you read my mind."

"Good." A waiter passed. "Champagne?" She grabbed two glasses and handed one to Royce.

"Here, let's slip out this way." He motioned toward the terrace, letting her lead the way. They weaved through crowds and got close enough to the doors to smell a warm, salty breeze floating in from the canals.

"Lord Brownell, there you are," Countess Capaldi said, grabbing his arm and bringing him to a halt.

"Countess," he gave an Italian greeting, "may I introduce my...my partner, Ms. Cordelia Dyer."

She gushed over Cordelia's dress, her beauty, and asked every social norm question. The Countess left little time for a reply, suggesting she had no interest in knowing Cordelia, only in appearing gracious.

"Now, have the Earl and Countess decided if they're hosting the hunt in October?"

Cordelia's back and shoulders shifted. "If you'll excuse me, Countess, it was lovely meeting you."

"You as well."

"I'll find you shortly," Royce said, releasing his hand from the small of her back. His eyes followed her as she disappeared onto the terrace.

"Do your parents approve?" the Countess asked.

"Pardon?" Royce circled his fingers around the glass stem.

"The American, does the Earl and Countess approve of her?"

"As a matter of fact, they adore her." He sipped the champagne. "Back to your question..."

"Yes, I hadn't received an invitation this year, and I wondered if they'd decided not to host the hunt."

"I believe so, but there's been a few delays. We've hired a new gamekeeper."

"Oh, what happened to Mr. Blair? The Count will be very disappointed to hear."

The conversation dragged—ten minutes felt like hours. He finally extracted himself and headed for the terrace, placing his empty glass on a table outside the door. He heard Cordelia talking before seeing her. He smiled, turned the corner, and his heart dropped. Evie. *Bloody hell...now what?*

"I owe you an apology," Evie said, her voice void of desperation, replaced with something genuine—a humility he'd never heard from her. "My behavior has been inappropriate and unfair...to you and Royce."

He leaned against the wall and listened. The level of Evie's voice dropped, making it difficult for him to hear everything. *The one time she speaks softly.* He strained to catch her words, grabbing only fragments: something about therapy and regressing. *What is she telling Cordelia?* He concentrated.

Cordelia laughed with a burst of energy. "Strategic swooning? Is that what you call it?" she said.

"I discussed it with James, and it wasn't right for me to interfere with Royce's life."

Sod it. He smoothed the front of his jacket and took a step forward.

"Bella, Cordelia." Lorenzo materialized from inside like a predator hunting its prey.

From the shadows, Royce watched as he moved toward Cordelia and Evie.

"May I say, you look beautiful tonight. That gown was made for you."

Every muscle in Royce's body went taut. He stepped forward, paused, and stepped back. It wasn't about trust, not this time. He hesitated because she didn't need rescuing from some medieval knight, that much he'd learned from their argument. Cordelia had made it clear--she needed room to rescue herself.

So, he held back, giving her the space to handle the situation on her own terms. Royce folded his arms and listened.

"Lorenzo. Still making the rounds, I see," Evie said with admirable coolness.

"Forgive the interruption." He held laser-focus on Cordelia. "Is Lord Brownell with you this evening?"

"He's inside."

"I see." Lorenzo looked toward the ballroom.

"No matter, I was hoping to steal you for a dance. Or perhaps...if you are..."

Royce's hands clenched as Lorenzo reached for Cordelia's arm. *I've seen enough.*

But she turned her body away from him, holding her purse in front of her chest. "Thank you, I'm flattered, but I need to go find Royce."

Well done.

"Come now, one dance won't harm anyone," Lorenzo's voice dropped, "I doubt he'll care. He left you alone while he negotiates."

"Oh, he'll care." Cordelia adjusted her mask and fidgeted with her necklace.

"Me, I would never leave a beauty, as yourself, unattended at a gathering like this."

"Well, you're not him. And I said, no thank you." Her voice emphasized each word.

Royce stepped out of the shadow and walked straight to Cordelia. "The orchestra is starting the next waltz. Shall we dance, love?"

Lorenzo held his chin high. "Lord Brownell. Cordelia and I were—."

"Saying goodbye?" Royce said.

"We were debating the possibilities—."

"I believe we were all saying goodnight, weren't we, Evie?"

Cordelia approached Royce and slipped her hand into the crook of his arm.

"Well, I believe I'll leave on that note," Evie said. "Royce, goodbye. Cordelia." She bowed her head to each of them and hurried away. Lorenzo chased after her, saying something that made her cackle.

"Lord Thornbury, if the offer stands, I'd love to dance."

"Always." Whatever came next, whatever they had to rebuild came after their dance.

Chapter Twenty

Cordelia and Royce reached the dance floor as the orchestra struck the opening notes of a famous waltz. Every time she heard the piece, it conjured a deep sense of beauty, mystery, and sensuality. "Do you remember the first time we danced to this song?"

"That would've been the symphony ball?" Surrounded by other couples, he led her into position, his hand molding around her shoulder blade. His palm supported her, a strength that tingled down her spine.

Resting her hand on his bicep, she felt the flex of his muscles through the jacket. His solidness, his *Royceness* erased her anger —the way he touched her, the way he made her laugh in the darkest moments, and even his contradictions of living as a noble and a rebel. It all dissipated the hurt. But most of all, it was the way he held space for her to be imperfect. "Do you remember what you said that night?"

"I've got you?" Royce said with a smirk as he twirled her and guided her back into position.

"You did say that, didn't you? Right after I tripped going up the stairs." She met his eyes through his mask, noting the soft smile lines at the outer corners. "You said, trust me, and I want you to know I do, even after..."

"I know." He guided her through a turn as piccolos transitioned the melody from sultry to sweet.

The box steps and turns escalated as the waltz unveiled its complexity, a melodic story. After eight charity events in one year, she'd memorized the standard orchestra playlist and dance steps.

"Royce..." Across the room, she spotted Evie dancing with Lorenzo. Her eyes narrowed and searched for James, noticing he chatted with a tall woman in a purple and gold mask. *Who knew?* Cordelia refocused on the dance, feeling his hand pull her slightly closer. "I should've trusted you that day at the university."

His fingers tightened around her hand as they spun. "I never should've gone."

"But you needed closure, and I let my imagination get out of hand."

They moved through a pattern that required repetitive spins —pushing away and pulling close. Perfect form. Perfect timing. *Feels like our relationship lately.*

The music softened into the sorrowful, expressive sounds of oboes and cellos. Despite their wide arms, Royce wrapped his arm across her back. "Cordelia, what are you afraid of?"

"Do you want the full list?"

"Yes, I do."

They passed beneath one of the massive chandeliers, its light fractured through crystals, painting rainbow patterns across their skin. Around them, other couples swirled, but the space around them felt vast and private.

"Here? Now?"

"Then one thing, tell me what you're most afraid of." He spun her and placed his hand at her waist.

She clasped his hand tighter. *Just say it.* Her palm pressed against his as they swept around the room. "I'm afraid of being her, and losing you."

"You're not your mother, Cordelia. And I'm sorry for what I said."

The music swelled to a crescendo, and their feet moved faster. She felt her toe throb, but she stepped wide, keeping the pace. Her heart raced. The orchestra stopped in a dramatic ending, bring dancers to a halt. Some couples clapped as they walked away. Cordelia stepped into Royce's arms. "I think I'm ready to have that conversation now."

"I'm here."

"At the apartment?"

"Even better. Shall we go?"

Cordelia nodded and kissed his cheek. "Royce, I'm sorry, too."

The orchestra began another piece, and they rushed off the dance floor. Her entire body pulsed with a rush of optimism as they walked down the palazzo stairs toward the dock. As they waited for their water taxi to arrive, Royce removed his mask, and kissed her. The heat of his mouth coaxed desire. She pulled back, fearful she'd forget everything she wanted to say, and realized she still wore her mask.

The water taxi's engine hummed beneath them as Royce settled into the leather seat, conscious of every inch between their bodies. With every rock of the boat, Cordelia's gown brushed his thigh—sheer and heavy—contrasting weights, opposites, like them in many ways. "Palazzo Li Fonti," he said to the driver, anticipation coursing through his body, despite the layers between them. The usual mossy scent of the canal carried a lighter jasmine fragrance, a breeze of change.

The same cheerful man who'd delivered them to the gala nodded, "Si, si." He guided the boat into the maze of narrow canals where ancient walls rose from dark water. "Beautiful party, no? You dance like lovers, yes?" The questions were more profound than he knew. As he sped up, water lapped against the hull as they glided past palazzo windows that flickered like thousands of candles in winter.

"Si, ci è piaciuto molto." Royce leaned closer to Cordelia's ear, feeling the heat of her skin. "I told him we enjoyed it. Would you agree?"

"It was lovely." She still wore her feathered mask, revealing little of her thoughts, and forcing him to interpret the glint in her eyes or the slight uplift of her mouth.

"That's very diplomatic of you."

"Hopefully, the party's not over."

What was she thinking behind her disguise? What exactly did she want to say? Her words echoed in his mind, *I have more to say*, causing his stomach to tighten with curiosity.

Out of his periphery, he caught her watching him. *Is she ready?* She sounded ready to commit to their future, to unpack and fully share their lives. Cordelia needed security, he needed certainty. They both wanted love. *But is she ready?*

When he found her hand in the darkness, her pulse fluttered against his wrist, and despite the warm evening, her fingers felt cold. As he warmed them, she didn't pull away. Instead, she interlaced their fingers and rested her shoulder against his. The electricity felt monumental—an opening in the wall, an offering of her heart.

Back in London, his grandmother's diamond engagement ring lay safe inside a vault. It had lived there for four years, since he'd inherited it from her. The ring had witnessed sixty-five years of marriage, through wars and scandals, doubt and devotion. And for the first time since inheriting it, Royce envisioned the next hand that would wear it. When and if he proposed to Cordelia, it wouldn't be out of duty, but from absolute certainty.

The boat glided through a narrow canal lined with darkened palazzos. Cordelia's breathing quickened, and Royce felt her pulse in the palm of his hand. He recognized the rhythm from late nights when she lay awake worried, working through problems in solitude.

Her thumb moved across his knuckles, sending heat up his arm. He wanted to pull her into his lap and admire her with his hands, but she'd asked for a conversation first. And he'd learned, Cordelia swung between cautious and devoted.

The boat approached a low bridge, plunging them into darkness. Its wake created soft ripples that captured the fading lamplight and turned it into a stream of liquid amber that trailed behind. Cordelia shifted closer, settling herself on his chest. He breathed in her perfume as she nuzzled her nose on his neck, kissing him just below the ear. She exhaled. The boat emerged on the other side, illuminated by muted apartment lights and street lamps.

Bloody hell. Royce pulled back, seeking her eyes. "You're teasing me."

"I'm communicating."

"Is that what you call it?"

Her hand slid to the inside of his thigh. Heat radiated through the wool of his trousers where her palm rested. His body stiffened.

"I think we need to talk first, isn't that what you said?"

They stared at each other, neither changing the position of her hand.

The boat rounded a corner, revealing their palazzo rising from the water like a promise. Soon they'd be alone, truly alone, with nothing but love and courage to bridge the gap their fears had created.

As the driver navigated toward their dock, Cordelia's hand retreated, clasping her palms in her lap. The night's sounds carried differently as they skimmed over the water: distant laughter from a late-night dinner party, the echo of footsteps on a nearby stone bridge, and the soft splash of oars somewhere in the maze of canals.

Royce embraced the sensual curve of her hips as he wrapped his arm around her waist. When he kissed her bare shoulder, a sweet taste lingered on his tongue.

The boat glided to a stop. Royce paid the driver and assisted Cordelia as she disembarked. Inside the palazzo foyer, they faced each other, both opening their mouths to speak, but they waited. He untied the ribbon of her mask, letting it fall into her hands.

"I had everything I was going to say planned out, and now I can't remember anything other than I love you."

"Then why don't we start there and see where it takes us?"

She nodded, took his hand, and headed toward the elevator. As they waited, footsteps shuffled in the corridor. They looked both directions, nothing.

"Do you feel that?" she asked.

"What?"

"The air. It's cold."

"Come on, Cordelia..."

"No, I'm serious, it's colder. See, I'm shivering." She held her hand up, showing how her fingers shook. The elevator doors opened, and the footsteps shuffled four doors away. "There's someone here." She grabbed Royce, causing him to startle.

He held open the elevator door while she boarded. "You know I'll get you back the next time we're at Hayton, and trust me, British ghosts don't play around."

"What are they going to do, startle me? Wake me in the middle of the night?"

Royce laughed. "They like to follow you, waiting until you're alone, especially if it's raining outside, and brush up against you." He grazed his fingers down her arm. "And sometimes, they'll kiss your neck, like this." His mouth nuzzled her neck, soft at first and then added a slight nibble. Her squeal echoed, bouncing off the elevator walls.

Chapter Twenty-One

The elevator doors whispered shut, surrendering them to the saffron glow of the palazzo's main living room. A moonless night meant that only Venice's shadowed lamps streamed through the tall terrace doors, transforming the apartment from battleground to refuge.

Cordelia made her way to a window, placing her mask and clutch on a side table. She traced a light pattern on the glass, hyperaware of every sensation: the silk of her gown pressed her skin, the cool marble beneath her sore feet, the sound of Royce popping open a bottle of wine, and the electricity of his eyes burning against the back of her neck. They were alone. No interruptions. No barriers. Nowhere to hide. Unless her stubborn fear decided to resurface. *Not this time.*

"Dance with me," he said, his voice edged with need. The same desire that drummed in her veins. His breath warmed the side of her neck as he handed her a glass of red wine, their fingers brushing in the exchange.

She turned to face him, her gown trailing on the floor. "There's no music." But even as she said it, an invisible thread drew them together.

Royce pulled out his phone, thumbed the screen, and played a song. A sultry saxophone wound through breathy notes while piano keys whispered their accompaniment. The song felt like a river float trip on a summer afternoon where time eases by.

"That's the song, the one from the Seine," her voice elevated, surprised he'd remembered. "How did you...?" Her second date in Paris, with the handsome author who happened to carry monogrammed handkerchiefs, had developed unexpectedly. Even she couldn't believe she'd entertained the idea of anything more than a glass of wine with him. "Seriously, how did you find those guys?"

"I assumed they frequently played there, so, I went by on my last research trip."

"Royce..."

He set their wine glasses down and tugged her closer. "That's Mr. Brownell to you."

"If you keep doing stuff like that, you just might reach Lord Thornbury status again." And there they were, the dimples she hadn't seen in days. Reality hit Cordelia, a thud in her chest. *That's what life would feel like without him.* Dreary.

Royce minimized the distance between their hips. Her arms wrapped around his neck while his encircled her waist. They didn't move, and the only thing between them was the weight of their nine months together.

"Have you figured it out yet?"

"What?"

"I'm a sap when it comes to you."

Cordelia placed her head on his shoulder and listened to the rhythmic pulse of his heart. "It's lovely."

The music wrapped around them, but his scent—dark cherries from the wine, spice from the cologne, and the soap on his skin created an intoxicating concoction. Her mouth watered. Her core craved. "I'm sorry," she whispered, tasting salt on his partially exposed chest where a hint of dark hair peeked through.

His hands slid lower, feeling the lines of her back and hips. "For what?"

Pulling back, she met his eyes. "For overreacting."

Royce touched the fine strands of hair beside Cordelia's cheek and cupped her face. His touch felt like absolution.

"I'm sorry for not trusting you."

"I'm sorry too. I shouldn't have—."

She silenced him with a kiss, insatiable and wild—pulling him closer, until the void between them had disappeared. All she felt was his heartbeat against her breasts.

The kiss ignited him, and his tongue moved past her lips. The taste of wine and passion.

Cordelia moaned.

Royce spun them until her back hit the cool marble wall, his body caging her in. She gasped. The cold stone, a shock against her spine, contrasted his heat. His mouth moved to her throat, finding the spot just below her ear that made her knees buckle— the spot he'd discovered that night at Hayton.

He murmured against her pulse point, his teeth grazing the skin. "Cordelia…"

Her hands worked at the buttons of his shirt, eager to free him from the restraining fabric—to feel the firmness of his chest. When the last button opened, he tossed the shirt to the floor.

Royce lifted her arm and drew down the hidden zipper of her gown with a deliberate slowness that made her want to scream. She wanted to be released from the refinement.

Soon, the gown pooled at her feet, a whisper of silk and tulle, exposing her to the night's air.

His gaze and fingers traced the black lace that covered her breasts. His eyes offered a sense of safety again. She felt beautiful in his eyes.

Cordelia unhooked her bra and let it slide off, watching his muscular chest rise with a sharp breath. An animalistic heat rose in her belly, but she wanted to savor things.

His hands framed her face, guiding her closer, and he kissed with the lightest touch, his lips moist and warm.

She recognized the tender restraint, a desire to explore rather than seize. Having come close to walking away from him, she herself wanted to stretch the moment—to sustain their appetites.

Slowly, he palmed her breasts. The warmth of his fingers contrasted with the cool hardness of her nipples. She arched into his touch and undid his belt. He groaned against her mouth when her hand found him, rigid and ready. A wanting took control, and what was left of their clothes fell onto the floor. Every nerve ending surged—hip to hip, their hands mapped each other. His body pressed into her, the chill of marble against her back.

"God...I missed that," she mumbled as his tongue grazed down her stomach, causing her to shiver. He seemed intent on relearning what made her tremble, creating fresh memories for future reference. She moaned, feeling greedy for more. She sought more of him, more of herself.

When his mouth returned to her lips, the broad expanse of his shoulders pressed into her, and his heart hammered against her chest. Cordelia wrapped a leg around his hip and pulled him closer.

He exhaled an impatient longing—gripping her thighs and lifting her onto himself.

All of her focus narrowed to the sensation of him entering her: slow, reverent, consuming. For a moment, neither moved. "I love you," she whispered, seeking trust in his eyes.

"And I love you...Cordelia." His hips moved rhythmically, increasing an urgent sensation. Her head leaned back, pleasure coiled in her belly. Royce's mouth found her throat, her collarbone, marking her with kisses and gentle bites.

Their love escalated and fragmented, his name on her lips. He groaned, a sound that emerged from his core. They stayed pressed together, trembling and gasping, held up by the wall and each other. Finally, he lifted his head from her chest and searched her face—so tender it made her heart swell.

Hours later, they lay tangled in sheets that revealed a story of reconciliation. The scent of passion lingered on their skin. Cordelia traced circular patterns on his chest while he played with her hair. Her thoughts scrolled through everything she still wanted to say to him, but her heart resisted breaking the spell.

She reached across him, grabbing her wine glass from the side table, and sipped. A drop of wine dribbled down the glass and landed on his chest.

Royce startled.

Cordelia glanced from the spilt wine to his face. Her mouth rested over the drop, licking and swirling her tongue over the wine. He watched. Playfully, she held her glass above him.

"What are you doing?" he said.

"Dare me?"

"Don't get it on the sheets."

She straddled him. "Oh, I have no intention of that." A thin stream of wine drizzled into the valley of his chest. Placing the glass onto the table, Cordelia tasted him—salty, earthy, blended with dark cherries. But what lingered on her tongue was the future, their future. She looked up, noting the candor in his eyes, *That's where I belong.*

Royce rolled them over. "Ms. Dyer, I'm completely and utterly yours."

"And what am I?"

"You're mine." The words settled into her chest like a vow. Her speech lingered in the back of her mind. Those words still needed to be said, but the night had softened the fears, the uncertainty. How they navigated the future would be decided later. She just wanted to remain lost in the feeling.

Dawn crept across Venice with a tentative vow—a hope that painted the Grand Canal in shades of rose and gold, a beauty that would make master painters envious. Royce stood on the terrace, wearing shorts and his dress shirt he threw on as he walked outside. Below, the city woke under layers of mist, a haze that rose off the lagoon. Back inside, he heard Cordelia moving about—footsteps on marble, coffee mugs clinking, her soft voice singing. There were two songs she'd sing when happiest: one by Ed Sheeran and the second by The Verve. Royce listened. Her voice tumbled over the words and lingered high over the last note. She sang about love.

Twice more that night, they made love, each time slower, deeper, an affirmation of the connection they shared through touch. But daylight brought a different kind of clarity, the type that requires talking. Honest conversations where feelings and truths were revealed, where compromise happened.

"You're thinking loudly," Cordelia said, stepping onto the terrace. She wore his yellow linen shirt, the fabric falling mid-thigh, with a messy updo that begged to be touched. He noticed she favored her sore foot, avoiding too much weight on the toe.

He opened his arms, inviting her to nuzzle up. "How's your foot?"

"It'll survive," she said, but she shifted her weight, telling a different story.

"I'll be right back," he said, pressing a kiss to her temple. "Do not move."

"I'm supposed to just stand here?"

Dashing inside, he said, "No, sit. I'll be back." He returned minutes later with a makeshift ice pack wrapped in a kitchen towel and found her posed on the edge of a chair. "This'll have to do." He knelt. "Just relax," lifting her foot onto his knee.

"Royce, you didn't need to—."

"Let me," he said, meeting her eyes. "It's my fault, let me take care of you."

Her expression shifted, and she settled back, relaxing the weight of her foot into his hand.

"Does it feel better?" he asked after a few minutes.

"Much. Thank you." She touched his cheek. "We need to talk, don't we?"

He stood, placing the ice pack on the table, and pulled her close. Cordelia fit perfectly in his arms, shorter than him, but tall enough that he could kiss her without overly straining her neck.

"We do." He ran a hand through his hair. "What I said the other night, about your mother—it was harsh, and I know on some level it's unforgivable."

"It was. Things get said in an argument, things we regret. You were so jealous..."

"Jealous?" The word left a bitter taste in his mouth.

"Lorenzo, your jealousy is what started the whole thing."

"Right. You're right, I was jealous. On some level, I probably still am. The looks you gave him were exactly how you looked at me in Paris, before you knew anything about my family. I was terrified that I might lose you."

"Royce..." Her arms hugged him tighter.

"I'm not making excuses. I couldn't believe my reaction either. I thought I'd lost you, and it deeply hurt. I'd never felt that level of loss before. I was shattered, Cordelia."

"Don't you know, he means nothing to me? He'd never be you, ever. There's no comparison."

"That's exactly what I've tried telling you about Evie." He exhaled slowly, locking eyes with Cordelia. "Speaking of her..."

Her back muscles tensed. "Please don't tell me you had an affair with her."

"Christ, no. You know the facts. But the truth is, I tried to protect her, and it was a mistake. I wanted to fix what had happened—."

"You mean, she was right?" Cordelia plopped into the chair.

Royce sat across from her. "What did she tell you?"

"That you collect broken women. That I'm part of your collection."

"No. Has anything about our relationship indicated that I think you're broken? And forget what Evie said." Nearby church bells rang. "This is about us."

Cordelia squinted, her eyes darted as if she recalled memories. "No, I don't think so. But she said you'd deny it, change the rules, and eventually discard me. Just like Katherine."

"Let's stick to the facts, not Evie's lies."

"Are they lies? Maybe to her they're facts."

"Facts, not perceptions, just facts."

She drew in a long breath, exhaling as she crossed her legs and arms.

Royce slid his chair in front of her, forcing Cordelia to face him. "We're not going anywhere until this gets settled. I'm not losing you, Cordelia Dyer. Not over malicious lies from a former student."

"Fine." She placed her hands in her lap. "I trust you. And

no, you've never indicated I'm broken…except for the other night, when you said, what you said."

He held her hand in his and kissed her fingertips. "I am sorry. I truly hope you'll forgive me."

"I am. But I need your assurance that you won't use my mother against me. I admit she left me scarred. God, there's so much I want to say to her…and ask her. But I don't want to be like her." A passing speedboat slapped water against the stone walls, and faint voices snapped in Italian.

Cordelia was quiet for a long moment, and when she spoke, her voice had softened, barely above a whisper. "I've carried my mother's abandonment like an instruction manual. Every relationship, other than my father and James, has been based on that one thing. It's like she couldn't stay, so she left a map for me to follow, her last-ditch effort, trying to instill something in me. And I followed it—distance, fierce independence, and never committing because that meant exposure, and exposure meant heartache."

He wanted to speak, to offer comfort, but her rigid posture suggested she needed to talk, and he needed to listen.

"And Daniel knew that. He'd feed that fear," she shook her head remembering, "He knew I wanted to be different. I tried, but I couldn't trust him, so we played the game." Her voice grew stronger. "It was strategic, you know. He'd leave for a tournament and then call begging me to be at his side. And if I did, he'd act indifferent. I already knew people left, so I kept one foot out the door myself, just in case. And he'd use that against me, just like you saw in London."

The sun climbed higher, burning off the mist and warming the terrace.

"But I've learned something new, not everyone leaves. You stayed." Tears tracked down her cheeks, and she uncrossed her legs. "Even this week, you could've left and gone back to London."

"So could you. Neither of us left." He placed his hands on hers. "Besides, where would I go? You're home, Cordelia. Everything else is simply geography."

She made a sound that was a half-laugh, half-sob. Her arms wrapped around his neck, and she buried her face in his shoulder. Royce held her, feeling tears soak through the shirt.

"I always wondered, if my own mother wouldn't stay for me," her voice broke, "then why would anyone else?"

The quiet admission hit him like a punch to the chest. He'd known about her mother's abandonment, but hearing the raw pain in Cordelia's voice grieved him—to tear the world apart and demand she apologize to the seven-year-old girl who missed her mother.

Instead, he clutched her tighter. "Because," he said, whispering in her ear, "It's not about your value, Cordelia, it's about her lack. You're worthy of loving every goddamn day, and that's what I'm trying to do. Just love you." He wiped the tears from her cheeks. "Ms. Dyer, if I haven't made myself clear, I'm not going anywhere. And for the record, you're not broken. But you have to believe that."

She searched his eyes, wiping remnants of mascara from under her eyes. "Sorry, I got some on your shirt."

"I'll take it to the cleaners when we get home."

"I didn't mean to dump all of that on you. I'm sorry."

"Do not apologize," he leaned toward her. "It's called vulnerability, something we're both learning to do."

Her hands fidgeted with her hair. "God, I have a whole speech planned, and now I can't remember it."

"I think I understand." Royce pulled her into his lap and kissed her. Her lips, salty, sweet, with a hint of coffee. "Did you have a cup already?"

"Only a sip, but I—." She started to stand, but he halted her leaving.

"Wait, I spoke to Jared, we can extend our stay for a few days, if you're interested. What do you think about an additional three days?"

"Really? Oh God, that would be fantastic. Are you sure? What about work? I mean, that would mean rescheduling meetings, but yeah, I'd love it. And your interviews, what about them?"

"I can reschedule."

"Then yes, I'd a few more days—before we're thrown back into routine."

"Perfect. Three days without interference."

"I'll need to call Jessica and let Bastien know," she made a mental list, "and I'll ask Sam to check on Jasper and Lucy for me. Oh, I also need to text Cassandra, she wanted to catch up when I got back." Her smile stretched wide, causing a glow across her face. Despite the smear of black under her eyes, she radiated beauty. "I love you, Mr. Brownell."

"Mister? I've been downgraded?"

"Never. But right now, you're just my Royce...Mr. Royce Brownell."

Chapter Twenty-Two

When they arrived at a small patch of grass alongside a canal, the early afternoon sun bathed the water in opulent light. The scent of wood-fired ovens drifted from nearby restaurants as Cordelia watched Royce adjust her life vest for the third time. His fingers brushed her collarbone as he tightened the straps and double-checked the buckles.

"You realize, I know how to put on a life jacket?" she said.

"When was the last time you were in a boat?"

She stopped him from checking the buckles again. "Royce, you're hovering."

"I'm looking out for you. You said it had been years."

"I doubt life jackets have become complicated in the last sixteen years." She released her jacket from his hold. "Besides, it's a canal, not the Atlantic."

"Famous last words, darling," he whispered in her ear. "And I'm not taking any chances."

Her head dropped. "Oh my God, Royce, it's a canal." Nearby church bells rang, signaling the top of the hour.

"Well, don't fall in."

"If I do, you'll be in the water with me." She patted him on the cheek. "You're the adventure guy, relax. This is supposed to be fun."

His arms tightened around her waist. "Just protecting my cargo."

"Cargo? I can pull my own weight, thank you." She gave him a kiss.

"Then shall we wager who carries the load?"

"Definitely."

Mano, their instructor, pushed the tandem kayak closer to the water. "Remember, whatever you do, do not drink the water. Understand?"

Cordelia and Royce acknowledged and walked to the canal's edge holding hands.

"Signora, you are in front, signore, you are in back. He steers, you provide the power."

"Hear that?" Cordelia grinned, "I'm the engine, and you're the navigator."

"We'll see about that." Roye offered his hand to her, helping her in.

The kayak wobbled when she stepped into the front seat. "Oh God, we're going to end up in the canal, aren't we?"

"Probably," he said, laughing and settling into the rear seat. "At least it's a hot day, and you needed a shower."

"Not funny, Brownell."

"We're down to last names only, must be serious." He tickled the back of her neck, laughing as she swatted his hand away.

The kayak teetered to the left, causing Cordelia to lean right. "We haven't even hit the water and we're about to tip."

Mano pushed them off with last instructions about paddle strokes and staying to the right in the narrow canals. He jumped into his kayak and positioned himself at the front.

Within minutes, they'd found their rhythm—Cordelia's paddle cut through the water while Royce steered them away from ancient stone walls. The first challenge was maneuvering under a bridge so low they had to duck and avoid turning sideways.

"Left side," Royce said as they approached a gondola. "That's it, easy strokes." Their paddles glided through the murky water.

"I know how to paddle," she said, not wanting to admit the mind might remember, but the hand-eye coordination seemed to be lacking. So, she followed his guidance.

Seeing the buildings from the water provided a different view of the Venetian architecture. She awed at the grandness of the buildings—compared to gondolas, they appeared regal and imposing. And the moss looked like little pillows, a reminder that the rare city was built on water.

They glided past a small square where tourists sat at caffe tables, some waved as they passed, including an elderly man who looked up from his newspaper and sipped espresso. Just past him, three children sat on the canal wall eating gelato, while their mothers rapidly gestured and talked to each other.

Mano rounded a corner, guiding them into a quieter canal lined with residential palazzos. Laundry hung from windows like colorful flags, and a cat watched them pass from a stone ledge.

"This is incredible," Cordelia said, her voice softer now. "I can't believe I almost talked you into a cooking class." She shifted, trying to look back at him, and caused the kayak to rock. Her hands latched onto the sides, almost dropping her paddle in the water. "Oops.... I'm okay."

"Are you sure?" Royce steered them further to the right.

"Yeah, I'm good."

"Getting tired of being the engine yet?" He asked, using his paddle to push off a wall as they navigated a narrow passage.

"I could go all day," switching the paddle between hands while rubbing her forearms. "What about you? Tired yet?"

"No."

"That's because you have the easy job." Cordelia stopped paddling for a moment, letting the kayak drift.

"You wanted the power." He chuckled, splashing water forward.

"Hey. That's dirty, don't get me wet."

"If you think this is filthy, wait until hunting season."

"What? I'm not going hunting."

"You have to do it once. It's an adventure." Royce held his paddle in the water, angling them past a gondola.

"Royce Brownell, I already told you, I don't hunt."

They emerged onto a wider canal where the midday light caught the water just right, giving it a mirrored quality.

"It's only quail."

"Doesn't matter."

Royce let the kayak drift closer to a quieter section near some steps. "Does that mean camping's out of the question too?"

"What gave you that idea?"

"No reason." His paddle stilled the surrounding water, keeping the kayak straight. "So, if I schedule a trip for September, you won't back out?"

"As long as there's no hunting. I'll camp, hike, and even fish, but no hunting."

"You're very opinionated about this, aren't you?"

"Yes, I am, and your sexy British charm won't change my mind."

A water taxi passed, leaving its wake behind. Royce used his paddle to steady them. Although she could only see him out of her periphery, his confidence had a seductive quality.

"You're good at this," she said. "I never knew you were so outdoorsy."

"Summer holidays in Scotland bred it into me. Pop believed fresh air cured urban angst, so he forced Marcus and me to spend half the summer in the highlands."

"You never told me this. Why didn't you tell me?"

"It never came up."

She crooked her neck as far as it would go. "Royce, that's your childhood. That's special. Did your father go or just you two?"

"Most of the time, he and Mum were there. Sometimes, they'd return to London for business or a charity event. He saw it as *learning self-reliance*." His voice held a sentimental tone. "Marcus and I spent weeks hiking, fishing, and we even learned to read weather patterns from Mr. Blair, the groundskeeper."

A sweet glow settled in Cordelia's chest. She paddled slower. It explained his confidence in nature, and the way he approached problems with a protective instinct. "When was the first summer you stayed up there?"

"The first time he and Mum went back to the city...I was seven, maybe eight." Royce's paddle cut through the water.

Seven...wow. He was in the highlands chasing clouds, and I was learning how to do laundry. "So you said your mom went too, did she hike with you guys?"

"Hiked, fished, camped..."

"Your mom camps?" Cordelia's voice echoed off the water as they passed through a narrow section.

"She did. I don't think they've been since Marcus left for university."

"My God, after nine months, and my mind's blown. I'm shocked...but in a good way." She still discovered new layers about him, giving her a deep understanding of how his childhood shaped him, beyond boarding school and family traditions.

Royce's laughter bounced off the walls. "It's good to know I can still surprise you."

"You do. You really do."

They paddled in silence for a bit longer, working together without coordinating their strokes. She loved the quiet moments with Royce as much as their conversations or sex. He never tried to diminish her competence, unlike Daniel, who rarely offered compliments.

As they cut through the water, the boat's movement combined with their rhythm felt natural, like when they made love—a conversation in motion.

"Over there," Royce said, directing her toward a small landing where Mano waited.

They dragged the boat ashore, sharing their enthusiasm with Mano, who suggested a nearby park that was perfect for picnics or aperitifs.

Two women pulled laundry from the lines above a small alley, distracting Cordelia from the conversation. Despite the space between them, they carried on a lively conversation— friends, neighbors, Venetians—they bonded through mundane tasks.

Royce squeezed her hand. "Ready to go?"

"I am," Cordelia looked back at the two women who leaned out their windows and gestured with bold hands at one another. Who had they loved? What were their fears and triumphs? And did they see the beauty around them or take it for granted?

"I'm ready to go home," she said, resting her head on his shoulder as they walked away from the canal.

Chapter Twenty-Three

Cordelia paced, fracturing the shadows that stretched across the living room floor. Her damp hair tumbled onto her shoulders and moistened the pink tank top's straps. "Right, ask Sam if he can stop by and see Jasper and Lucy. I don't want them to think we've forgotten about them."

She ran her fingers through Royce's thick hair, still wet from their post-kayaking shower. "Yeah, I'll just text Sam myself. Don't worry about it...but listen—."

Royce looked up from his book, a spy novel he'd picked up at the airport, and motioned for her to sit. She nodded, but walked closer to the terrace doors.

The evening light hit her eyes. "No, I'll email the couples myself. But let the team know our meeting's postponed. I'll send a group text in a couple of days. I'm thinking we should do some team building, like maybe paintball one evening." Royce whipped around, looking over his shoulder.

"Right...exactly. Feel free to think of some ideas, otherwise, I'll research it on the flight home." Cordelia finished the call and joined Royce on the sofa. She positioned herself between his legs, resting her head on his chest.

"Sounds like Jessica's handling everything."

"Yeah, I'm surprised."

"You sound worried." He tossed the book onto the coffee table and wrapped his arms around her.

"No, not really. I mean...do I want to be pushed out of my job? No. But at least if she's more competent, then I can focus on bigger projects."

"What does Bastien say?"

"You know him, he supports me as long as the patisserie thrives. And he thinks my success benefits BL London."

"It does. Everything you're doing brings attention to him."

"I know, that's why I can screw up."

"And you won't. I've never known you to make a bad career decision."

She rolled onto her belly and kissed him. "You've only known me nine months, give it time."

Royce traced her chin with his thumb. "I want to talk to you about something. Something I've been thinking about."

Her stomach tightened. "That sounds ominous."

"Not ominous, but important." He rubbed her shoulder and arm. "Move in with me. Properly. Permanently." They'd danced around the conversation for two months, and he'd never fully asked—instead letting it progress slowly. But Venice had taken him full circle, and at thirty-seven, he was ready to commit.

"I practically live there already," she said.

"No, you sleep there. Your life is still packed in boxes in your apartment."

"That's not—."

"What do you call those three boxes in the corner of your living room, that haven't moved since you arrived in London?"

"I haven't had the time."

His raised eyebrows, a look that questioned her honesty. "Didn't you show me those boxes seven or eight months ago?"

"Maybe, I don't remember." Cordelia recalled the night—an evening at her place with butternut squash risotto and binging on Netflix. He'd questioned the boxes shoved in the living room corner, wondering why she hadn't unpacked them. *Something else to open up about.*

"They're just old photos and stuff. Nothing important."

"Then why is it stored in the living room?" His voice elevated with curiosity.

"I just haven't moved them." She pushed away, about to stand when Royce pulled her back.

"Wait, don't run off. If you're not ready to talk about it, that's fine. But I'm asking you to move in with me."

She tucked strands of hair behind her ear. "I'm flattered—."

"Flattered. That's not the response I expected."

"You know I love you."

"Then say yes."

"First let me ask, can I bring the boxes?"

"Of course, it'll be your home."

"What if I wanted to put stuff out, like a photo of my dad?"

"We'll add it to the family photos in the study."

"You want to combine them?"

"Why not? It would be your home too.

Her eyes gazed at his chin, feeling the days-old stubble he maintained. She traced the lines of his lean jaw. "I can't even remember everything in those boxes."

"Cordelia, did you ever unpack those boxes when you lived with Daniel?"

She fidgeted with the collar of his T-shirt. "No."

"In eight years, you never unpacked those boxes?"

"No. That would've meant it was permanent."

Royce shifted her, bringing her face within an inch of his. "Is there something wrong with permanency?"

Quietly, she traced the collar on his shirt. "No. I just don't know what it feels like to know that that's home. That place, that person, that life. We moved a lot, sometimes annually, depending on my dad's work. And with Daniel, it was about being what he needed rather than what we needed together. So, I never saw it as home. Deep down inside, I knew it wasn't permanent."

"And London?"

"The people are home...the city's home—."

"But?"

"But, I lived with those boxes for so long, they're just a part of me." She hesitated. "They used to be a reminder of our mobile life, and then they were part of an escape plan just in case. Now, they're a fixture, and in some odd way comforting."

Royce caressed her hand. "What if, when we get back to London, we unpack them together, in our home?"

"But it's your property, I'm just living there."

"That doesn't matter to me. It would be our home, with our things."

Cordelia tapped her fingers against his chest. "What if I wanted to set out my kindergarten ceramic handprint?"

Royce's face scrunched. "A shelf in my... our office?"

"And what if I wanted to set out the flower pot I painted with a rainbow of colors?"

"How old were you when you painted this flower pot?"

"Six."

"Let's think about that one. I thought you said they were full of photos?"

"And stuff."

He paused. "Bloody hell, why not. If you want it all out, we'll turn the office into your room of mementos."

"Really? You'd give up your office for my stuff?"

"If it means we're properly living together, then yes, I will."

"Well, lucky for you, I was only joking."

Royce appeared confused, propping up on his elbows.

"I won't unpack the boxes."

"But you'll move in? Permanently, full time?"

"Yes, I'd love to. Permanently."

He cupped her face and kissed her. "You really had me worried there."

Her giggle grew into full laughter as he pinned her to the sofa and tickled the spot under her arm that made her squeal. "Okay, okay, I'm sorry. I just wanted to see what you'd say."

"You, Ms. Dyer, have an evil streak." He nuzzled her neck, causing her to squeal more.

"But I said yes." She wrapped her legs around his. "That makes it worth it, doesn't it?"

"It depends on what you say next."

She waited, studying his eyes.

"Cordelia, do you promise to move in and not unpack your rainbow flower pot?"

"But it'll add fresh style and personality..."

His fingers found another spot on her side that made her flinch and laugh uncontrollably.

"All right, I promise," she gasped for a breath, "but you have to promise you'll give up some closet space so I can store the boxes, other than in the living room."

"Agreed." Royce rested his hips against hers, and ran his fingers down her side, grazing the edge of her breast.

Royce insisted on celebrating, convincing Cordelia they should make pasta, drink wine, and watch Italian TV.

"I'll be right back," he said, rushing toward the elevator. When he returned, he found Cordelia in the kitchen, apron on, and kneading dough. Next to the sink was a yellow ceramic colander overflowing with basil.

He whistled, opening a bottle of Brunello wine he'd found in Jason's guest cellar. "Marcus called."

"Just now?"

"Yes, I was on the elevator."

Cordelia folded the dough and covered it with a cloth. "How are they doing?"

"Well." The cork popped, releasing a bold fragrant scent. "Nothing new."

"You told him, didn't you?" She said, washing her hands.

"Told him what?"

"That I'm moving in."

"Oh, that. Is that big news?" He handed her a glass of wine.

"Obviously it is." She brought the glass to her lips, but paused before sipping. "You called him, didn't you?"

Royce wrapped his arm around her waist, whispering in her ear, "Can you blame me for being happy?"

"No. Are you sure this is what you want?"

"Very."

Four hours later, after dining on homemade pasta and a bottle of wine, Royce fumbled with the remote.

"Just pick something," Cordelia said, burrowed into his side.

"I'm trying. The programming isn't like home."

The screen flickered through channels: game show, news, what looked like a parliamentary debate, and what could've been an outdoor cooking competition in the mountains. Royce finally landed on a black and white movie.

The woman clutched her pearls. The man wore a fedora, gripping her shoulders. The street lamp illuminated them. Rain fell with cinematic perfection.

"Ooh, Italian melodrama, perfect," Cordelia said. "What are they saying?"

Royce listened. "She's upset about... Thursday?" He nestled with Cordelia, propping his head on a throw pillow. "And possibly anchovies?"

"A Thursday anchovy crisis. That's serious."

On screen, the woman pressed a letter to her chest. The man removed his hat, revealing gelled hair that held its style despite the rain.

Cordelia deepened her voice, adopting her film accent. "Well, obviously, my dear," and then pitched higher, "Antonio, you promised to take me away from all this."

Royce said, "But Francesca, what about your husband's anchovy empire?"

"I never loved him. I only loved his fish," Cordelia flung her arm across the sofa and feigned distraught.

On the TV, the woman slapped the man. He caught her wrist, yanked her into an embrace that defied both respect and the laws of physics.

"Kiss me, you fool, before the anchovies spoil," Cordelia demanded, in her high-pitched Italian accent.

"But what about your cousin Luigi?" the words rolled off Royce's tongue.

"Luigi was just a distraction. His pizzeria means nothing to me."

Royce laughed, his hand stroking her back. "They're passionate about their food."

"Hey, don't knock it."

"I'm simply pointing out their food obsession."

They continued creating dialogue for the characters, developing the food passion storyline. Soon, Cordelia began analyzing props and secondary character motives: a newspaper left in a chair, the open train station door despite the snow outside, and an obscure small dog that seemed invisible to the characters.

"The dog represents capitalism," Cordelia said during a lingering close-up of its lonely face.

"No, it represents man's isolation."

"No way, that's the newspaper. See, it's ignored and isolated in the corner chair."

"But what's your reasoning for saying the dog represents capitalism?"

"Because, the dog belongs to the anchovy guy, but shows more loyalty to whoever feeds it. It's literally selling its affection to the highest bidder. Pure capitalism."

"I disagree. If the dog represented capitalism, it would get fatter, but it's gotten thinner. It's wasting away because everyone's ignoring it. That's isolation."

"Fine, you win...again."

On TV, the lovers climbed into a boat and sped through the Grand Canal, while gondolas rocked in its wake.

Cordelia grabbed Royce's shirt, as if she were the woman, and said, "Take me away from all this pescatarian madness." She flung her hand into the air, gesturing wildly.

Her voice deepened, her interpretation of an Italian man. "My darling, I'll give up everything to have you—my barber shop, and my timeshare in Sicily."

She clutched her chest and elevated her voice. "Not the timeshare." Cordelia gasped and plopped onto Royce.

"Bravo," Royce said. On screen, someone produced a gun. The dog barked. The woman fainted on the boat. "Why is the dog on the boat?"

"See, capitalism. It followed the highest bidder, which obviously wasn't the anchovy king."

"I concede, I'll give the win back to you," Royce said.

They missed the gun climax and never saw the dog again. A kiss escalated, and when they finished making love, another film had started. It appeared to be about a wedding with people on bikes, and a business hostile takeover.

Cordelia pulled on her tank top and noticed she had a voice message. "Marnie called, twice."

"Can you call her back tomorrow? It's late." Royce flipped off the TV, pulling her into his lap, wanting to sustain their intimacy longer.

"Yeah, but what if she needs me?"

"You're thousands of miles away, what can you do for her right now?"

"I can listen and make her feel better."

Royce glanced at the TV and watched a woman driving too fast on a cliff-side road. "All right, well, I'll clean the kitchen."

"Are you sure? I won't be long." Cordelia said.

"Who am I to come between best friends?"

"I love you," Cordelia said, "and thanks for understanding."

Royce pecked her lips, picked her up, and placed her back onto the sofa. "Me too, darling, me too."

From the kitchen, Royce heard Cordelia's animated conversation about Marnie's split from Edward Gild. She had a particular cadence to her words when comforting people—the same tone she used with Jasper and Lucy—patient, warm, fiercely protective.

Darius might have a chance now. He smiled and scraped the last of the pasta-making flour from the counter.

It had been a day of revelations. Finally, he understood about the boxes, a symbol of loss and control. Her childhood, neatly packed into cardboard and carried with her—both a burden and comfort, was foreign to his own. Despite their differences, they complemented each other. She balanced him.

In a few days they'd return to London, and real life would return—boxes and all. A warm contentment settled over him as he wiped the dust from the cold stone. Everything had been worth it: the randomness of Paris, the secrets in London, and the miscommunication there in Venice. He'd face jealousy again, as long as he still woke by her side.

"Babe," Cordelia stood in the doorway, wearing his green shirt, with a bit of black lace peeking from underneath. The fabric shielded her breasts, but exposed enough to entice. "Mind the interruption?"

Royce tossed the cloth into the sink. "Not when you ask like that."

She met him halfway, snaking her arms around his neck, as his hand slid between the lace and her skin. Her eyes drifted closed, and she exhaled.

The following morning, they lay in bed reading news on their phones. Cordelia scrolled through her social media feed, pausing on a photo of her four-year-old nephew, Jackson, climbing advanced playground equipment.

"Look at this," she showed Royce the screen. "James and Savannah are letting him climb on a rock wall."

Royce glanced and shrugged his shoulders. "The kid's impressive."

"Are you kidding? That's dangerous."

"I was that age when my parents first put me on a horse."

"You were four when you started riding?" Cordelia turned toward him, phone in her lap. "That's terrifying."

"Not really. Children don't develop fear until they're older. It's safer to start them young—they're more flexible, less resistant." His eyes crinkled with amusement.

"Less resistant? That's your approach? Start them young so they bend easier when they're tossed?"

"Well, when you put it that way..." Royce set his phone aside. "What's your solution? Keep them wrapped in cling film until they're teenagers?"

'Cordelia sat up, adjusting her tank top. "I'd wait until they were old enough to understand the consequences. Old enough to be afraid when they should be—maybe ten or twelve for something like horseback riding."

"By then they would've developed all sorts of fears. That can be prevented if you start them young."

"Yeah, but look at Marcus, he gets injured all the time, and he's a pro. Imagine if that were your child."

"Marcus has always been fearless, partly because he started riding young. He learned early to respect the horse and trust his own abilities. That's what I want for my children."

She located Marcus' page and tapped on a photo. "This is the risk you want your children taking?"

Royce chuckled, "He's an adult. He wasn't doing that when he was four. Besides, riding is a tradition for us, everyone learns."

"I understand, but I can't imagine watching my child on a horse and not feeling afraid for them. I don't know if I could allow it...and I still think James and Savannah are letting Jackson do something too dangerous."

He stopped and rubbed his eyes. "Right. Well, I suppose we see childhood quite differently. And we should probably discuss it when the time's right. Maybe get you comfortable on a horse first." He threw back the covers, pressed a soft kiss to her check. "I'm grabbing an espresso. Would you like one?"

She nodded, scrolling through James' photos of Jackson on the rock wall.

Chapter Twenty-Four

Venice shrank into a postcard as the boat cut through the smooth water, leaving foamy waves behind. Royce, still on vacation mode, debated football in Italian with their driver. Their hands waved dramatically, emphasizing their opinions with grunting sounds.

Cordelia envied him, the way he could mentally disconnect and ignore the flood of responsibilities waiting back in London. Her to-do list ran rampant. As much as she already missed Venice, before it had even faded out of sight, she looked forward to their routine life.

She reached into her tote for her calendar book, discovering an unexpected piece of paper—another folded note from Royce.

Tesoro mio, I saw you this morning on the terrace, watching Venice slowly wake. And even though you didn't know I was there, I savored your smile, the way you glowed as the sunrise bathed you in warmth, and the gondolier serenaded from below. You fill the gaps in my life.

I love you.

Forever yours, R

Cordelia looked up to find him still engaged with the driver.

She reached up and squeezed his hand, memorizing the way his fingers wrapped around hers—skimming across the back of her hand, as if to say, "I love you."

The note joined the others in her journal. But soon, they'd be treasures in a new box she'd begun, one filled with mementos of their life together: the handkerchief from their first meeting, the wine cork from their date at Darius' restaurant, and Old Harry Rocks postcards from their first weekend getaway.

She looked at Venice as it dissolved into the morning mist. The boat approached the airport docks, and Cordelia knew she left with more than photos and recipes. She carried a confidence that love could survive transparency.

Royce stared out the window, listening to the steady hum of the plane's engines. At cruising altitude, they lived in a liminal space between Venice and London. In three hours, routine life in Mayfair would resume.

Cordelia rested her head on his shoulder, having fallen asleep moments after takeoff. Strands of hair escaped her ponytail, little wisps resting on her cheek. Her hand curled around his arm. *So beautiful.* Royce loved those moments—simple things that created big memories.

His thoughts drifted to Christmas and the plans already forming in his mind. He had five-and-a-half months to prepare for the most important conversation they'd have.

He shifted, hoping not to disturb her. In his leather journal, he wrote:

Scotland - Christmas - ring
1. Talk to Pop - tell Mum, Marcus
2. Talk to James - coordinate visit
3. Plan: What to say? Timing? How? Make it special.

4. Size ring - how??

Closing the notebook, he tucked it into the seat pocket—unable to hide his smile. Outside the plane, clouds stretched like an endless white blanket, carrying them home and to their future he was ready to build.

A Gift

A Thank You from Me to You

Dear Reader,

You have made this story complete by choosing to continue Cordelia and Royce's journey with me. Thank you for spending time in their world, from the shimmering canals of Venice to the marble halls of Palazzo Li Fonti, and of course, the magical Venetian masquerade.

Your Exclusive Gift Awaits

As a special thank you, I've created a downloadable bookmark featuring Cordelia and Royce on the book cover.

Download Your Free Bookmark Here: https://Book Hip.com/CWCGWWN

For best results, print on cardstock, and let it transport you back to those Venetian nights and gondola rides every time you open your next book.

*P.S. Keep an eye out for **Book Three**, where we follow Cordelia & Royce to the highlands of Scotland for some holiday adventure. **Release date - November 6, 2025***

Stay Connected

Stay Connected for More Sweet Escapes

Loved Cordelia and Royce's continuing story? Their journey continues in Scotland, and I'd love to share what's next:

Join my Reader's Club for exclusive bonus scenes, author's musings, recipes, and be the first to know about upcoming releases.

Sign up at: https://shannonsteevesauthor.substack.com/subscribe

You'll also receive:

• A bonus chapter of Cordelia's life in New York

• Cordelia's recipe for those irresistible orange-cardamom madeleines

• Early cover reveals and pre-order pricing

• Monthly letters with behind-the-scenes stories, research, travel, and more

Reviews

One More Thing...

If Cordelia and Royce's story touched your heart, please consider leaving a review on Amazon, Goodreads, or your favorite book platform. Your words help other readers discover their next favorite escape, and they mean the world to me as I write the next book in this series.

Amazon: http://bit.ly/45VRo5V
Goodreads: http://bit.ly/3URlQYu

Thank you again for choosing this book and The Hayton Collection series. Like a perfect macaron, the best stories are meant to be savored and shared.

With heartfelt gratitude and warmest wishes,

Shannon Steeves

Acknowledgments

Acknowledgments

Every book is a journey, and I'm grateful to the incredible people who helped me navigate the journey, from that first spark of an idea to the story you hold in your hands.

First and foremost, you, the reader. You make sharing these stories exciting and fulfilling.

My deepest gratitude goes out to Tom Bromley and the incredible writing group I've discovered through Reedsy. You all have provided feedback, support, and encouragement while helping me to develop as a writer. Langdon—you keep me from wandering into the world of cliches and BS. Thank you.

To my editor, Steffi Waters, whose keen editorial eye and unwavering belief in Cordelia and Royce's story made this book infinitely better. Thank you for pushing me to dig deeper and for knowing exactly when to add "more interiority." Your patience is legendary.

Special thanks to Katarina (nskvsky) for creating a cover that captures the romance and style perfectly.

Additional special thanks go out to my social media manager, Adriana Bernal, for putting up with my revolving ideas. You've been a blessing all these months! Thank you.

To my brilliant beta readers and critique partners who provided insight and honesty, pushing me to challenge myself. You remind me that the writing process may be solitary, but the journey is never lonely.

My husband, Ford, deserves medals for living with a writer. Thank you for supporting and encouraging me to never give up! To my children and grandchildren, you inspire me daily and remind me why happily-ever-afters matter.

To every librarian, bookseller, book blogger, and bookstagrammer who champions romance novels, you are the true heroes of the literary world.

Finally, to you, my readers, thank you for choosing Cordelia and Royce's story. Thank you for believing in second chances, romantic moments, and the transformative power of love. Your support makes this journey possible. I'm thrilled to have your support, and you all encourage me every day!

Any errors in aristocratic protocols or ping-pong scoring are entirely my own, probably because I was too distracted imagining the next undressing scene.

With gratitude and love,
Shannon

About the Author

About the Author

Shannon believes every great love story requires passion, trust in the characters to guide the story, and the right amount of spark to make it unforgettable. She writes stories that transform through romantic love, that offer hope.

A double major in English and History turned romance author, she's a lifelong student of England's past, from pre-Roman Celts, to the Norman invasion, and Victorian society, which she weaves into her contemporary love stories. When she's not crafting strong feminine heroes and new book boyfriends, you'll find her in her kitchen attempting to perfect the elusive croissant or planning her next historical research trip.

An avid tennis and F1 fan with a bucket list that includes all four Grand Slam tournaments and the Monaco Grand Prix, she brings the same passion for competition and precision to her writing that she does to the court, though she admits she's better at writing match points than scoring them.

She currently lives in Atlanta, GA, where she treasures time with her husband, adult children, and four grandchildren who keep her young at heart and provide endless inspiration for storytelling. Her German Shepherd serves as both hiking companion and patient listener during plot brainstorming sessions. Between researching and planning her next adventure, she's working on her next romance because she firmly believes that love is the element that carries us through life's journey.

Connect with her at shannonsteeves.com or shannon steevesauthor.substack.com/subscribe for updates, bonus scenes, Cordelia's recipes, and tales from Royce's latest historical discoveries.

Find her on Instagram *@shannon.steeves.author* or TikTok *@s.steeves.author*

Also by Shannon Steeves

We Met in Paris

We Wandered in Scotland - _Coming November 6, 2025._

Sweet Surrender - The Hayton Collection Cookbook